Wake

Wake

A Novel

Anna Hope

McCLELLAND & STEWART

Published in Canada by McClelland & Stewart,
a division of Random House of Canada Limited,
a Penguin Random House Company

Library and Archives Canada Cataloguing in Publication available upon request.

ISBN: 978-0-7710-3966-9

Typeset in New Caledonia
Text design by Caroline Cunningham
Cover design by Kathleen DiGrado
Cover art © Susan Fox / Arcangel Images and Stephen Youll

Printed and bound in the United States of America

McClelland & Stewart,
a division of Random House of Canada Limited,
a Penguin Random House Company

www.randomhouse.ca

1 2 3 4 5   18 17 16 15 14

For my parents, Tony and Pamela Hope

wake /wāk/

1. Emerge or cause to emerge from sleep.

2. Ritual for the dead.

3. Consequence or aftermath.

Wake

Day 1

Sunday, November 7, 1920

Three soldiers emerge from their billets near Arras, northern France: a colonel, a sergeant, and a private. It is sometime close to the middle of the night and bitterly cold. The men make their way to a field ambulance parked next to the entrance gate; the colonel sits in the front with the sergeant, while the private climbs into the back. The sergeant starts up the engine, and drives them out and onto the road beyond.

The young private holds on to a strap dangling from the roof, as the van lurches over the rutted road. He feels shaky, and this jolting is not helping things. The raw morning has the feel of a punishment: When he was woken, minutes ago, he was told only to get dressed and get outside. He has done nothing wrong so far as he can tell, but the army is tricky like that. There have been many times in the six months since he arrived in France when he has transgressed, and only afterward been told how or why.

He closes his eyes, tightening his grip as the van pitches and rolls.

He had hoped he would see things over here. The sorts of things he missed by being too young to fight. The sorts of things his older brother wrote home about. The hero brother who died taking a German trench, and whose body was never found.

But the truth is he hasn't seen much of anything at all.

In the front of the van, the sergeant sits forward, concentrating hard on the road ahead. He knows it well but still prefers to drive in the day, as there are several treacherous shell holes along it. He wouldn't want to lose a tire, not tonight. He, too, has no idea why he is here, so early and without warning, but from the taut silence of the colonel beside him, he knows enough not to ask.

And so the soldiers sit, the engine rumbling beneath their feet, passing through open country now, though there is nothing to show for it—nothing visible beyond the headlights' glare, only an occasional startled animal scooting back into darkness on the road ahead.

When they have been driving for half an hour or so, the colonel rasps out an order. "Here. Stop here." He hits his hand against the dash. The sergeant pulls the ambulance over onto the shoulder of the road. The engine judders and is still. There is silence, and the men climb down.

The colonel turns on his flashlight and reaches into the back of the van. He brings out two shovels, handing one each to the other men. Next, he takes out a large burlap sack, which he carries himself.

He climbs over a low wall and the men follow him, walking slowly, their flashlight beams bobbing ahead.

The frosted ground means the mud is hard and easy enough to walk on, but the private is careful; the land is littered with twisted metal and with holes, sometimes deep. He knows the ground is peppered with unexploded shells. There are often funerals for the Chinese laborers who have been brought over to clear the fields of bodies and ordnance. He saw five dead last week alone, all laid out in a row. They end up buried in the very cemeteries they are over here to dig.

But despite the cold and the uncertainty, he is starting to enjoy himself. It is exciting to be out here in this darkness, where ruined trees loom and danger feels close. He could almost imagine he is on a different mission. Something heroic. Something to write home about.

Soon the ground falls away, and the men stand before a ditch in the earth, the remains of a trench. The colonel climbs down and begins walking along it, and the others follow, single file, along its zigzag lines.

The private measures his height against the side. He is not a tall man, and the trench is not high. They pass the remains of a dugout on their right, its doorway bent at a crazed angle, one of its supports long gone. He hesitates a moment before it, shining his flashlight inside, but there is nothing much to see, only an old table, pushed up against the wall, a rusted tin can still standing open on the top. He pulls his light back from the dank hole, and hurries to keep up.

The colonel turns left into a straighter, shorter trench and at the end of that, right into another, built in short, zigzag sections like the first.

"Front line," says the sergeant, under his breath.

After a few yards, the colonel's beam picks out a rusted ladder slung against the trench wall. He stops before it, placing his boot on the bottom rung, pressing once, twice, testing its strength.

"Sir?" It is the sergeant speaking.

"What's that?" The colonel turns his head.

The sergeant clears his throat. "Do we need to go up that way, sir?"

The private watches as the colonel swallows, his Adam's apple moving slowly up and down. "Have you got a better idea?"

The sergeant seems to have nothing to say to that.

The colonel turns, scaling the ladder in a few swift jerks.

"Fuck's sake," mutters the sergeant. Still, he doesn't move.

Standing behind him, the private is itching to climb. Even though he knows that on the other side there will only be more of the same blasted country, part of him wonders if there may be something else—something close to the thing he came out here for: that vague,

brave wonderful thing he has not dared to speak of, even to himself.
But he cannot move until the sergeant does, and the sergeant is fro-
zen to the spot.

The colonel's boots appear at the height of their heads; light is
flung into their faces. "What's the holdup? Get yourselves over here.
Now." He speaks like a machine gun, spitting out his words.

"Yes sir." The sergeant closes his eyes, looking almost as though
he may be saying a prayer, then turns and climbs the ladder. The
private follows him, blood tumbling in his ears. Once over, they
stand, gathering their breath, their beams sweeping wide across the
scene before them: great rusting coils of wire, twenty, thirty feet
wide, like the crazed skeleton of some ancient serpent, stretching
away in both directions as far as the eye can see.

"Bloody hell," says the sergeant. Then, a little louder, "How're we
going to get through that?"

The colonel produces a pair of wire cutters from his pocket.
"Here."

The sergeant takes them, weighing them in his hand. He knows
wire, has cut it often. Apron wiring. Laid enough of it, too. They
used to leave gaps, when they had time to do it right—gaps that
wouldn't be seen by the other side. But there are no gaps here. The
wire is tangled and crushed and bent in on itself. Ruined. Like every
bloody thing else. "Right." He hands his shovel to the private. "Make
sure you light me, then." He bends and begins to cut.

The private, trying to keep his beam straight, stares at the wire.
There are things caught and held within its coils, things that look to
have been there for a long time. There are tattered remnants of cloth,
stiff with frost, and the light catches the pale whiteness of bones,
though whether human or animal it is impossible to tell. The country
smells strange out here—more metal than earth; he can taste it in his
mouth.

On the other side of the wire, the sergeant straightens and turns,
beckoning for the men to follow. He has done a good job, and they

are able to pick their way easily through the narrow path he has made.

"This way." The colonel strides out across lumpy ground that is littered with tiny crosses: crosses made from white wood, or makeshift ones made from a couple of shell splinters lashed together. There are bottles, too, turned upside down and pushed into the mud, some of them still with scraps of paper visible inside. The colonel often stops beside one, kneeling and holding his light to read the inscription, but then carries on.

The private searches the man's face as he reads. Who can he be looking for?

Eventually the colonel crouches by one of the small wooden crosses, set a little way apart from the rest. "Here." He motions for the men to come forward. "Dig here." A date is written on the cross, scribbled in shaky black pencil, but no name.

The private does as he's told, lifting his shovel and kicking it into the hard ground. The sergeant joins him, but after a couple of spades of earth he stops.

"Sir?"

"What?"

"What are we looking for, sir?"

"A body," says the colonel. "And bloody well get on with it. We haven't got all day."

The two men lock eyes for a moment before the sergeant looks away, spits on the ground, and continues to dig.

Beneath its frosted crust the mud is softer, clinging, and they do not have to dig for long. Soon metal scrapes on metal. The sergeant puts down his shovel and kneels, clearing the mud from a steel helmet. "Think we might be there, sir."

The colonel holds his light over the hole. "Keep going," he says, his voice tight.

The men crouch low, and with their gloved hands, as best they can, they clear the mud from the body. But it is not a body, not *really; it is only a heap of bones inside the remains of a uniform. Nothing is left of the flesh, only a few black-brown remnants clinging to the side of the skull.*

"Clear as much as you can," says the colonel, "and then check for his badges."

The dead man is lying in the earth, his right arm beneath him. The men reach down, lifting and turning him over. The sergeant takes his pocketknife and scrapes away at where the shoulder should be. The man's regimental badges are there still, just, but they are unreadable, the colors long gone, leached into the soil; it is impossible to tell what they once were.

"Can't see them, sir. Sorry, sir." The sergeant's face is red in the flashlight beam, sweaty from effort.

"Check around the body. All around it. I want anything that might identify him at all."

The men do as they are ordered, but find nothing.

They stand slowly. The private rubs the small of his back, looking down at the meager remains of the unearthed man lying twisted on his side.

Then a thought rises in him, unbidden: His brother died here. In a field like this in France. They never found his body. What if this was him?

But there is no way of knowing.

He looks back up at the colonel. There is no way of knowing if this is the body the colonel's looking for, either. This has been a waste of time. He waits for the colonel's reaction, bracing himself for the expected anger on his face.

But the colonel only nods.

"Good," he says, chucking his cigarette on the earth. "Now lift him out and put him in the sack."

. . . .

Hettie rubs her sleeve against the misted taxi window and peers out. She can't see much of anything; nothing that looks like a night-club anyway, just empty, darkened streets. You wouldn't think they were just seconds from Leicester Square.

"Here, please." Di leans forward, speaking to the driver.

"That's a pound, then." He turns his light on, engine idling.

Hettie hands over her ten-shilling share. A third of her pay. Her stomach plummets as it's passed to the front. But the taxi's not a luxury, not at this time; the buses aren't running and the tubes are shut.

"It'll be worth it," whispers Di as they clamber down. "Promise. Swear on my life."

The taxi pulls away and they find each other's hands, down an unlit side street, dance shoes crunching on gravel and glass. Despite the cold, damp pools in the hollow of Hettie's back. It must be way past one, later than she has ever been out. She thinks of her mother and her brother, fast asleep in Hammersmith. In not too many hours they'll be getting up for church.

"This must be it." Di has stopped in front of an old, three-story house. No lights show behind the shuttered windows, and only a small blue bulb illuminates the door.

"Are you sure?" says Hettie, breath massing before her in the freezing air.

"Look." Di points to a small plaque nailed to the wall. The sign is ordinary-looking; it could be a doctor's or a dentist's even. But there's a name there, etched into the bronze: DALTON'S, NO. 62.

Dalton's.

Legendary nightclub.

So legendary some people say it doesn't exist.

"Ready?" Di gives a blue, spectral grin, then lifts her hand and knocks. A panel slides open. Two pale eyes in an oblong of light. "Yes?"

"I'm here to meet Humphrey," says Di.

She is putting on her posh voice. Standing behind her, Hettie is filled with the urge to laugh. But the door opens. They have to squeeze to get around. On the other side is a small entrance area, little bigger than a cupboard, where a young doorman stands behind a high wooden desk. His gaze slides over Hettie, in her brown coat and tam-o'-shanter, but lingers on Di, with her dark eyes, the shorn points of her hair just showing beneath her hat. Di has this way of looking, down and to the side, and then slowly back up again. It makes men stare. She's doing it now. Hettie can see the doorman goggling like a caught fish.

"You've to sign in," he says eventually, pointing at a large book lying open before him.

Di pulls off her glove, leans in, and signs with a practiced sweep. "Your turn," she says, handing the pen to Hettie.

From below comes the throb of music: a giddy trumpet. A woman whoops. Hettie can feel her heart: *thud-thud-thud.* The ink of Di's signature is glistening and has sprawled out of its box and onto the line beneath. She takes her own glove off and scratches her name: *Henrietta Burns.*

"Go on, then." The man pulls the book back, gesturing behind him to unlit stairs.

Di goes first. The staircase is old and creaky, and as Hettie puts a hand out to steady herself, she feels damp wall flake beneath her fingertips. This is not what she imagined; it's nothing like the Palais, where the glamour is all out front. You wouldn't think these musty old stairs led anywhere much at all. But she can hear the music properly now, people talking, the sound of feet fast on the floor, and as they reach the bottom, a wave of panic threatens to take her. "You'll stay close to me, won't you?" she says, reaching for Di's arm.

"Course." Di catches her, gives her a squeeze, and then pushes open the door.

The smell of close, dancing humanity assails them. The club is no bigger than the downstairs of Hettie's mother's house, but it is packed, each table crammed, the dance floor a roaring free-for-all. Most people seem to be in evening clothes—the men in black and white, the women in colored gowns—but some look as though they have come in fancy dress. Most astonishing of all, the four-piece band crashing through a rag on the tiny stage has a Negro singer, the first she has ever seen. It's dizzying, as though all the color missing in the city up above has been smuggled underground.

"Killing!" Di grins.

"Killing!" Hettie agrees, letting out her breath.

"There's Humphrey!" Di waves to a fair-haired man weaving his way through the crowd toward them. Hettie recognizes him from that night at the Palais two weeks ago, when he hired Di for a dance—and then another, and another, right up until the end of the night. (For this is their job: *Dance Instructress, Hammersmith Palais. Available for hire, sixpence a dance, six nights a week.*)

"Capital!" says Humphrey, kissing Di on the cheek. "You made it. And this must be . . ."

"Henrietta." She holds out her hand.

He is not much older than them, has an easy handshake and a pleasant, freckled face. He looks nice, at least. Not like some of the ones Di has been with in the past. After a year at the Palais, Hettie has a compass for men. Two minutes in their company and she can tell what they're like. Whether they are married, sweaty-guilty, sneaking out for an evening alone. That glazed look they get when they're imagining you without your clothes. Or sometimes, like Humphrey, when they're actually sweet. "Come on," he says with a grin, "we're over here."

They follow him, picking their way as best they can through the crowded tables. Hettie makes slow progress, since she keeps fall-ing behind, twisting to see the band and their singer, whose skin is so astonishingly dark, and the dancers, many of whom are moving wildly in a way no one at the Palais would dare. Eventually they arrive at a table in the corner, not far from the stage, where a short man in tails scrambles to his feet.

"Diana, Henrietta," says Humphrey, "this is Gus."

Hettie's companion for the evening is thickset and doughy, barely taller than she is. His hair is thinning, his scalp shiny in the heat. Her heart sinks behind her smile.

"May I take your coat?" He hovers around her, and she shrugs it off. Her old brown overcoat is bad enough, but beneath it she is wearing her dance dress, the only one she has, and after a double shift at work already tonight it is none too fresh.

On the other side of the table, meanwhile, Di unwraps, revealing the dress she bought with Humphrey's money just last week. Hettie sinks into her seat. *The dress.* This dress has a physical effect on her; she covets it so much it hurts. It is almost black, but covered with so many sequins, so tiny, so dazzling in their iridescence, that it is impossible to tell just what color it is. She was there when Di bought it, in the ready-made at Selfridges. It cost six pounds of Humphrey's money, and she had to swallow her envy and smile when afterward, for fun, they rode up and down in the lifts.

Both men stare until Gus, remembering his manners, takes the seat beside Hettie's, pointing to a plate of sandwiches in the middle of the table. "They're rather grim," he says with a smile, "but they have to serve them with the drinks. No license, you see. We'll just pile them up on the side." He lifts them away, and she watches them go. She could murder something to eat. Hasn't had a thing since a ham-and-paste sandwich in the break between shifts at six.

"So"—Gus pours from a bottle on the table and hands her a glass—"I s'pose you're awfully good, then. You pair, Humph told me, dance instructresses at the Palais, aren't you?"

"Oh . . ." Hettie takes a sip. The drink is fizzy and sweet. She can't be sure, but she thinks it might be champagne. "We're all right, I suppose."

They're better than all right, really, she and Di. They've been practicing their steps for years, in carpet-rolled-back living rooms, singing out the tunes they've memorized, poring over the pictures in *Modern Dancing*, taking turns being the man. They're the best two dancers at the Palais by far. And that's not boasting. It's just the truth.

"I'm a terrible dancer," says Gus, sticking his lower lip out like a child.

Hettie smiles at him. He may not look like much, but at least he's harmless. "I'm sure you're not."

"No, really." He points downward, grimacing. "Left feet. Born with two."

There's a raucous cheer from the dance floor and she turns to see the singer goading his band, urging them on. They are American, they must be. No English band she knows looks or plays like this; definitely not the house band at the Palais, not anymore, not since the Original Dixies left, with their cowbells and whistles and hooters, to go back to New York. And the crowd—they're dancing crazily, as though they don't care a fig what anyone thinks. If only her mum could see this. *Respectable* is her favorite word. If she could see these people enjoying themselves, she'd throw a fit.

Hettie turns back to Gus. "It's just practice," she says, taking another sip of the drink, her body itching with the beat.

"No, no," he insists. "I'm *terrible*. Never could get the hang." He gives his glass a couple of brisk twists, then, "Up for a go, though," he says, "if you'd like a turn round the floor?"

"I'd love one," says Hettie, throwing a quick glance at Di, whose dark head is bent close to Humphrey's, deep in a whispered, intimate conversation that she cannot hear.

The crashing chords of the rag are fading now, and the band is moving into a four-four number, something slow. They shoulder their way through the crowd and find a spot on the edge of the packed dance floor. Gus takes her hands in his and then looks up to the ceiling, as if the mysteries of movement might be written out for him there. Then he bounces a bit, counting under his breath, and they are off.

He was right. He is a terrible dancer. He has no sense of the music, is already two beats ahead, snatching at it, not letting it guide him at all.

Listen! Hettie wants to say. *Just let it move you. Can't you hear how killing they are?*

But it won't help, so she tries to fit her feet to his awkward steps.

(They have a rule at the Palais: Never dance better than your partner. You're hired to make them feel good. If they feel good, then they'll hire you again. As Di is fond of saying, *It's all just economics in the end.*)

After a few bars, Gus's grip loosens and he looks up, delighted. "Damned if I'm not getting the hang of this!" They go into the turn, Hettie exaggerates her movements to flatter his, and as the number comes to a close, he takes a victory lap around the floor. "Humph was right!" He beams, coming to a breathless stop. "You girls are really something. Damned thirsty work, though." He takes his hankie from his pocket and mops his face. "Hang on a tick, I'll fetch us something cold from the bar."

He disappears into the crush, and Hettie finds a spot close to the damp wall, happy for a moment to be alone, just to take it all in. A couple squeeze past her, giggling, holding each other up. The girl is young and elegant, her body wrapped in blue silk, her long neck trailing pearls, but her lovely face is blurry, and she keeps slipping off her partner's arm. It is a moment before Hettie realizes she is drunk. She stares after them, half-expecting someone to come and tell them off. But no one seems to bat an eyelid. She's not at the Palais now.

Just then someone knocks into her, hard, from behind, and she almost falls, catching herself just in time.

"Sorry. My *God*. Sorry."

Hettie turns to see a tall man beside her. He seems distracted, an apologetic smile on his lips. "*So* sorry," he says again. One hand tugs at his hair, the other grips an amber-colored drink. "Are you all right? Thought you were a goner, then."

"Yes . . . fine." She gives a small, embarrassed laugh, though whether for him or herself, she cannot tell.

The man's eyes land on her properly, taking her in, and Hettie feels herself flush. He is a very good-looking man.

"My God," he says. His smile fades, and a different, shrinking expression takes its place.

Heat stings her cheeks. *What? What is it?* But she says nothing, and the man carries on staring, as though she is something awful from which he cannot look away.

"Sorry," he says, shaking his head as though to clear it. An echo of the smile is back. "Thought you were—" He holds up his glass. "Drink? Must let me get you a drink. Say sorry and all that."

She shakes her head. "Thank you. I'm . . . Someone's already buying me one."

She steps away, wanting to put distance between them, to find a mirror, to check that everything is all right with her face, but the man has his hand on her arm. "Where are you from?"

"Pardon?" she says. His grip is tight.

"I only meant, are you English, then?"

"Yes."

He nods, releases her. Is it disappointment she can see on his face?

"Excuse me . . ." She ducks away, escaping him, threading

through the crowd, which is even denser now, looking for the lavatories, finding them through an archway, small and damp-smelling,
a dark spray of mold clinging to the walls.

She examines herself in the mirror, breathing hard. There is
nothing particularly terrible to see, other than a red blotch of embarrassment on her neck and that two of her bobby pins have come
loose and her hair is threatening to unravel. She pushes the offend-
ing pins back into the bristling porcupine it takes to hold it up. Her
long, stupid hair that her mother won't let her cut.

*If you come home looking like that friend of yours, you'll catch
it. Filthy little flapper.*

Her mother doesn't know a thing. Di has the best haircut of any
of the girls at the Palais. They are always trying to get her to let on
where she has it done.

Hettie steadies herself against the cold rim of the sink. It's late.
She's been on her feet for hours. The night, which had been filled
with promise, is curdling somehow, and the same old doubts are
rushing in. She is from Hammersmith. She is too tall. Her dress is
old and she cannot afford another since she gives half her wages to
her mother and her useless brother every week. She's scrubbed
cleaning petrol and scent on the armpits more times than she can
count, but it still stinks and she'll probably never have a dress like
Di's as long as she lives. She's got to be nice to Gus. And to top it
all off, her breasts stick out, no matter how much she tries to strap
them down.

It is that man's fault, she thinks, finding her eyes in the mirror.
The way he looked at her, and his questions. *Where are you from?*
As though he could tell she didn't belong, here in this club with
these people who act so freely in their drunkenness and dancing,
as if whatever they do, their life will hold them up.

Come on.

She splashes water on her cheeks, checks that her petticoat isn't slipping, and stabs a last stubborn pin in her hair. The red blotches on her neck have calmed a little now.

Back out in the fray, she scans the crowd, relieved to see that the tall man has disappeared. There is no sign of Gus either, and when she finally spots him, his shiny bald head is still bobbing in the queue at the bar. Over at the table, Di and Humphrey haven't moved. Except, perhaps, a little closer together. Hettie can see Di laughing at something Humphrey has said. They don't look as though they'd welcome an interruption. For a moment, as she stands there alone, her fragile resolve threatens to falter. But something is happening over on the dance floor. People have stopped moving, and the band is slowing, the instruments dropping out one by one, until only the drummer remains, keeping the beat with a lone, shivering snare. Then he, too, comes to a stop, and a hush descends on the club. Over at the table, Di and Humphrey look up.

Hettie, breath caught, steps away from the wall.

For an electric moment it feels as though anything may happen, until the trumpeter moves forward and lifts his instrument to play. It flashes in the low light. A flare of purest sound fills the room. Hettie closes her eyes, letting it in, letting it hollow her out, and then, when the man begins to play in earnest, the notes drip molten gold into the space he has made. And standing here, full of this music, it hits her with the force of revelation that *it doesn't matter*— none of it, not really: She is young, she can dance, and it was worth her ten shillings just to *see* this place, to hear these musicians, to tell the girls at the Palais on Monday that it's true—that there *is* a club in the West End, buried underground, with the best jazz band since the Dixies left for New York.

"Are you lurking?"

She snaps open her eyes. The man from before is a few feet away, leaning against the wall, smoking a cigarette.

"I'm sorry?"

"You're lurking," he says.

"I'm not lurking." Her heart thuds dangerously against her chest.

"You are. I've been watching you for two whole minutes. Two minutes constitutes a lurk."

She can feel that awful flush creeping back up her neck. "I'm not, actually—I'm watching the band." She crosses her arms, looking away from him, trying to focus on the trumpeter's fingers, trying to remember how good she just felt.

From the corner of her eye she sees the man push himself away from the wall. "You're not one of those anarchists, are you?" he says.

She turns to him, incredulous.

His gray eyes are steady. This time he doesn't smile. "I've read about your sort. You go into public places like this." His hand sweeps over the club. "Hundreds of innocents. Bomb in your coat. Leave it in the lavatories. Lurk a bit, then . . . *boom.*" He mimes something exploding. As his hands move up and away from each other, ash falls, scattering in the air. A few flakes land on her dress.

For a moment, she is too surprised to speak. Then, "My coat's over there," she says, gesturing to the table in the corner. "And there's no bomb inside. Anyway, if I were going to blow something up, I wouldn't *lurk.* I'd leave."

"Ah." He nods. "Well, perhaps I got you wrong."

"Yes," she says. "You did."

They hold each other's gaze. She tries to keep steady, to read him, but her compass is haywire and she cannot fathom him at all.

Then his face cracks open with a smile. "Sorry." He shakes his head. "Terrible sense of humor."

Her heart skips. It is disconcerting, the smile; so sudden, as though there were another person entirely hidden underneath. He looks respectable enough, dressed in white shirt and tails, but there is something odd about the way he wears them. She can't say just what it is. Indifference? His hair is unslicked. There are purple shadows beneath his eyes.

He reaches into his pocket, takes out a flask, and lifts it to her mouth. "Here, have a bit of this while you wait."

"No, thank you."

She half-turns from him, cringing as she hears her voice in her head: *No, thank you*. She sounds so Hammersmith. So up-past-her-bedtime. So prim.

"Go on. It's good stuff. Single malt."

His eyes are laughing now. Is he laughing at her? He is the sort of man who could talk to anyone. So what is he doing hanging around here? It feels like a trick.

She should go and find Gus; he must have been served by now. She should. But she doesn't.

Instead, she reaches for the man's flask, takes it, lifts it to her mouth.

Because she's only here for tonight, and her companion is use-less and elsewhere, and her friend is otherwise engaged.

And so what has she got to lose?

She is unprepared for the sharp hit of the drink, though, and she chokes and coughs.

"Not much of a whiskey girl, then?"

She takes another, deeper pull in reply. This time she swallows it down. "Thanks," she says, pleased with herself, handing it back.

He looks out over the dance floor. "Are you here to dance, then?" he says. "Or have you just come to lurk?"

"I've come here to dance," she says, as the whiskey flares in her blood.

"Glad to hear it." He crushes his cigarette in an ashtray nearby then turns to her. "How would you feel about dancing with me?"

"If you like."

Fewer people are dancing now, and they can walk straight out to the middle of the floor. Once there, the man holds up his hands. It is an odd gesture, not quite the gesture of a man beginning a dance, more that of a man who is unarmed. Hettie puts one hand in his, the other on his evening coat, which is fitted tight against his back. The crease of his collar touches her ear. His hand is cool. He smells of lemons and cigarettes. She feels a bit dizzy. Perhaps it's the drink.

The soulful, gorgeous trumpet has faded now, and the band is picking up again, the music moving into a rag, a one-step.

One-two, one-two.

The floor is filling, people pressing all around them, cheering, clapping, stamping the music back into life.

One-two, one-two.

He steps toward her.

Hettie steps back.

And it's there; it's in that first tiny movement—the flash of rec-ognition. *Yes!* The rare feeling she gets when someone knows how to move. Then the music crashes in, and they are dancing together across the floor.

"Good band tonight," he says, over the music. "American. I like the Americans."

"Me, too."

"Oh?" He raises an eyebrow. "Who've you seen, then?"

"The Original Dixies."

"The *Dixies*? Damn." He looks impressed. "They were the best." He puts his leg between hers as he goes for the spin. "Where'd you see them?"

"The Palais. Hammersmith." She comes back to face him.

"Really? I went there once—saw them there, too!" He looks eager suddenly, like a boy.

Hettie considers this, wonders if they danced near each other. They definitely didn't dance together. She'd have remembered.

"What was your favorite number, then?" he says.

She laughs; that's easy. "'Tiger Rag.'"

"'Tiger Rag'!" He grins. "Crikey. That one's dangerous. So damn fast."

The fastest of all. Even she used to get out of breath.

"What was he called?" His face creases. "That trumpeter—Nick something or other."

"LaRocca."

Nick LaRocca—the world-famous trumpeter from New York. He used to make the girls go barmy. He'd smiled at her once, in the drafty backstage corridor: *Hey, kid!* he said, and winked as he was doing up his bow tie. She's had his picture above her bed ever since.

"La*Rocca*! That's it." He looks delighted. "Crazy man. Played like a lunatic."

They are on the edge of the dance floor now, where the noise isn't quite so loud. "So, then," he says, "tell me. An anarchist with a love for American jazz."

"But I'm not—" Their eyes catch, and something passes between them, a silent understanding. *This is all a game.*

"What's your cover?" he says, leaning close—close enough for her to smell the whiskey on his breath.

"Cover?"

"Day job."

"Oh, it's dancing. At the Palais. I'm a dance instructress there."

"Good cover." He smiles, then his forehead creases again, as though he's remembering something. "Not in that awful metal box thing, are you?"

She nods, feels the familiar wince of shame. "Afraid so, yes."

"Poor you."

The Pen. *That awful metal box.* Where she and Di sit, trapped, along with ten other girls, till they are hired, while the men without partners shark up and down, deciding if they want you, if you are worth their sixpence for a turn around the floor.

He leans back, as though to see her better. "You don't look like the sort of girl who's for hire."

Is he making fun of her again? It could be a compliment, but she can't be sure.

"I'm Ed, by the way," he says. "Terribly rude of me. Should have introduced myself before."

She hesitates.

"Right, then," he says with a grin. "You can tell me your name when I get the thumbscrews out later."

She laughs. The dance is almost finished. Over his shoulder she can see Gus standing on the edge of the floor, staring out at them forlornly, two drinks in his hands, and as the music comes to its close she is clumsy suddenly, aware of her body, of the parts where it is close to Ed's. She takes her hands down, steps back.

"Wait." He catches her wrist. "Don't go," he says. "At least, not before you've told me your name." His face has changed again. The smile has gone.

"It's Hettie," she says. Because whatever game they were playing is clearly over and, all told, she's not the sort of girl to lie.

"Hettie," he repeats, tightening his grip. Then he leans in close. "Don't worry," he says, "I won't give you away. I know how much these things matter. I want to blow things up, too."

Then he lets her go, and turns and walks, without stopping, without looking back, through the crush of people, across the floor, up the stairs, and out of the club.

The room wheels, a queasy kaleidoscope around her.

And here is Gus, crossing the floor toward her, sagging now, all jubilation spent. "Who was that, then? Someone you know?"

She shakes her head. But she can feel him still, this Ed, this man she doesn't know, a Chinese burn scalding her wrist.

"You looked as though you knew him," says Gus. He sounds aggrieved.

Hettie is furious suddenly. With poor, bald Gus. His awkward dancing and that half-cringing look on his face. And then, seeing that he sees this, she is sorry for him. "Perhaps I knew him," she says quietly. "Perhaps I met him before."

He seems a little appeased. When she doesn't say any more, he nods. "Lemonade?" he says, holding out her drink.

. . . .

"Evelyn."

Someone is calling her name.

"*Evelyn,* turn that bloody alarm off, would you? It's been racketing for an age."

Evelyn opens her eyes to darkness.

She reaches from under the blanket and gropes for the clock on her bedside chest. There's a sudden shocking silence, until Doreen grunts on the other side of the door. "*Thank* you."

Evelyn curls onto her side, her knuckles in her mouth, biting down, as Doreen's slippered footsteps retreat.

She was having the dream again.

She lies there for a moment more, then takes her fist away, sits up, and pulls the curtains aside. Thin light touches the face of her clock. The immovable realities of morning make themselves known. It is eight o'clock. It is Sunday, her mother's birthday, and she has to be in Oxfordshire by lunch.

Bloody hell.

In the bathroom, the pipes clank and creak. She hauls herself out of bed, the soles of her bare feet cold against the floor, and while Doreen hums and splashes next door she dresses in the half-light, choosing her least tatty blouse and her longest serge skirt, slipping into her stockings and shoes and pulling her cardigan tight.

The light is stronger by the time she has finished dressing; still, she avoids her reflection in the mirror on the wall.

Outside, in the scrubby patch of grass that passes for a garden, she pushes open the door of the damp lavatory and squats, shivering as she pees, before pulling the chain and stepping out. There's a battered packet of Gold Flakes in the pocket of her cardy and she coughs as she lights one up. She looks up at the trees, at their wet black bare branches latticing the lightening sky. As she stands there, a single, tired leaf detaches itself, twirling down onto the path. After a couple of drags she throws the cigarette onto the path beside the leaf and puts her foot over them both, grinding them into the ground at her feet.

In the kitchen, she boils water for her coffee, then pours the coarse grounds straight into her mug, taking it to the table, where she sits and lights another cigarette.

"Good morning." Doreen's smiling head appears around the door.

"Morning." She dumps two heaped spoonfuls of sugar into her cup and stirs.

"How's you?"

"A-one, darling." Evelyn salutes. "A-one."

"Breakfast?" Doreen disappears into the pantry to root around.

"God, no."

"Off to the country?"

"Paddington. Ten o'clock," says Evelyn.

Doreen emerges with bread and butter. "Better get a move on, then."

As much as Evelyn loves Doreen, as much as sharing this flat with her is the calmest, least troubling living arrangement that she can imagine, just now, just this morning, she really doesn't want to talk. She would rather sit here alone, with the remains of her dream wrapped around her like a stole against the gray morning air.

Doreen pulls out a chair and begins slicing bread. She is humming. Dressed to go out: wearing a pretty frock, her cheeks scrubbed and powdered, her hair up. Though it's hard to tell in this light, she may even be wearing rouge.

"What are you up to, anyway?" says Evelyn. "It's Sunday. Shouldn't you be in bed?"

Doreen looks up from her slicing. "I'm off today, too. The man, remember. I told you last week. He's promised to take me out of London. Said I was languishing in the smoke."

"Ah."

"I know he'll drag me up a godforsaken hill somewhere and make me look at a view. Still . . ." Doreen smiles, apologetic, flushed.

Evelyn crushes her stub in the ashtray. "You're right. I do have to get a move on." She pulls on her coat. "You look lovely. You are lovely. Have a lovely time. Say hello from me." She goes to the door, then turns back. "And wish me luck."

"Luck," says Doreen, grinning, holding out her buttery knife. "And remember, don't let the old girl get you down."

Evelyn stands beneath the clock, tapping her foot against the ground, scanning the Paddington crowd for her brother. No sign. She checks the departures board a last time and then heads off across the station, moving through wide slices of morning light. Irritating. It's irritating he should be late.

The engine is spitting ash when she arrives at the platform, and she just has time to jump on the last carriage before it pulls away. She walks the length of the swaying train, checking each compartment for her brother's tall, rangy shape, the welcome of his smile.

He is nowhere, though, and the train is full, but in the last carriage of second class she finds a compartment to herself.

Where the hell is he, then? They've had this arrangement for weeks.

She feels a brief, worried contraction on his behalf—but then pushes it away. She doesn't want to think about her brother. Her brother can more-than look after himself. She wants to think about her dream. About how it begins.

It begins like this: She's in the sitting room of the house she grew up in, and she is reading a book. The doorbell rings; she marks her place and stands, moving across the carpet to the door. Now all she has to do is turn the handle and step into the hall, and Fraser will be there, waiting for her on the other side. Her hand is over the doorknob, and she is touching it, can feel the cool brass of it sliding into her palm; she presses down, the door swings open, and—

She never gets any further than this.

These are things she remembers: Light, a morning in summer, Fraser beside her on the bed. The shifting patterns across his face.

The train rattles through a tunnel. When it emerges again into the unpromising morning, Evelyn catches sight of her reflection in the mirror above the seat. Because of the way it's angled, slightly downward, she can see her hair parting clearly. She hasn't seen her hair in daylight for a while, and in among her dark hairs are coarse white ones—too many now to count.

And here is the truth of things, she thinks. Even if the dream were real, if he could assemble himself from his thousand scattered parts; if she could open the door and find him standing before her, whole; he would be horrified: She will be thirty next month. She has betrayed him. She has become old.

Outside, London's suburbs slide on. She thinks of all the people, in all of the houses, waking to their gray mornings, their gray hairs, their gray lives.

We are comrades, she thinks, in grayness.

This is what remains.

When Evelyn wakes, there's a small boy on the knee of a large woman sitting on the seat in front of her. Both of them are staring. The child has a headful of orange curls and a round, pasty face. The woman turns immediately away, as if caught in the act of something shameful, but the child carries on looking, mouth open, with a thin silver slug trail from his nose to his chin. Three more people sit in the carriage, too: a man and two elderly women over by the door. Evelyn looks out the window. They are pulling away from a station. READING, halfway there.

"That lady's got no finger."

"Shh," says the woman with the child. "*Shh*, Charles."

Evelyn raises an eyebrow.

"Look out of the window, Charlie," says the woman in a high, strangled voice. "Can't you see the sheep?"

"*No*," says Charlie, wriggling and squirming on the woman's lap. "*Look*." He appeals to the man next to him. "Lady's got no *finger*." He is leaning forward now, the line of drool almost touching his mother's skirts.

Evelyn looks down at her hand. She has indeed got no finger. Or half a finger. Her left index finger ends in a smooth rounded stump just after the knuckle.

"Good gracious, Charlie," she says, looking across at him. "Do you know what? You're quite right." She waggles her stump in his direction. "Did you eat it while I was asleep?"

Charlie jumps back. The rest of the carriage takes a sharp breath, and then, as if in a game of Grandmother's Footsteps, everyone freezes their gaze straight ahead.

"You can touch it if you like," says Evelyn, leaning toward the little boy.

"Can I?" the boy whispers, reaching out.

"No!" manages his purple-faced mother, yanking Charlie back. *"Absolutely not."*

"Well," says Evelyn with a shrug. "Let me know if you change your mind."

Charlie slumps back onto his mother's lap. His eyes flicker from the stump to Evelyn's face and back again.

"And where are you going to, Charlie?" says Evelyn.

"Oxford," says Charlie, punch-drunk.

"Perfect. Me, too. You can wake me up when we arrive."

At Oxford, Evelyn waves good-bye to Charlie, changes trains, and takes the branch line that leads out to the village. She still half-expects to see her brother, emerging sleepily from farther up the train, but she is the only person to alight on the tiny platform. The small ticket window is shuttered up; a few straggling remnants of geraniums survive in the hanging baskets, the brittle skeletons of foxgloves in the beds. She walks out over the crossroads, where the butcher's and the post office face each other with blank-eyed Sunday expressions, and passes the low, five-housed terrace that leads to the green.

There was a boy who lived here, Thomas Lightfoot, the son of one of the men who worked for her parents; her brother played with him sometimes when they were children. She always liked his name. He was the first person she knew to die. She remembers her brother telling her, one sunny afternoon in London, in the spring of 1915. He had a wife and a child and he lived and died and all before he was twenty-three. She looks into Thomas's house as she passes now, sees a young woman through the window, back turned, scrubbing at something in the sink.

Evelyn walks on, her feet the only sound on the road, leaving the village behind, until she is passing open fields, where scattered crows pick at the stumps of the crop. The sun is out. She shuts her eyes against it, letting the light dance orange on her lids, and takes a lungful of pure air: glad, despite herself, to be out of London. Ahead of her, the low stone wall that marks the boundary of her parents' land comes into view; behind it are clusters of high firs, their branches dark against the bright sky.

She takes the road that leads behind the house, so she can approach without being seen. Opening the gate in the wall, she enters and stands on the lawn. In front of her is the house, seen from the side, its Cotswold stone deep golden in the sun. As she stands there, a black-clad maid comes running out of a side entrance and scoots around a tree trunk to where she is lost from view. Soon a small cloud of smoke rises into the air. Evelyn smiles: *Good for her.*

She sets off across the lawn, heading for the back of the house. The grass is surprisingly tall for November, and by the time she reaches the steps her shoes are soaked. She pushes the door open with her hip and swears under her breath as she reaches to unbuckle her shoes. They are suede, thinly strapped—the only vaguely ladylike pair she owns and a rare concession to her mother's tastes—but they are too wet, now, to wear. She kicks them off and takes them to the cupboard by the back door, where a familiar smell greets her: damp and cobwebs and the close winter-rubber smell of stored galoshes. She chucks her shoes in between the umbrella stand and an old tennis racket, considers for a moment the merits of wearing galoshes to lunch, thinks better of it, then pads in damp stockings on cold flags down the corridor past the kitchen. A quick glance through the interior window tells her that they are buzzing: a platoon of servants scurrying to and fro.

When she reaches the end of the corridor she stops, puts her hand to the wall.

Once she turns the corner, she will be in the main hall, at the end of which is the front door, and behind the front door is where Fraser stands in her dream. And she knows it is stupid, but still . . .

She closes her eyes, letting the feeling of his nearness fill her, fill her chest, her arms, the air before her face, until—

"*Evelyn.*"

She snaps open her eyes.

"*What* are you doing?" Her mother, trussed in cream and gold, rears before her. "*Where* are your shoes?"

"I"—Evelyn looks down at her stockings, clinging wetly to her toes—"I came in around the back. They're in the cupboard," she adds. "Under the stairs."

Her mother makes that noise: that special, back-of-the-throat click.

"Well, it won't do. And neither will that blouse. You look like a shopgirl. Is this your latest pose?"

"I—"

"Your *cousin* is here." Her mother leans forward, hissing. "And your old dresses are upstairs. Now *go at once and change.*" She steps back, narrowing her eyes. "Where is your brother?"

"I—don't know. We were supposed to come together but then—"

"But what?"

"But then he wasn't there."

"He wasn't there? Well, *where is he, then*?"

Evelyn shrugs, defeated. "I'm sorry, Mother. I really don't know."

Her mother pulls herself up to her full height—she is magnificent, really, even Evelyn has to admit—and steers her great Edwardian bosom into the wind.

Evelyn grits her teeth. Occasionally, just occasionally, she can muster the strength to pick her battles. "Mother?"

Her mother turns back toward her.

"Happy birthday."

Her mother nods once, swiftly, as though acknowledging something painful but necessary, like the removal of a tooth, then pushes open the door to the kitchen. As the door swings shut, the hubbub within dies. Her voice barks out an order—something about fish.

Evelyn turns back again and closes her eyes. But it is useless. The feeling has gone. She walks around the corner. The front door is there, ten feet of impassive wood, but behind its panels: nothing. No one is waiting for her on the other side. There is nothing but the brightness of the day and the dancing patterns made by the sun as it hits the bubbled glass.

. . . .

Jack pushes his breakfast plate away and stands, then, "I forgot this yesterday," he says, taking a squash from the bottom of his haversack. "It's a good-looking one, I think." He puts it in the middle of the table and shoulders his empty bag. "Right, then. See you tonight." He stays there a moment, as though there is something more he wanted to say.

Twenty-five years.

Ada stays seated. His wide-shouldered bulk fills her view. He is wearing his old Sunday clothes, allotment clothes, softened and worn with use. She can still see the young man in his silhouette. Just.

"Yes," she says. "See you tonight."

He nods, goes, the back door shuts behind him and his footsteps disappear down the path.

Twenty-five years tomorrow. Twenty-five years since they went into the round chapel and said their vows. The day was as warm as springtime as she walked the uneven stone path to the door. Then, in the cool darkness within, she gasped, as though she had been plunged into water. She could hardly breathe, she was laced in so tight. For a moment she had the sense she was alone, until she saw the shape of him, standing next to the minister at the top of the aisle. Slowly, she could make out their guests, too, scattered in the rows on either side. She set her course for Jack and tried to walk straight.

"All right, there." He took her hand in his and winked. "Here goes nothing, then."

The morning kitchen is dim, but the squash he left her is a bright orange-yellow color, its skin seeming to pulse with the memory of sun. It will be one of the last pickings before winter attacks the allotment with frost. It fairly hums with life.

She picks up the breakfast plates, puts them in the sink, and goes outside, filling the kettle from the pump in the yard, then coming in and putting it on the range to boil.

From the back window she can see the fences and gardens of seven houses. She knows the names of all the mothers in this street and the next, all the children, all the men, alive and dead. She has lived in this house for twenty-five years. Jack even carried her over the threshold, the neighbors gathered, laughing, delighted at the unexpected show.

When the kettle is whistling she pours half the water into the washing-up bowl and the rest into the teapot, then scrubs the congealed remains of breakfast from the plates. She'll use the squash tomorrow. A dinner to celebrate. Stew and dumplings. Buy some good meat to go in it. It pleases her, this plan.

When the plates are dried and stacked, she goes to move the squash from the middle of the table and put it in the pantry, and a sound comes from the front: a scuffling almost, as though an animal has come to the door. At first she thinks it must be Jack, come back for something he's forgotten. But he'd never come to the front. A neighbor, then? Ivy? But she wouldn't come to the front, either, not on a Sunday. Not on any day.

There's a knock, and Ada jumps, moving quickly, taking off her apron, smoothing her skirts, and then going to open the door.

"Yes?"

A young man stands on the step. Thin sandy hair, pale eyes, an attempt at a mustache struggling over his top lip. Where his fresh-shaved skin has met the morning air his face is raw. He looks surprised, as if it were she disturbing his peace, rather than the other way around. He takes off his hat, holding it close to his chest. "Morning, missus."

"Good morning."

His eyes flicker over her face and shoulder to the hall beyond. He clears his throat. "Do you live here, missus?"

"Yes."

"Then—w-would it be possible to trouble you for a minute?" He seems relieved when the words are out. What can he want? Then she sees the heavy bag at his feet. They are everywhere now, boys with bags like these: on every street corner, peddling everything from matches to bootlaces. Or begging. Knocking and asking for cast-off jackets or shoes.

"We don't need anything."

The boy stares. "Pardon, missus?"

"We don't need anything," she says, moving to close the door.

He steps forward, and there's panic in him. "Can I come in? Just for a minute? Please?" His voice is wheedling. He moves slightly, revealing his left arm beneath his jacket. She catches sight of the yellowed edge of a sling. She stays where she is; the door open a crack, the boy shifting his weight from foot to foot. Then something in her softens, and she steps back, opening the door a touch wider, letting the young man slide round.

The two of them are standing close. She can smell him, sour beneath the clean hard smell of the outside air. There are white flakes scattered over the shoulders of his jacket. They stand there for a couple of awkward seconds. She doesn't want to take him into the parlor, but one of them needs to move.

"In here, then."

He follows her into the kitchen. At the sink she turns to face him, arms across her chest. The boy hesitates at the door, seeming to wait for permission, and when she inclines her head slightly, he comes into the room in a series of odd, lurching movements. When he reaches the table he holds on to the back of the chair.

"Nice place you got here." He is out of breath, as though the small effort has exhausted him. "Nice and quiet." He stares at her as though he is expecting her to make whatever move has to be made.

"You'd better show me what you have," she says eventually.

"Sorry?"

"In your bag?"

"Oh, right." And he bends, lifting brown paper packages onto the table, each movement with a similar careful intensity, as if he cannot rely on his body to carry out the small commands he gives it. He reminds her of her son, when he was small: the jerky unpredictability of his limbs.

Shell shock.

One of those.

She looks at the well-thumbed packages in his grubby hands and knows that there will be nothing but cheap rubbish inside. "I'm sorry," she says. "We don't need anything after all."

He looks up at her, pale face tight, and nods briefly, as though acknowledging the futility of their exchange.

She waits for him to gather his things, but he makes no move to do so. Instead, he carries on, his voice rising a couple of desperate notches. "Dishcloths?" He opens one of the paper parcels to reveal a pile of loose-woven sandy cloths. "Everyone needs those."

"I'm fine for dishcloths, thanks."

"What about a tea towel?" He leans toward his bag.

The bag is large. They could be here all morning. "How much are the dishcloths, then?"

He jerks back up. "Dishcloths?" He looks surprised. "They're—tuppence. Tuppence for five."

"I'll take them. Five. That'll do. I'll just get my purse." She goes toward it but then realizes she is trapped—cannot get to her money without showing him where her purse is kept.

"Would it be all right if I had a smoke?" he says; that wheedling voice again. "Just a quick one? I'm fairly done up with the cold." He moves quickly, before she can say no, taking out a packet with his good arm, shaking a cigarette into his mouth, and reaching into his pocket for a light. "Like one?" He holds them out toward her.

"No, thank you."

He nods and puts the pack on the table. "Can I sit down?"

Something strange is hovering in the air between them, something beyond the brazenness of this boy. Ada feels a thin sense of dread. But she nods, slowly, and he pulls out a chair.

"Thanks." There's the scratch of a match against the box, the small fizz of the flame in the room.

She goes over to the fire, gives it a quick stoke, then walks quickly behind him, toward the drawer that contains her purse. She turns to see if he is watching, but he has his back to her, smoking in quick, jabbing drags. She slides the drawer open as soundlessly as possible, is lifting the purse out and searching inside when there's a sudden noise, a sort of strangled cry. She turns to see him staring at the air in front of him, curled forward, his whole body straining toward something she cannot see.

"Michael?" he says. Then his head jerks once, twice, as though caught in a fierce current, and is still.

Ada drops the purse back into the drawer. "What did you say?" She moves over to face him.

"Nothing," the boy flinches, shaking his head. "I never—I never said nothing."

"You did." She speaks slowly, though her heart is pounding. "I heard you."

"I never." He stands up. Stabs out his cigarette. Takes a couple of crablike steps away from her.

"You said 'Michael.'"

Then the boy begins to twitch, and the twitching spreads, until he is having a fit, almost, in awful spasms, and it is awful, and she should help him, but he is terrifying, and she cannot, and so she stands, stranded, until the fit has passed and he is still. It is a moment before she can speak.

"Why did you say 'Michael'?" She tries to make her voice light, easy. She wants to keep him here.

"I never," the boy says, snatching up his packages. "I never did. I just knocked on your door. I'm just selling stuff, aren't I?" And he holds his hopeless little packages out to her, before stuffing them back into his bag.

"You said 'Michael.' You knew him."

"No, I never." His head swings violently from side to side. "I don't know any Michael. No."

"Stop it," she says. "*Stop that.* You knew him. You knew my son."

But the swinging movement only gets faster and faster, until he takes a couple of steps toward her, grabs one of her hands in his and puts it on his head. "I'm sorry," he says, pressing her hand hard against his skull. "I'm sorry, missus." Then he stumbles from the room.

For a moment she is still, feeling the burning, buzzing touch of him against her. Then she runs, down the hall, out of the house, calling after him to stop.

But there is no one on the quiet Sunday street. The boy has disappeared.

As though he were never there at all.

. . . .

Just outside the small town of Saint-Pol-sur-Ternoise, near Agincourt, on the road that leads to the coast, from her room in the bar-

racks of the British Army, a young nurse watches a field ambulance arrive.

It is very odd; it is the fourth such ambulance she has seen today.

The nurse blows her nose. She has a cold and is out of sorts. She has been reading a letter from home, trying to stay as close as possible to the tiny little stove. The letter is from her fiancé. It is a perfectly pleasant letter, full of perfectly pleasant things. He is a perfectly pleasant man.

And yet.

She had her demob papers last week. One of the last left over here. She hadn't been in a rush to go. Soon she will have to face him. This small, uninspiring man who was wounded in 1918 and whom she tended, and felt sorry for, and agreed to marry when all of this was done.

Since then the nurse had fallen in love. A French captain. She met him at a social. He calls her "Chérie." It sounds a lot like the fruit.

She knew the French captain was married. He never lied about that. But he did promise he would leave his wife. Then, last week, when she was out shopping on her day off in Saint-Pol, the ugly, bruised little local town, she saw them: the whole family. Two dark-haired little children, the Frenchman, and his pretty young wife. All of them laughing, holding hands, jabbering away in a language she couldn't understand. She hid in a doorway, mortified, till they were gone.

The nurse puts down her letter and goes over to the window, pulling her cardigan closer against the cold. A coffin is being unloaded from the ambulance by four men. All the other ambulances today have held coffins, too. She watches as the men lift the plain box and carry it into the small chapel that went up last week. That, too, was strange, since no one said why they were building the little Nissen hut, or nailing a cross above the door. They've managed perfectly well without a chapel until now.

She wonders who is inside the box.

It is odd to see a coffin nowadays. Not like before, when they loaded and unloaded them like so many loaves of bread. The nurse reminds herself to ask around—find out what might have happened that four bodies have been brought here today.

When the ambulance has gone she goes back over to the stove and picks up the letter. Then puts it down again. She will write to him later. For now, she cannot think of what she might say.

. . . .

In her old bedroom at the very top of the house, Evelyn sits on the edge of the bed and smokes. She stares balefully at the rack of dresses in the open wardrobe in front of her, tipping the ash into her palm. Then she pulls open the window sash and throws the butt out.

In the distance she can see the blue-gray waters of the lake. It's not really a lake; she grew up calling it a lake, but really, from up here, it's an overgrown pond. She can just about make out the red roof of the two-room summerhouse that stands on the reedy little island in the middle. There's a fireplace in one of the rooms. She could sneak downstairs to the kitchen now and steal some wood, take the little rowing boat over there, light herself a fire, and spend the day hidden and reading. It wouldn't be the first time she's ducked out of a family gathering in the same way.

Rather that than enduring her mother's birthday lunch; rather that than her cousin Lottie and her tiny bites of food, her tiny nibbles of conversation from her tiny, tidy mouth.

It'll be ten times worse without her brother, too.

There's a knock at the door. She pulls herself back from the window as a uniformed young woman enters the room. Evelyn doesn't recognize her. She must be new. Her mother has always gone through maids like other people go through handkerchiefs.

"Yes?"

"I was sent to ask if you want any help."

"Help?"

The girl blushes. "With changing, miss."

"Oh, right. No. Thank you." She waves a hand. "Please tell my mother I'm more than capable of choosing a dress."

The girl, looking relieved, disappears, and from somewhere deep in the house a gong sounds, insistent and low. Evelyn goes to the wardrobe and runs her palm along the rack of dresses, which bob and jingle on their hangers, pretty, pliant as puppets. She plucks out the most muted dress she can find, a green silk day dress she hasn't worn for years, and pulls it over her head. It smells of must and mothballs. The color is all wrong, draining her already pale skin.

Bright chatter from the morning room spikes the hall as she makes her way down the wide main staircase of the house. She listens but cannot hear her brother's voice, and so she heads across the hall to the dining room instead. They'll all be in here soon enough.

Two young men, little more than boys, are putting the finishing touches to the place settings. They must be new, too, as she doesn't recognize either of them. They nod at her, then bow and turn and slide away.

She walks to the window, looking out to where the lawn slopes down to the lake. She can just see the little boat, tethered up against the deck, and conjures the damp wood and varnish smell of it, the friction of the oars against the heels of her palms.

"*Here* she is."

Evelyn turns to see her aunt Mary, Lottie's mother, plump and bejeweled, leading the march. She submits to being kissed, and then scrutinized at arm's length.

"You look tired. Are you still *working*?"

"Mmm." Evelyn nods.

Her aunt's face wrinkles. "And are you still in that *horrible* little flat?"

Despite herself, Evelyn smiles. "Yes, Aunt Mary," she concedes, detaching herself gently from her grip. "I'm afraid I am."

Then here they come, the rest of them, Uncle Alec, Cousin Lottie, Anthony—*Lord* Anthony—Lottie's husband. All of them pink and smug and smiling. No sign of her brother. For a brief moment she wonders if something is really wrong, but then they are upon her, and she steels herself, arranging her face to meet them, making the right noises as she progresses down the line, the sudden, reluctant welcoming committee to her mother's birthday lunch. Her father nods at her, chin set, eyes locked, as ever, somewhere to the left of her head. But next to him, her mother's gaze strafes her, head to toe. And in it is the inevitable, the illimitable disappointment. *Better,* says her expression, *but still not good enough.*

The family members take their places around the table, and the two young men reappear with the soup trolley, moving quietly around the room. Anthony takes the seat across from Evelyn. The space to his right is free.

"So," says Lottie, to Evelyn's left.

"So," says Evelyn, turning to her cousin, who is resplendent in yellow lace.

"How's London?" Lottie tilts her head to one side, as if London were a wayward old acquaintance she used to run around with but with whom she has lost touch. When she married, two years ago, Lottie moved from a short-lived flat share in Chelsea into Anthony's ugly, crenellated Victorian pile. She is a Lady now. *Lady Charlotte. Lady Lottie.* Evelyn can only guess at the fury that engendered in her own mother's breast.

"London seems well," says Evelyn, taking a sip of wine. "Bearing up. Shall I pass on your regards?"

Lottie gives an indulgent smile. "And are you still living with Doreen?"

They were all at the same school: Lottie, Evelyn, and Doreen—Evelyn and Doreen three years ahead, fused in friendship by their mutual loathing of everything the school stood for. When Evelyn inherited a small sum from her grandmother at the age of twenty-one, she bought a flat in Primrose Hill and invited Doreen to live in it, too. Her family couldn't have been more scandalized if she'd announced that the two of them were planning to keep a brothel.

"Still living with Doreen," says Evelyn.

"And is she still"—Lottie pauses delicately—"*unattached,* too?"

Evelyn meets her cousin's watery gaze. "Yes," she lies. "She is."

There's a flurry in the corridor. Her brother's voice. *Finally.* She looks up to see him handing his coat to one of the young men.

"Edward!"

"Sorry, Ma. Got caught up. Missed the train. You're looking divine."

As Ed embraces their mother, her skin registers pink delight. He's not looking his best—his jacket is creased, and his hair looks as though he wet it in the kitchen on the way through—yet, somehow, he carries it off. As the ripples from his arrival spread across the smiling room, Evelyn is struck, not for the first time, by her brother's easy grace, his seemingly limitless ability to dispense charm. If it were she, late for a family gathering in this way, she'd have been cut out of the will.

She is the last to be reached. When he leans in to kiss her he smells of alcohol—not fresh, but saturated, as though he's been drinking for a long time.

"I thought we were supposed to be coming down together?" she hisses into his ear.

"Sorry, Eves."

"Where've you been, anyway? You look like hell."

"Out." He shrugs.

She rolls her eyes as he takes his place diagonally across from hers. Her mother knows better than to seat her two children together. The young men resume wheeling the soup trolley and start to serve.

"And what about you?" Evelyn says, turning to Lottie. "Country life treating you well?"

Lottie picks up her spoon. "I *am* rather well, actually. I mean, in a manner of speaking. I've been a little sick, too."

"Excuse me a minute." Evelyn tries to catch her brother's eye, but he is already in conversation with Anthony, so she leans forward and steals a cigarette from his case on the table in front of him. She turns back reluctantly to Lottie. "What was that you said?"

"I'm going to have a child." Lottie's wispy little voice rises at the end of the line, as if she is unsure herself about this state of affairs.

Evelyn lights up.

"I'm going to have a child," says Lottie again, a little louder.

"I heard." Evelyn blows out a lungful of blue smoke. "Goodness me."

To her right, at the top of the table, she can feel without looking that her mother's eyes are upon her. She turns properly to Lottie, giving her mother the back of her head. "That's wonderful," she says, too loudly. "Congratulations. What do you think you'll have?"

"Excuse me?" Lottie looks confused.

"What do you think you'll have? Cannon fodder? Or the other kind? What shall we call it? Drawing room fodder? *Tedium* fodder?"

Lottie puts down her spoon. "I'm not sure I quite know what you mean."

"Boy," says Evelyn slowly, "or girl?"

On the other side of the table, as though alerted by some chivalrous instinct, Anthony and Ed look up. Anthony clears his throat and leans forward. "So. How are you, Evelyn old thing?"

He looks even plumper, thinks Evelyn, while Lottie looks thinner than ever. Perhaps they've got things confused and it's Anthony that's eating for two. For a brief, horrible moment an awful mental picture assails her: Lottie and Anthony, deep in the act. He smiles encouragingly. "Coming along with us on Thursday, then?"

"Thursday?"

"The burial. Westminster Abbey. Got a friend with a place on Whitehall," says Anthony. "Good view of the Cenotaph. We'll be having some drinks. You're most welcome."

The burial. Few drinks. He makes it sound like a trip to the West End.

"I'm not sure," she says. "I'm not really one for funerals."

Anthony looks at her, seeming to weigh the relative truth of this.

"Still fighting the good fight?" he says eventually. "What is it again? The labor exchange?"

"Pensions, actually," says Evelyn.

She knows that he knows this. They have had this conversation before.

"Pensions." He shakes his head. A loose flap of skin already hangs beneath his chin. Soon he will be one of those men with necks like farmyard fowl.

"I don't know how you stand it," chimes in Lottie, giggling, braver now that the reinforcements have arrived. "I'm sure I never could."

"I know why she does it." Anthony leans forward.

All the other conversations around the table appear to have ceased.

"And why's that?" says Evelyn.

"Men," Anthony cackles, leaning back in his seat. He slaps his leg and holds out his arms. "All of those *men.* Just the thing for a girl like you. Cripples, most of them—can't run away. Must be able to just pick them off." His lifts both his hands and mimes shooting. "Fish in a barrel, what?"

Lottie sniggers.

Evelyn feels her skin flare. "Hardly," she says. And finally, now, she manages to catch her brother's eye. He is smiling, but the look is a faded version of the one she has seen so often before: of mingled awe and humor, that dares her to go on. He looks tired, as though he hasn't the strength for whatever is about to unroll. And she is furious then, more furious with him than with the whole lot of them put together. "Hardly," she says again, a little louder this time.

"And why not?" Anthony smiles encouragingly.

"I think we all know where I stand on this."

"And where is that, Evelyn?" says her mother from the head of the table. "Where exactly is it that you *stand*?"

Evelyn turns toward her mother. "Why, on the shelf, of course."

"The shelf?" says Lottie.

"Yes. The shelf. You know the one. The dusty old shelf." She looks around the table, none of them quite looking at her, none of them quite looking away. "Haven't you heard of it? It's quite comfortable up here, I assure you. The view's not bad. You wouldn't understand, though, any of you." She lifts up her fish knife. "You're all on the other side. What's the opposite of the shelf? *In the mix?* In the cake mix? Look at Lottie." She waves her blade at her cousin, who gasps. "Isn't she lovely? She's a veritable little currant, wouldn't you say?"

"Evelyn," says her mother slowly.

She turns her head. "Yes, Mother?"

"Would you like an ashtray?"

She looks at the cigarette in her other hand, whose precarious length of ash is on the cusp of falling into her soup. One of the young men slips an ashtray under her arm.

"Evelyn?" repeats her mother.

"Yes?"

"When are you going to learn?"

"Learn what?" She crushes out her cigarette.

"Bitterness is simply not very attractive."

Evelyn opens her mouth. Closes it again.

When she was growing up, she used to imagine her mother as a savage with a blowpipe, dispensing poison darts. She never missed. One had to learn to duck.

She puts down her knife, lining it up with the side of her plate. *Bitter?*

She isn't bitter.

Bitter is the last thing she is.

. . . .

Ada is on the other side of the small park when she sees Jack heading home, his back slightly hunched, head bent against the cold. She has been out here longer than she intended, trying to calm herself, breathing in the chill afternoon air, walking looping circles of the patchy grass, one end to the other, avoiding the piles of fallen leaves. She sets off toward him now; if she walks fast enough she can catch up.

Jack lifts his head as she approaches. "Ada." He looks surprised. "What are you doing out here?"

"I just"—she tries a smile, but her cheeks are numb—"fancied a bit of air."

"You could have come to me." He adjusts his pack. "There was plenty to do on the allotment today."

Is his tone resentful? She cannot tell, but they fall in step beside each other anyway, crossing the park toward home. Ahead of them the sun is hanging low, in a sky the color of tin. Between them is the slight, constant distance—the distance they cannot name or broach. She takes a breath. "Jack?"

He slows, turning to her. "What's that?"

She comes to a stop, hands clenched in her pockets.

"What is it, Ada?" His eyes seek hers out. "What's wrong?"

"Earlier. Just after you left, a boy came. He knocked on the door."

His brow creases. "Who?"

"I don't know. He was—just one of those boys, selling things. Rubbish, most of it. But I—let him in."

"You let him in?"

"He was wounded," she says.

He nods, accepting this. "What was it? Did he do something to you?"

"No, nothing like that. No."

"Well, what then?"

She breathes in the scent of the leaves held in piles around them, the sweet beginnings of their decay. "There was something about him," she says. "Something not right. I said I'd buy some dishcloths, just to make him go. But when I went to fetch my purse, when I was standing in the corner . . . he said it."

"Said what?"

The old flicker of danger.

Their marriage is trip wired.

You can still stop.

"Michael," she says.

The fuse is lit. She can feel it, fizzing in the air between them.

Jack is suddenly very still. "He said 'Michael'?"

"Yes."

"Michael Hart?"

"Just 'Michael.'"

He takes a step away from her. "Well, who was he? Did he give you his name?"

"I didn't ask."

"What did he look like, then?"

A young couple walk past, heads bent toward each other. Ada waits until they have gone, and then speaks in a low, urgent voice. "He was small. Wounded. Had his left arm in a sling. I was standing with my hand on my purse and—he said 'Michael,' and when I turned around he was looking in front of him. As if he could see something."

The wind troubles the plane trees. A shower of leaves falls to the ground around their feet.

"He was sitting in your chair."

"What happened then?"

"Nothing."

"Nothing?"

"I asked him why he'd said it. He said I'd imagined it. He said I was wrong. But I wasn't wrong." She feels her heartbeat increase. "I heard it," she insists. "Plain as anything. 'Michael.' That's what he said."

Jack holds her gaze a moment more, his eyes searching, his face lined and reddish in the afternoon light. Then he looks away.

"What?" Ada says. "Say something. What?"

"It's cold." His voice is flat, controlled. "I'm going to go inside. Are you coming?"

She is silent, furious.

"Right, then." He walks a couple of paces away from her.

"Jack! He said his *name,* Jack."

He doesn't reply, only shakes his head before setting off across the park.

Ada takes one breath. Two. She looks up, to where the sun is setting, bleeding into one of those glorious autumn sunsets that stain the sky. Then she puts her head down and follows her husband inside.

. . . .

For some reason the light in their compartment doesn't work. Evelyn fiddles with it, growing increasingly cross, and then goes out into the corridor. The lights are off there, too. There's no sign of the conductor, but the next carriage is bright. The middle-aged man occupying it looks up from his crossword, catches her eye, and smiles out at her. Frowning, she turns and goes back to her carriage, and sits back down in the dark.

There isn't even any decent conversation to be had, since in front of her Ed sleeps, just as he has since the train left Oxford, with his mouth open and his face slack. From the look and the smell of him at lunch, he probably didn't sleep at all last night. She thrusts her hands into her pockets. It's freezing in here; the heat must be run on the electric, too. The fields beyond the window are blue in the fading light. She used to like this time of year. The run-up to Christmas. Now it makes her uneasy. There's nothing but darkness till spring.

The train jolts and Ed wakes. He rubs his face, giving her a vague, sleepy smile, before turning to look out of the window. "Where are we?"

She peers out. They haven't passed a station for a while. "No idea." Her breath is beginning to cloud in front of her face. "Sleep well, then?"

"Fine, thanks."

"So." She can't help it. "That was well played."

"What's that?" His eyes find hers.

"Turning up late."

He chuckles. "I wasn't really late though, was I? Not in the end."

"Where did you get to, anyway?"

"When?"

"This morning. You were supposed to meet me at ten, remember? Paddington Station? Under the clock?"

He yawns. "Sorry, Eves. Had a late one."

"Whereabouts?"

"About."

She thinks of what she did last night. Came back from a walk to

an empty flat, read till her fire gave out, and went to bed. He has
never invited her on one of his nights. She can only imagine where
he goes. She studies his silhouette in the gathering dark. The easy
lines of him. For years they were close. Now they rarely speak. She
wonders what goes on beneath the surface. Even the war has
hardly seemed to scar him; he barely appeared to miss a step, his
face and body unblemished—his charm, if anything, increased.

He turns back, catches her looking, and smiles, taking out his
cigarette case and offering one to her. "Funny," he says.

"What? Your night?"

"No. Well—" He rummages in his pocket for a light. "It was,
sort of, but that wasn't what I meant. I meant today."

"Really? What was funny about it?" She can't think of very
much that was funny at all.

"I remembered something, when I went for a smoke, in the
garden earlier on."

"And what was that?"

A flame flares, hollowing his face. She leans in to light her cigarette.

"The summerhouse. On the island," he says. "Remember when
you hid there for a night?"

"It was two actually." She feels a small sting of pride.

"You're right." He chuckles. "I remember now. They were beside themselves in the house."

"I was only eleven. There were hardly many places I could go."

"I knew you were there, though, all along."

"Really?"

"Yes."

"Well, why didn't you come sooner, then?"

"I thought you'd rather be on your own."

She pulls her coat tighter around her. "I'm sure I probably did."

She didn't use to mind, then, being on her own. She used to do
things like that all the time.

"Eves?"

"What?"

He stretches. "You all right, old thing?"

"Fine. Why? Shouldn't I be?"

"You just seemed a bit . . ."

"What?"

"I don't know. Just a bit—offish at lunch."

"*Offish?*" She bridles. "That's rich. Coming from you. You looked like death warmed up."

"Fair enough." He holds up his hands. There's a silence, then, "Come on, Eves," he says quietly. "How long can you be like this for?"

"*This?* What does 'this' mean?"

Someone passes in the corridor outside.

Am I bitter? Am I?

Tell me. Please. I'll listen to you.

Ed leans forward, and she can just see his eyes in the plummeting light, the halo of blue smoke around his head. "It's just—it's not a crime to be happy, you know."

She whistles. "Really? Gracious. What an incredibly facile thing to say."

"I'm sorry." He sits back. "Sorry, Eves. I suppose it is."

She turns away to the darkness thickening outside.

Easy.

Easy for you to say.

Everything's always so bloody easy for you.

. . . .

"Di?"

"Mmmm?"

"You awake?"

"Mmm."

There's no fire here in Di's small room, and Hettie's nose is cold.

"What's the time?" Di yawns, her voice thick with sleep.

"Don't know. But it's getting dark."

Di rolls onto her back, and Hettie has to shift. Her right arm is dead anyway. She dangles it down the side of the bed, and the blood returns in pricks and swells of pain. "I'll have to get back," she says. "My mum'll kill me if I'm late."

Their breath blooms in soft clouds above their heads.

"You could just stay here instead."

Hettie brings her arm back under the covers. It's tempting. Given the choice, she would. Stay here in Di's rooms above the furniture shop, where there are no mothers to look you up and down, or sniff out the traces of the night on your clothes.

"Can't. Told her I'd be back for dinner, didn't I?"

But she doesn't move. Not just yet. It's cozy under the covers, here in their body-scented warmth.

"It was a killing night." Di stretches, and Hettie can hear her smile.

They stayed for hours, and when they left it was morning: startled pigeons eyeing them, the men in overalls sprinkling the roads. Humphrey gave Di the money for a taxi, which they rode through half-deserted streets, upon which the pink autumn sun was just starting to rise.

There's a silence, then, "Humphrey wants me to go away with him," says Di.

"*What?*" Hettie turns so they are lying face-to-face. "When?"

"Next weekend. To a hotel."

It is too dark to see Di's expression, but Hettie feels something cold take possession of her insides. "And will you go?" she whispers.

"Yes," says Di. "I think I will."

Hettie's heart thuds into the space between them. They have spoken of this, endlessly. Of what it would mean, to finally be with a man. Not the boys they grew up with, or those they work with at the Palais, who are always trying to get them round the back of the stage door for a cigarette or something more. Not most of the men who hire them, in their shabby lounge suits, pressing themselves up, always that bit too tight. But a real man. Someone you liked. Two girls they know have done it already—one with a soldier in the war, who had to give the baby away, and another, Lucy, from the Palais, who did it with a man from Ealing, for five quid—the deposit on a sealskin coat.

It is here, then. The future, come for Di.

"But what if you . . . you know . . . what if you get caught out?"

"I won't," says Di, lightly. "I know what to do."

Hettie closes her eyes and sees a darkened hotel room, a bed. A girl and a man. But it is not Di and Humphrey inside.

I've been watching you for two whole minutes.

A sharp ache floods her. It frightens her, the force of it.

"What about you?" says Di. "Did you like Gus?"

Hettie opens her eyes, breathing out into the dark. She danced with Gus for hours in the end but can barely resurrect him now—the pieces of him indistinct, the shape of him too blurred. "He was"—she searches for the word—"nice."

"He liked you," says Di. "I could tell."

"Mmm."

There's a silence.

"I'd better go." Hettie slides reluctantly from the bed.

She slept in her dress, since it was freezing when they got back, and so has only to put her feet in her shoes and pull on her hat and coat. "I'll see you tomorrow, then."

They hug, briefly, Di's body warm and heavy, already slipping back into sleep.

Hettie makes her way to the door, where Di's dress is tossed carelessly over the back of a chair. She reaches for it, lifting a section of its black, diaphanous material, feeling the delicious crunch of sequins beneath her fingertips. Behind her, Di turns in the bed.

"Ta-ra, then," says Hettie, bringing her hand away.

Outside, she pulls her scarf tight, passing the plate-glass windows of the furniture shop, eerie in the twilight, its beds and chests and chairs in small, clannish arrangements, as if they didn't need humans to intrude in whatever dark business they are upon. At the end of the street she turns left onto the Goldhawk Road, where the tang of fish and the iron smell of meat, and the soft, sweet pall of vegetable decay still hang over the shuttered-up stalls. Then, hurrying now, she walks the low-housed streets that separate Shepherd's Bush from Hammersmith. She can see people sitting down to dinner, house lamps spilling light as curtains are closed against the coming night. Everything in its right and proper place, everything with that ordered, stultifying Hammersmithness that sometimes, in her darkest thoughts, makes her wish that the zeppelins had dropped their bombs here rather than carrying on to the East End.

It is because she doesn't fit. Ever since she can remember, she has felt it, this hunger for something more. Something that thought it would be happy with the job she used to have at Woolworth's, but wasn't, no matter how well paid or how smart the uniform she was given to wear. That thought it would be happy at the Palais, but instead feels she is just going in circles, round and round the floor. Di has it, too, this same desire; Hettie knows she does. But Di has transformed it into angles of the head and lowerings of the eyes that bring her men and money and means of escape. Hettie doesn't have those skills—doesn't know how to flatter and flirt, doesn't even know if she wants them—and so it stays inside her, this hunger, ragged and raw.

The smell of boiled mutton hits her as she opens the front door, and she checks herself in the mirror in the hall, sending up a small, silent prayer that the adventures of last night will not be written on her face.

"Het? Is that you?" Her mother's querulous voice comes from the kitchen.

"Coming." She takes off her hat and goes down the narrow passage to the kitchen. Her mother is standing by the stove. Her brother, Fred, is in shirtsleeves, leaning his elbows on the table, the windows are misted with cooking and heat, and a thick mutton smell lies over everything. Fred lifts his head, giving her the usual glassy-eyed, empty stare.

"Hello, Mum. Fred."

Her mother gives her the up-and-down. Fred murmurs hello.

"You're late."·

"Am I?"

"We were wondering where you'd got to."

"I was at Di's." She picks one foot up, touches it to the back of her opposite calf. "I said, remember?"

"You took your time coming home. We thought something might have happened. Didn't we, Fred?"

Hettie casts a look at her brother, who doesn't seem as though he's wondering much at all.

"Why didn't you come home earlier? I don't like to think of you coming through that market at night."

It is safer to say nothing.

"Take off your coat, then, and carry these over for me."

She does as she's told, taking two plates and putting one in front of her brother's place.

"Thanks," says Fred softly.

Thanks, he can manage. *Please* and *thank you,* and sometimes, if you're lucky and you ask him a direct question, *yes* or *no.* Anything else is a push. Ever since he came back from France. He speaks enough at night, though. Cries and shouts out the names of men in his sleep. She can hear him through the walls.

"So," says her mother, taking her seat, "shall we give a bit of thanks?"

Hettie rests her chin on her clasped hands.

This was what her father used to say. *Shall we give a bit of thanks, then?*

He was Irish, and kind, and he used to look at them sometimes in a startled way, as though astonished he should have washed up here, with this English wife and these English children, sharing a life with strangers masquerading as his kin.

Hettie closes her eyes, and for a flashing moment she is back in the club, as though it were projected there on the back of her eyelids—the Negro singer, the frenzy of the band, the way they all danced as if they truly didn't care.

"For what we are about to receive."

Are you here to dance, then?

"May the Lord make us truly grateful," mumble Hettie and her brother.

She opens her eyes. On the plate in front of her a piece of mutton sits beside a lump of marbled bubble, the lot of it surrounded by a pool of sticky gravy. Her mother makes her gravy on a Sunday night with the bones of the joint, so that by next Sunday dinner, having been eked out over the week, it mostly resembles what it mostly is: glue.

Her mother takes up her knife and fork and quiet descends, lumpy, Sunday silence, broken only by the squeak of knife and fork on plate.

"Saw that Alice at mass. The one you used to work with at Woolworth's."

Hettie pokes at her food.

I've been watching you for two whole minutes.

"Hettie?"

"What?" She looks up. Her mother is staring over at her.

"That Alice? The one whose sister died of the flu, same time as Dad?"

Hettie sees her father, lying on the bed. One day he was fine, the next he was dead, his skin shining and purple, a terrible blooming; the color of the heliotrope flowers in the garden out back. She misses him. He more than made up for her mum. "I remember," she says quietly.

"She's married. Expecting now."

"Oh." She knows what's coming.

"Says her job's coming up."

Her mother has never forgiven her for leaving the household goods section of Woolworth's, where she'd worked since she was fourteen, and taking the job at the Palais. It was as though she had bought a ticket for the next train to hell. Nonstop, no changes. *All the way down.* Her mother wasn't interested, or happy, or proud when Hettie told her how many other girls had gone for the job. *Five hundred, for eighty places,* whittled down in the course of a day. All she said was, *No respectable girl would be seen dead in a place like that.*

"I've got a job, thanks, Mum."

Her mother grunts.

Hettie pokes at her mutton with her fork.

"How's Di?"

"Fine." Hettie sighs. "Di's fine."

A well-rehearsed conversation:

But why's she got to live alone?

She doesn't live alone, Mum. Her landlady's in the room next door.

Still. There's something about it. It's not right, is it? Anything could happen.

There's no use in explaining that was the *point*; and if Hettie had her way she'd be living there, too.

She looks up at them: Her mother, thin hair pulled back in a bun, wearing the wraparound overall that Hettie hates, because it makes her look like what she is—a charwoman who has to go out every morning and clean other women's homes. The tidy little kitchen. And Fred, chewing, eyes glazed—so pale you can almost see the wall behind.

For this she has to give over half her pay. Fifteen shillings a week for this. On the table on a Monday night. Every week since her brother came back useless and her dad died and left them in the lurch. She'd be able to board at Di's for less. And have some money left over for clothes.

You're not one of those anarchists, are you?

They're not real, she thinks. Neither of them. Her mother or her brother. Neither is this kitchen. None of this is real.

I want to blow things up, too.

Hettie imagines an explosion, enormous, the house made rubble, the street in flames, the wide sky and stars above her, and walking out into the vastness with ashes fluttering in her hair.

"What?" says her mother.

"What?" says Hettie.

"You were smiling."

"Was I?"

Her mother's face darkens. "What's so funny?"

"Nothing," she says, shaking her head.

Then she looks down at her plate, and lifts a forkful of mutton to her mouth.

Day 2

....

Monday, November 8, 1920

In Saint-Pol-sur-Ternoise, just past midnight, Brigadier General Wyatt climbs down from a military car. He is the director of the Commonwealth War Graves Commission, the man charged with organizing the burial of the dead of the British Army. Beside him is his deputy, Colonel Gell. The men walk toward two soldiers standing guard in front of a makeshift hut. The more senior of the soldiers steps forward and salutes. "They're ready for you, sir."

"And have the selection parties gone?"

"Yes, sir, they have."

"And their arrivals were staggered as ordered?"

"Yes, sir, they were."

"Very good." Wyatt steps around the man and through the corrugated metal doorway. Beyond a small paraffin lamp, barely visible in the dim light, lie four stretchers. He stands, listening to the wind as it lifts and whistles through the sides of the hut. To his left, standing open and empty, its lid beside it on the ground, is the shell of a plain wooden coffin. On the stretchers before him are four shapes, each of them covered with a Union flag.

They are very small bundles. These cannot be bodies. These are just scraps of things; they look like little more than rags.

He is seized with the sense that something has gone terribly wrong.

But then he shakes his head. Of course they are not bodies. They have been in the ground for far too long for that.

He thinks of what has brought him to this spot, barely three weeks since the Cabinet's decision to go ahead: of the flurry of tele-grams; the brief, rushed meetings of the emergency selection com-mittee; the work it took to persuade a reluctant king that this might be a good idea.

He hopes it is. He very much hopes that they have judged the country right, and that, in four days' time, this will be seen to have been worth it, after all.

Outside, he hears one of the soldiers cough.

Wyatt gazes out over the stretchers as though to fix this moment in his mind. Then he closes his eyes and, very briefly, reaches out, touching his hand to one of the stretchers. He knocks on the wall of the hut, and the colonel steps inside. Without speaking, Wyatt indicates the stretcher he has touched. The two men lift the bundle, still wrapped in its sack, each end tied up with string, and lower it into the waiting coffin. They screw the lid in place and cover it with its tattered flag. Then they leave, climbing back into their regimental car, which backfires once, twice, into the night, and drive away.

. . . .

In the early hours, while the sky is still dark, two more men ap-proach the hut. They exchange salutes, and the guards stand aside.

The men see the closed coffin with the tattered flag draped across. They pause for a moment before it, and then move to the other stretchers, the three that were not picked. They lift the first and load it into the ambulance. Then they come for the second stretcher. Then the third.

A chaplain, roused from sleep, an army greatcoat thrown hastily over his robes, joins the men in the front of the ambulance. They drive south along the road leading to Albert. When they have been driving for twenty minutes or so they stop. By the side of the road is a large shell hole. The men came past here, earlier in the day, and marked the place.

They light a storm lamp and place it on the ground, where its flame illuminates a medium-sized hole, about ten feet wide. A sharp wind cuts across their faces. They are eager to be back inside, in bed. They slide the first sack into the hole. It hardly makes a sound as it falls. When all of the sacks are lying in the earth the chaplain climbs down from the vehicle. He stands beside the shell hole with his leather-covered Bible in his hand. The shapes of the sacks are just visible at the bottom of the pit. Standing at the lip of the hole, the wind whipping his hair across his forehead, he says a short prayer. When he has finished, the soldiers take up their shovels and hastily cover the bodies with earth. Then the three men climb back into the ambulance and drive away.

. . . .

Ada rises and dresses quickly, going over to the window and pulling the curtains wide. The street below is quiet, the sky brightening. It is early, and though Jack has left already, some of the last men are still making their way to work. The light of morning fills the room, finding familiar things to fall on, lifting the shadows of the night before.

She has hardly slept. All yesterday evening, she and Jack circled each other, and it seemed to her as though that boy were there still, in the room between them, as well as their son, Michael, his name echoing in the space, the first time it has been spoken in more than three years.

But there is something about standing here, in this ordinary light.

Perhaps she heard the boy wrong. Perhaps she heard only what she wanted to. It wouldn't be the first time.

Whatever the explanation, from the way he left, the boy isn't likely to come back.

She turns to the dresser, where there's a photograph of her and Jack, taken twenty-five years ago today. The pair of them are staring straight at the camera and laughing. She picks it up and brings it closer. It had been her idea to have it taken. In giddy spirits, straight after the ceremony, she'd dragged him into the studio on the High Road, where a fussy young man showed them into his back room and held things up for them to look at: a stuffed teddy, a feather duster, a bicycle horn. When he honked it they laughed out loud, as the camera exploded in a burst of light.

They look so young. She brushes the top of the dresser lightly with her sleeve and puts the photograph back. She remembers how she felt, walking up this street for the first time, toward their house: the future unrolling before them, waiting to be stepped into, sunlit, wide.

Twenty-five years of marriage. Of learning to live with someone. Learning to love them. Learning to bury the things they cannot bear to face.

It is Monday, and so, as she does every Monday, she strips the bed down. But today, before lifting the sheets, she stops, caught again by memory. They would spend whole mornings here, Sundays, when they should have been in church, his fingers twined in her hair, their legs wrapped around each other, speaking low. She gave birth in this bed, with a midwife from the next street. The shock of it. The astonishing, red-bawling jubilance of her son.

She turns, catching herself in the mirror. The sideways light from the window is not kind. What does he think, her husband, when he looks at her now? She puts her hands to her face, pulling it so that the heavy skin around her jaw tightens, briefly, before she allows it to fall.

What is wrong with her today? It is the anniversary, making her remember, keeping her from her work. She bundles the laundry into her arms and goes downstairs, filling the buckets at the pump in the yard, putting the sheets into the copper to boil. She makes up the starch, stirring it first with cold water, then hot, then rinsing the sheets, and turning them through the mangle. It's hard work, and as she turns the handle, another sudden memory assails her: her son, as a small boy, standing beside her, helping her, holding the sheets as straight as he can, while she turns the roller, feeding the sodden cotton through.

Michael.

It winds her, this memory.

After a moment, forcing herself to breathe again, she pushes it away.

. . . .

The queue is a long one this morning. Evelyn can see it as she passes the entrance to the Underground, all the way around the corner and halfway down the street. She needs to cut through the line to reach the back door of the office, so she pulls the brim of her hat down and lifts up the collar of her coat. "Excuse me."

A fair-haired man makes room to let her through, and she squeezes past him, shoulders hunched. She's relieved when she reaches the office door; sometimes some of the repeat visitors see her, and it doesn't do to be recognized in the street. She takes off her hat and coat and hangs them in the hall, then goes through to the cramped little kitchen. Despite the chill of the day, she opens the sticky window that gives out onto the courtyard at the back. For a moment, in the quiet, she thinks she must be the first one in, until she hears the door from the office open and Robin moving down the corridor toward her.

"Good morning." She turns to see Robin standing in the doorway, his broad frame encased in a tweed jacket and trousers, smiling, as though he knows something pleasant about what today might have in store.

Irritating. Immediately irritating.

"Good morning." She makes her voice as neutral as she can. There's little point making much of an effort. He is still quite new—has only been here a week or so. There have been many Robins. They come for a month, for two; sometimes, the sturdy ones, for as many as six, armed with their smiles and their good intentions, and then, after a month or two, they leave, defeated by the monotony, the misery, and the men. One of them lasted only a day, a small, red-faced man who'd been a teacher before the war. Someone had made him cry. As he was leaving, he turned at the door and told her she was a fool, that this was worse than being in France.

Robin picks up the battered kettle and leans over the sink to fill it. "Nice day," he says, nodding appreciatively at the open window. "Good and crisp."

"I'm not sure that you have enough time for that."

He looks surprised. "I suppose not." He puts the kettle down on the other side of the sink. "How are you this morning?"

He looks so fresh and rested. So *friendly*. He actually seems as though he'd like to know.

"Fine," she says. "I'm absolutely fine." She leaves him standing by the window, picks up her satchel, and makes her way into the small office, where the hunched shapes of the waiting men are visible outside. The first few in the queue are slumped on the ground, asleep most probably; they will have been there for hours. When she switches on the light those who are sitting on the ground haul themselves to their feet amid a general pushing and jostling about. She can hear their muffled expletives through the glass.

As Robin enters the room behind her, she checks she has everything she needs for the morning's work: pens and enough of each of the differently colored forms that she must fill in for each case, each comment, each complaint. Pink for officers, green for the other ranks. Then she looks at her watch. Three minutes to nine. She takes her bundle of keys from the top drawer of her desk and goes over to the door.

"Early," says Robin.

"Yes, well." She turns back to him. "Are you ready, or not?"

He maneuvers his tall frame around his desk, and when he's settled in his seat, salutes her. "Ready or not."

She rolls her eyes and opens the door.

There's a surge from the back, and some of the sleep-dazed men at the front topple, before regaining their balance. Evelyn steps out into the chill morning air. "Any men caught making a nuisance will be asked to leave or go to the back of the queue. Is that understood?"

A bit of heckling rumbles from farther down the line.

"Is that understood?"

The heckling quiets. A few sheepish *Yes, miss*es float toward her. Evelyn goes back to her desk, feeling the familiar tug of concern for this shabby bunch of men. But compassion is a swamp. It's better not to get stuck in it. Especially not at nine on a Monday morning. She'd never get through the week.

As her first man makes his way over toward her desk she gives him a swift look. *Amputee.* From the way his right trouser leg is pinned it looks as if it has been taken off all the way to the hip. There's no false leg; the stump was probably too small to fit against.

He takes his place on the seat before her. It's a game with her, to guess a man's rank before he speaks. In this post-khaki world, the extremes at either end of the scale are easy to spot, and have remained, so far as she can see, as rigid as they ever were, but the middle ground is different; it has not yet settled. The temporary gentlemen are the trickiest: those who were promoted from the ranks for their service in the field and are now stuck between society's strata. *Temporary gentlemen:* such a mean-spirited little phrase; still, it just about sums it up. This one, she is sure, is no gentleman, temporary or otherwise; from his dress and bearing, he is a private through and through.

She dips her head and takes out the first of her forms.

When her fourth man approaches the desk, she knows that he's trouble without looking twice. "You ready for me now, then?" he says, sitting down before her.

There's something about him, a confidence, a posture. *Officer?* His accent is indeterminate. She lines up the form against the side of her desk. *Rank?* Difficult to say; she can't call this one.

"Name?"

"Reginald Yates."

"Rank?"

"Second lieutenant, as was."

She writes "Reginald Yates" on the top of a pink form.

"And is this your first visit to the Ministry?"

"No," he snorts. "I'll say it's not."

He has a sharp face, brown hair greased tightly back from his forehead, and a neat mustache. It's difficult to tell his age. He could be twenty-five, but he could be ten years older. There's something restless, something bristling, about him. Evelyn is used, now, to assessing the potential danger that might come her way; a woman was attacked once, a year ago, by a man with a knife. Her last female colleague. The woman spent the night in hospital and never came back.

"I'm getting less," he says, extracting a packet of shag from his pocket and rolling himself a quick, expert cigarette.

She slides the ashtray in front of him. "Less money, you mean?"

"Yes." He lights up and blows smoke into the air between them.

"This happens I'm afraid, Mr. . . . Yates."

His eyes find hers through the smoke.

"May I ask what your injury was?"

"No, you may not."

At this, she sees that the sheen has come off his cockiness somewhat. "All right," she says. "That's up to you."

Buttocks then, or groin; those are the ones that never want to say.

He leans forward, jabbing the air with his finger as he speaks. "The only thing you need to know is I was on seventeen bob a week, and now I'm getting less." His accent, she notes, is slipping a little now.

"Well," says Evelyn, "you should know, Mr. . . . Yates, that for what the department calls second-grade injuries—and these are any injuries that do not include the loss of a limb—the payment drops after three years. Can I ask when the injury was sustained?"

"Nineteen seventeen."

She opens her hands. "There we are, then. I'm sorry, Mr. Yates. You're welcome to file an appeal."

The man spits a stray piece of tobacco out onto the floor. "Is that it?"

"That's it, I'm afraid."

"You're not going to tell me if I'm going to get more?"

Evelyn sighs. It astonishes her still that she is here, the mouthpiece for a committee that regards every claim as suspect, every man a malingerer, guilty until proven innocent, forced to plead for scraps from a government that has long since ceased to care.

"I'm sorry, Mr. Yates, but we're only a first port of call. If you wish to file an official complaint, then we are able to register that complaint and forward it on. You should have a date for reassessment, which will include a medical examination, within the month."

"Within the *maaanth*?" He leans forward, mimicking her accent. At this he is, she notes, not bad at all. "What about the benefits, then? How come if I'd stayed a private I'd be drawing more? *Land fit for heroes, is it?*"

He's right. In a way, the ex-privates are the lucky ones; they have been given a small unemployment benefit. No such benefit has been given to the commissioned classes; they are supposed to have friends, or means. Temporary gentlemen have come down to earth with a bump. He leans back in his chair, pointing his cigarette at her as though deciding whether to fire. "Fucking woman."

"Yes, well," she says. "I'm afraid unemployed women haven't been given any benefit, either."

He looks as though he could spit.

She shoots a quick look over to Robin, but he is deep in conversation with a redheaded man in front of him. Something the other man has said has made him laugh.

"I'm sorry, Mr. Yates," she says, turning back. "Now, if you'll—"

"How many kids you got at home, then?"

"That's none of your—"

"Five," he says. "I've got five." He coughs, then leans forward, lowering his voice. "You haven't got any, have you?"

She says nothing.

"Spinster, aren't you? I'll bet you're dry as a bone down there."

Whatever sympathy she may have had is long gone. She imagines hitting him, or stabbing him in his hand with her pen.

"I bet you love this, don't you? Up there on your high horse."

"Of course I do," she says, leaning back in her chair. "Do you want to know why?"

"Why?"

She leans forward again. "Because I'm a sadist."

He opens his mouth, then closes it again. "Bitch," he swears, under his breath, standing up, his chair legs scraping against the floor.

"That's right, Mr. Yates. I'm a sadistic bitch."

Then she reaches out a hand and, without looking up, puts the pink slip on the pile to be filed.

"*Next!*"

. . . .

Thick bars of morning light stripe Hettie's bed, touching the faces on the pictures above her, tacked in a careful arrangement on the wall: Vernon and Irene Castle in the middle of a fox-trot, Theda Bara, and, in a still from *Broken Blossoms,* Lillian Gish. Beside them are the Dixies, in a photo cut from the paper just before they left London: Billy Jones, Larry Shields, Emile Christian, Tony Spargo, and Nick LaRocca, brandishing his trumpet like a lethal weapon.

They all look happy this morning, grinning in the unexpected sun.

In the room behind her she can hear Fred getting ready to go out. Her mother has already gone to work, long before the light. Once Fred has gone the house will be hers for a few blessed hours till she has to leave for the Palais at twelve. She'll boil some water and have her bath. First, though, she wants to lie here, in this lovely bit of sun, and think about the man from Dalton's: *Ed.*

She closes her eyes and tries to conjure him. The smell of him. The way he danced. The way he talked, as though everything were a game: *Two minutes constitutes a lurk.*

No one has ever talked to her like that.

Behind her head Fred's wardrobe opens with a judder she can feel through the wall. Hettie snaps her eyes back open, defeated. She can't concentrate on anything good with her brother rooting around in there.

Fred woke her up again last night. It was just a few short shouts this time, and then he must have woken himself, because everything went quiet after that.

Clothes hangers clatter as he takes his jacket out. He gets dressed every morning and goes out, even though he hasn't anywhere to go. Hasn't got a job. Not since coming home from France, two years ago in December, just after their father died. For weeks after his demob, he didn't leave the house; he just sat there, in their father's armchair in the parlor. She would come back from work at Woolworth's and he would still be in the same position as when she had left. Often, the dim light and something about the way he sat made her think it *was* her dad, come back from the dead. It gave her the creeps. But Fred just stayed there, hour after hour, as if that old armchair might tell him where to get a job.

That was when she had to start handing over half her wages. And there was Fred, just sitting there, doing nothing about it at all.

He wasn't like that before. You couldn't shut him up. He was annoying. He took up room. He would spread his bicycle bits all over the kitchen table and tease her about her dance classes and her film cards. He worked at the lamp factory down at Brook Green with their dad. They both used to set off together in the morning on their bicycles. *Peas in a pod.* Sometimes after work he would go to the pub and come back singing, and their mum would pretend to be angry, but you could tell she wasn't really, because Fred was always her favorite. He had a girlfriend called Katy—who had hair so fair it was almost white and who smelled of pencil shavings since she worked at the stationer's down by the tube.

He could be kind, too. Once, when he came back on leave from

France, it was over Hettie's birthday, and he wrote and asked her what she wanted. She'd asked to go to the theater, and he bought tickets for Her Majesty's to see *Chu Chin Chow*. It was the first time she'd been to the West End, and the show was full of musical numbers and dancing and real animals on the stage. In the middle there was a zepp raid, and instead of going into the cellar with everyone else, they both went out on the street and shared a cigarette and watched the airships as they floated past in the late evening light, their bellies swollen like giant whales.

"Don't tell Mum." Fred had winked, as though they were in on it together, and she'd felt excited, and grown-up, and grateful for it all.

But the next time he came back from France he had changed. It was as though all of the noise and mess and life had been blasted out of him and only the empty, silent shell remained.

Hettie hears his footsteps pass her doorway now, his soft tread on the stair.

"Fred?" she calls out. He doesn't reply, and she slides out of bed, goes over to the door, and opens it.

He is standing halfway down the stairs.

She leans on the banister above him. "Going out, then?"

He nods, cringing, as if caught in the act of something shameful.

"Where you off?"

"I'm just—" He shrugs, clears his throat, turning his hat in his hands. "Going down to the labor exchange. To have a see what's what."

"Going to try to get a job?"

There's a horrible, stretched silence in which Fred's cheeks flare a painful-looking red. He seems about to say something—but busies himself instead with straightening the brim of his hat. "'Spect so," he says eventually. "Yes."

Then he puts his hat on and almost runs down the stairs.

Hettie goes back into her bedroom, closing the door behind her and leaning against it.

He doesn't go down to the labor exchange.

She saw him once, when he was out for one of his walks. Just shambling along, like an old man. He has become like those men from the Palais, the quiet ones: the ones who hire you and then shuffle around the floor, their silences like the thin skin on blisters, covering the things they cannot say.

Her eyes light on her dance dress, discarded by her bed.

If Fred got a job, at least she'd have a bit of money for clothes. Why can't he just move on?

Not just him. All of them. All of the ex-soldiers, standing, begging in the street, boards tied around their necks. All of them reminding you of something that you want to forget. It went on long enough. She grew up under it, like a great squatting thing, leaching all the color and joy from life.

She kicks her dance dress into the corner of the room.

The war's *over*. Why can't all of them just bloody well *move on*?

. . . .

"Morning, Mrs. H. What can I get for you today?"

The butcher boy's apron is red with wiped fingerprints. The smell in here is strong today, hitting Ada like a wall as she steps inside.

"What have you got that's good, then?"

"This liver's grand." The lad presses the purple meat with his finger, and a small puddle of blood oozes onto the silver tray beneath.

"I'll have some, and about half a pound of that beef."

"Right-o." The boy, whistling, turns around for his knife.

Ada takes her purse from her bag. There's a cage of ribs laid out on the counter in front of her, the whitened bone sticking out of one end of the marbled flesh. The heavy smell seems to increase. She looks away, out onto the street, to where the sun is striking the ground. Two women stand beneath the awning of the fishmonger's and a young man is walking past them, his head turned away from her.

The boy is slim and brown-haired. He looks like Michael. He looks like her son.

"Mrs. Hart?"

The butcher's boy is handing the parcels of wrapped meat over the counter. Ada doesn't take them. Instead, she rushes out onto the street. At first she can't see him but then catches sight of the back of his head, fifty yards in front of her on the other side of the road. He is walking briskly, his arms swinging at his sides. She shouts after him, but he is too far away and doesn't hear. A van makes its way up the road between them, cutting off her view with an advertisement: SUNLIGHT SOAP FOR MOTHER; a shy-looking girl in a blue pinafore and hat holds out a box of flakes. Ada weaves behind it. Her son is still there, walking steadily up the street in the sun, heading toward the park.

"Michael!" she calls, quickening her pace, but he seems to be moving faster than before. She tries to close the gap between them, keeping him in her sights. He looks well. She can see this, even from behind. He has both of his arms and both of his legs. He walks strongly and easily and his head is not bowed, and his hair is clipped just as it was the last day she saw him; and the sun is touching the tips of his ears, and whatever has happened to him, wherever he has been, he has come through it and is alive and well. She shouts his name again.

A small queue is gathered outside the grocer's, but she pushes her way through it, feeling heads whipping around to stare. Her heart is racing now, sweat breaking at her hairline, on her back, and it is difficult to catch her breath, but the gap between them stays the same. He must feel her behind him, because he seems to be varying his pace to hers, as though they are playing some kind of torturous game.

When he reaches the top of the street, she sees him hesitate, finally, standing beside the ironmonger's, as if deciding where to go, as if he is unsure, suddenly, of the way.

Turn left.

Go home.

He turns left, and she shouts after him as he disappears from view.

She lets herself slow a little, now that she knows he is heading home, but when she reaches the ironmonger's, she sees the road to her left is empty. Her son has disappeared. An old man comes down the street toward her, moving slowly, a boxer dog snuffling the pavement at his side.

"Excuse me?" She goes to him and grips his arm. "Did you see someone come up here?"

"What's that?"

"*Did you see someone* come this way? A boy? A young man?"

The old man, looking frightened, shakes his head. "No one, love. No."

She releases him and leans back against the wall, gathering her breath.

"You all right?"

"Yes." She nods. "Fine. I'm fine."

She pushes off, hurrying, heading up the street that skirts the park, her thoughts jagged. Then it comes to her, and she could almost cry with relief, because she realizes he must have been *running*, when he saw where he was, when he knew how close he was, he must have run the last distance home. And she wants to run, too, but makes herself walk; she doesn't want to be a hospital case when she reaches him, out of breath, unable to speak. Still, when she reaches the kitchen door she is shaking so much she needs both hands to turn the key.

Inside the house, everything is as she left it. The mangle in the corner, the air still heavy with heat and soap, the washing draped on the fireguard and hung on the dryer above her head. "Michael," she calls, her voice deadened by the damp air. Then louder, "Michael? Are you there?"

She lifts the damp sheets. Looks behind chairs in the parlor. Stands at the top of the cellar steps and calls down into the musty dark.

Upstairs, the bedroom she shares with Jack is empty. She steps onto the landing and waits, outside the door of Michael's old room, her heart hammering. Nothing but silence. Heavy silence. Thick. She pushes open the door with her hip.

The room is empty. She hesitates on the threshold, and then steps inside.

Months have passed since she has been in here. It is hard to breathe. She lifts the blanket and sees only unused sheets. She gets down on her hands and knees and stares at the empty air beneath his bed. Now there is only the wardrobe in the corner left. When she opens it, it smells woody, unused. There is nothing inside. Nothing but two empty hangers and a small cardboard box, tied tightly with string: a box tied so that no one would open it in a hurry; a box that hasn't been opened in years.

. . . .

Evelyn pushes Reginald Yates to the back of her mind and works steadily: each man a new piece of paper, each complaint copied down and registered on the correctly colored form. At a quarter to eleven she rings a bell and locks the door for a break. There's a groaning from the men outside. It's not too bad today, though. After the chill start the weather is mild, unseasonably so; the sun has been pouring through the front window of the office all morning, making the room stuffy. She could do with some air. She snatches her cardigan and cigarettes and pushes her way out into the dirty little courtyard at the back, where she leans against the wall and tips her head to the sky. Her neck is still sore from sleeping upright on the train last night. She puts her hand on her head and cricks it from side to side.

"Mind if I join you?"

She turns to see Robin in the doorway.

"I didn't know you smoked."

"I don't. I'm having a fresh-air break," he says with a smile. "If I'm not disturbing your peace?"

She shrugs.

Fresh-air break. Trust him to say something like that.

He takes a place against the wall beside her. "How are the troops, then?"

She lights up, blows out smoke, shrugs. "Same as ever."

There's a slight pause before he speaks. "I had rather an interesting one."

"Oh?"

"Someone I'd known a little, before the war."

"Really?" She looks up at him. "How?"

"We used to climb together."

"Climb? Climb what?"

"Mountains." He gives a brief, rueful smile. "We met in Wales. The hostel at Pen-y-Pass."

She takes a drag of her cigarette. "That must have been nice."

He either misses or ignores the sarcasm in her voice. "It was," he says. "We were there in 1912. Again in '13. We'd climb in the day and drink and talk at night. It sort of felt as though anything was possible." He is staring straight ahead, as if his past is somewhere there, hovering in front of him, instead of a scrappy courtyard and a soot-blackened wall. "He lost a leg," he says, "same as me."

She looks up at Robin, properly, for the first time. He isn't unattractive. Lots of people might even think him handsome. He is well built, with a broad body, a pleasant face. The sort of man that's made for mountain peaks. But there's something about him: his health, his *niceness*. The very idea of him exhausts her. She looks at her watch.

"Time to go back already?" He sounds disappointed.

"Yes." She rubs her cigarette out on the wall behind her and pushes past him, back to her desk.

. . . .

The cardboard box is beside her on the blanket. Ada isn't touching it, though. Her hands are in her lap. But they are itching and her head is buzzing as though a swarm of bees is trapped inside.

Why has she seen him again? Why now?

Is it her? Conjuring him? Making her mind play tricks?

No. It is that cold, stuttering boy.

Reaching out for her.

Scuttling like a crab across the floor.

She lifts her head. The room around her is empty; the only signs left of her son's habitation are the slight differences in color, the faint shadow of the paste Michael used to stick his football pictures to the wall. She puts her fingertips to them now, tracing their pattern.

Test me on the players. Go on, Mum.

Her son's twelve-year-old face, screwed tight with concentration, as he sits in the kitchen after school, uniform on, with the door open to the garden and the summer afternoon outside:

Parker,

Jonas,

McFadden,

Scott.

Clapton Orient. *The O's.*

Jack started taking Michael along to home games when he was six—his small hand clasped tight in his dad's—and neither of them ever missed one after that, not as far as she can remember, right until they stopped the football in 1915. By that time all of the first team had joined up. Their picture was on the front of the newspaper, smiling away in their uniforms. That was the year of Kitchener, his image plastered everywhere: omnibuses, tramcars, vans; his finger accusing you from every last patch of wall. YOUR COUNTRY NEEDS YOU! Wherever you moved, he held your gaze. Guilty. That's what he made you feel. She used to wonder how on earth they made it work.

At the last football match of the season all the players processed around the stadium, then walked down the High Road to show themselves off. Ada stood and watched with the rest of them, Michael in front of her, all of them waving and shouting themselves hoarse, cheering with the crowd.

The next day Jack found Michael down at the recruiting station, standing in the queue trying to join up. He pulled him out of the line by his ear and marched him up the road to their house. Michael was spitting. He couldn't understand why they were making him stay at home when he had the chance to fight alongside his heroes.

The rows they had, after that.

Once, when Michael had stormed out of the house, she went up to Jack, who was standing by the sink, staring out the window. She touched him on the arm and he jumped as though he'd been burned.

"What?"

"Perhaps we should let him go," she said. "The war will be over soon enough."

Her turned on her: *"You believe what you're told, do you? That the war will be over? With Kitchener's brave men?"*

His contempt shocked her. Because she did believe it. It was everywhere that summer—a growing feeling of optimism, of hope.

They were all training: Parker, Jonas, McFadden, Scott, and the rest of the Clapton O's. Joe White, Sam Lacock, and Arthur Gillies from their street—boys Michael had grown up with, just a little older than him. They and a million other young men were training, turning into the soldiers who would win the war.

The whole country was waiting that early, lovely summer of 1916, waiting for them to be ready, as though everyone was holding their breath.

The guns started in the last week of June. Ada could feel them from her Hackney kitchen, a sort of low booming, just on the edge of hearing, day and night for a week. Then they stopped. Half past seven in the morning, the first of July. She walked out onto the street of brown-bricked terraces, in the sudden silence of a mid-summer morning in which the sun was already high. Other women were out there, too. Ivy White was there. She crossed the street toward where Ada was standing. "That's it, then," she said. "Isn't it?"

She gripped Ada's hands in her own slick wet ones. They were covered in suds. "They'll be going over now, won't they? It's the end of the war."

But it wasn't the end. Jack was right. It was the beginning of something terrible and new. The papers printed the casualty lists, longer and longer each day. Ivy's son Joe was missing, pre-sumed killed. Ada would see her sometimes, at the end of the day, standing at the front window, looking out onto the street, expec-tantly, as if Joe were going to appear there, whistling on his way home.

Even Kitchener was killed. Drowned on his way to Russia. Sunk by a German mine.

Sometime at the end of that July she came home to find Michael sitting at the kitchen table, a newspaper open in front of him, his head in his hands.

"What is it?" she said. "What's wrong?"

He looked up at her, his face white, shoved the newspaper toward her, and went outside.

At first she couldn't see what he had been looking at. Then she saw the photograph: PRIVATE WILLIAM JONAS, CLAPTON ORIENT. His black hair was plastered down into a smart parting, his young face serious above the deep V of his strip. The paper said he had died in a trench alongside Sergeant McFadden. Beside his picture was a list of his football record: CENTER FORWARD—73 APPEAR-ANCES, 23 GOALS.

Outside, there was the sound of a ball being kicked angrily against the wall.

She went outside, the paper held in her fist. "Look," she said. "Look at me."

Michael carried on kicking.

"Aren't you glad you're here?" her voice was high, uncontrolled. She didn't care. "Aren't you glad your dad brought you home that day? That you're safe? It could have been you."

He stopped the ball beneath his foot, and turned on her.

"*Safe?*" her son spat. "There's no such thing, is there? Not for anyone, not anymore."

She went inside, sat down, and held her shaking hands in her lap.

He was right.

And she knew then it was coming. That it was coming for them all. It was like the Bible, the stories she remembered from child-hood, as though an order had been issued for all the boys to be killed.

The autumn came, the days began to shorten, and conscription began to take hold. She began to pray then—something she hadn't done in years. She prayed selfishly, frantically, for herself, for Michael, for the war to stop at her door. She didn't know who she was praying to, didn't know who was more powerful: a distant God, who may or may not be listening; the hungry war itself, growling, just beyond the gates; or Kitchener, his weather-faded face half-covered over by adverts for Ovaltine and cigarettes, but his finger still pointing, still accusing from beyond the grave.

Michael's birthday was February 20, 1917. The recruiting letter came in the first week of March.

The afternoon before he left for France, when he had finished his training and was home at the end of a week's leave, she knocked on the door of his room. He was packing the last of his things, his big bag and greatcoat already waiting in the hall. He had his haversack open in the middle of the floor, and laid out around him in a fan shape were bits of his kit. She walked around the neat half circle he had made. Toothbrush, soap and small towel, two spare bootlaces, mess tin, fork and spoon. The window was open, and pale sunshine was filling the room. He looked up at her, squinting in the light. "You inspecting me, Mum?"

"Might be."

He sat back on his heels. "Proper sergeant major you are."

She crouched down beside him and picked up a small sewing kit, turning it around in her hands. "They teach you to use this, then?"

"Just a bit."

She put it back in its place on the floor and went over and sat on the bed, watching her son. He was stronger-looking than when he'd left for his training. The soft, changing shapes of his boyhood were settling, the lines emerging of the man he would become. She watched his head as it bent and dipped, his long narrow back, the sunburned skin moving across the bone at the top of his spine. There was something hanging from his neck. "What's that?" she asked, pointing.

He looked up at her and then followed her gaze down. "It's my tag."

"Can I see?"

He brought it out of his shirtfront, stood up, and walked over to her. "That's my name," he said, pointing at the brown fiber disc. "My regiment there. And my number."

She stared at the number. Six digits. His pulse in the vein beside it, keeping time. Her son.

"You all right, Mum?"

"Grand." She nodded, tucking the tag back into his shirt, doing the button up.

He left in the morning, before the sun was fully up. They had offered to walk him to the station, but Michael hadn't wanted them to. They didn't argue. They just stood together at the door and watched as he shouldered his pack, then waved his funny, overladen silhouette off, his tin hat bumping against the back of his neck. He turned, once, at the bottom of the road, and lifted his arm in the brightening morning, before he disappeared from view.

A train passes on the tracks outside, making the windows rattle in their frames.

Ada reaches out and brings the box into her lap. She tries to pick at the knot, but it is stubborn, tied so tightly that she'll need something to open it with. She hesitates, briefly—but it is only brief, the hesitation, before she goes downstairs to fetch a knife.

. . . .

"Afternoon, lovely." Graham the doorman salutes Hettie with his good arm. "How's my favorite dancer, then? You on a double today?"

"'Fraid so." She leans into the little hutch where he sits by the door, oil heater on. It smells cozy—of warm wool and pipe. Graham is a fixture of the Palais. A brawny Cockney with an accent to match, he used to work on the railways before the war, and his stories are legion. It is said you can lose hours in his cubbyhole, emerge blinking in the light, and be ten years older, your youth stripped away:

One of the last to be called up.

Didn't want an old bugger like me.

Proud to lose it in the end.

Two days till the Armistice!

Saw it there, twitching on the ground. Hand still moving.

Knew it was mine from the tattoo on the wrist!

"Commiserations," says Graham.

"Need the money." Hettie shrugs.

"Don't we all. Hang on a sec." He reaches into his pocket and pulls out a tin, opens it and takes a tablet out. "Here you go." He passes it over the hatch toward her, a Nelson's meat lozenge, brown-red. "Keep your strength up." He winks. "Kept us going for hours, they did. Route marches. All the way 'cross France."

This is what he always says.

"Thanks," says Hettie, tucking it into her cardigan pocket. "I'll keep it for later."

This is what she always does. This is their little routine.

Does he suspect that she keeps the stinky little tablets only long enough to put them in the dressing room bin?

But it is their ritual, and she supposes it makes both of them feel good.

"I don't know how you girls do it," he says, shaking his head. "Dancing for hours. I really don't."

Hettie shrugs, as if to say, *What's to do?*, then pulls her cardy round her, heading down the long, unheated corridor to the strip-lit dressing room at the end. The scattered girls turn to greet her, and they exchange hellos as she hangs her corduroy bag on the rail. Those girls who are changed already are sitting, chattering, puffing on illicit cigarettes despite the NO SMOKING signs nailed to the walls.

The chilly Palais dressing room is one of the dubious perks of the job. It's not what you'd expect, though, from the ones out front, which are all decked out with Chinese wallpaper covered in pagodas and birds. The walls back here are just covered in paint, and a dismal green color at that. Some of the girls have scratched their initials into the plasterwork, which is already starting to peel. Some wit has even written a poem at knee height:

> *Beware old Grayson*
> *If he thinks that you're late, son*
> *He'll take behind and*
> *He'll give you what for.*

When Hettie first started, she had to have it explained it to her: Grayson, the thin-lipped floor manager whose hard line on tardiness is legendary, is rumored to live out with another man somewhere in Acton Town. The boys swear he's forever giving them lingering looks.

She takes off her cardy, blouse, and skirt, hangs them on the rail, and pulls on her dance dress, shivering in anticipation of the cold to come. Without the press of bodies that fill the Palais later in the week, the vast dance floor will be freezing. The management doesn't allow you to take your woollies inside, so the girls try all the tricks they can, sewing extra layers under their dresses, or wearing two pairs of stockings, but nothing much will work on a frigid Monday afternoon; your only hope is to be hired and keep moving so you don't have to sit still for long.

"Hey, Hettie!"

"Did you get in, then? Did you see it? Dalton's? Saturday night?"

She turns to see that a ring of girls has gathered behind her, their faces expectant; hungry animals, waiting for the scraps. "Yes, we did."

"So it's real, then?"

"It's real, all right. It's so hidden, though, you'd never know it was there."

The girls seem to exhale as one, and she can almost feel their breath alight on her, gilding her with their envy. She thinks of telling them about the dancers, about the way those people moved, as though they didn't care, but it's just too tricky to explain.

"And what about the band? Were they as good as the Dixies?"

"The band was *killing*."

"And Di's man? What's he like?"

"Smitten. And rich."

The girls sigh and draw away, back to the mirrors, their powder and cigarettes, giving last-minute adjustments to their faces, their hair. Hettie pulls her dance shoes out of her bag and sits down to buckle them on, warmed by a rare glow of satisfaction. She is envied for once. It may not be nice but it still feels good.

Di rushes in, just in time, pulling a face, whips off her coat, and changes at lightning speed, as the door opens and Grayson's head appears around it.

"Time, ladies." He claps his hands. "Out onto that floor." He puts his head into the room and sniffs theatrically. "And if I catch *any* of you smoking that'll be pay docked for a week."

The girls move out into the chilly corridor, Hettie and Di at the back, the boys coming out of the dressing room opposite. Twelve of them, all dressed in their suits, ready for the afternoon shift.

The usual mix of feelings compete in Hettie as the dancers pass through the big double doors onto the floor. There is no doubt that the Palais is spectacular. Everything out here is Chinese: the whole dance floor covered by a re-creation of a pagoda roof; painted glass and lacquer panels showing Chinese scenes are hung around; and the ceiling is supported by tall black columns, all of which are decorated in dazzling golden letters. In the middle of the floor is a miniature mountain, with a fountain running down its sides, and beneath one of the two smaller replica temples, the band is warming up.

The first time she saw the Palais was when she came down for her audition on a cold day in January. Parts of it were still roped off, then, and the sound of hammering and sawing formed a background to the thumping piano accompaniment as Grayson drilled the hopeful dancers in front of a severe-looking woman who barked out orders and culled the men and women from five hundred to eighty during the course of the day.

Even then, in the club's unfinished state, smelling of shavings and planed wood, you could feel it was going to be something special.

There were the adverts placed in all the local newspapers:

Palais de Danse

THE TALK OF LONDON!

Largest and most luxurious dancing palace in Europe!

Two jazz bands.

Lady and Gentleman Instructors.

Evening Dress Optional

Hettie used to cut them out of the paper and leave them on the kitchen table for her mother to read.

Six thousand people turned up that first weekend, and when Hettie stepped out onto the dance floor that first time, seeing the Palais in all its glory, it truly did seem like a palace.

But what Hettie soon came to realize was that none of its splendor was meant for the staff. It was all for the punters, for the ones who had paid their two and six. For Hettie and Di and the other dancers, the Pen waited. As it still waits.

They file in now, boys on one side, girls on the other, heads bowed as Grayson inspects the line for any cardigans or visible hankies, anyone slouching, any contraband cigarettes or knitting needles that might while away the dances that you spend unpicked. His gaze rakes them. *General Grayson:* That's what the boys call him, especially the ones who were out in France.

Twelve boys and twelve girls a shift.

Twenty dances in the afternoon (3–6) and twenty-five in the evening (8–12).

Sixpence a dance.

"Bloody freezing in here tonight," hisses Di, as Grayson stalks past.

Grayson stops. He turns, slowly, and Di looks down at her hands. But there's no time for reprimands since the heavy door is opening and the punters are streaming through; hundreds of them, even on a Monday night, heavy-footed on the sprung wooden floor.

The band makes a bit of a ragged start and the first few couples brave it out. It's always a waltz first at the beginning of the shift. Hettie surveys the scrappy scene, hands in her armpits against the cold. If people ever bother to wear evening dress to the Palais they definitely don't on a Monday, and the dance floor is a sludge of brown and black and gray, the men in lounge suits, the women mostly in blouses and skirts.

An upright matron trussed into a woolen two-piece is crossing the floor with a determined stride, heading toward the male Pen. Di nudges Hettie and giggles. "Here she is." Across the aisle, Simon Randall sits up straighter, spits surreptitiously onto his hand, and smooths down his hair. The woman stops before him, holding a ticket coyly in her hand. Simon, smirking, takes it and lets himself out. *Hired.* Simon is one of the most popular men, rented out two afternoons a week by this same woman at eleven shillings a time. Not including tips.

The crowd is scattered now, some of them sitting at tables, a few buying drinks from the little cabins around the sides of the floor. The cavernous room is filling up, the dance floor thickening, the band sounding stronger, the afternoon starting to find its shape.

Hettie's eye catches a tall man, moving slowly among the crowd on the other side of the floor, and she sits up, heart hammering. It looks like him, the man from Dalton's: Ed.

The Palais? I went there once.

She grips the rail. Would he come here looking for her?

The man steps out onto the dance floor, and she leans forward, the better to see. She's almost standing in her seat, but as he comes closer she sees it isn't him. This man, other than being tall, is nothing like him; this man has the hesitant, shuffling gait of the false-legged. You can tell them a mile off. You have to be careful with them; they can trample all over you and not even know.

"What was that about, then?" whispers Di.

"Nothing." Hettie, feeling cross, shakes her head.

But the man has had his attention caught and is making his way across the floor. She knows the look: a little vague, half-whistling through his teeth, as though he is pretending not to know how this business works. "Afternoon," he says, hands in his pockets.

"Good afternoon."

"How much is all this malarkey, then?"

"Sixpence," says Hettie.

"Sixpence?" The man looks aggrieved, his voice rising a notch. "But I've just paid two and six to get in."

"Come with a partner," Di chimes in, "if you don't want to pay."

The man flushes crimson.

Hettie feels immediately terrible. Her heart wilts, for him, for her, for the whole damn business. "You buy your ticket over there," she says gently, indicating the cabin to her left. "It's a fox-trot next."

The man swallows. "I'll come back," he says, "shall I?" His *Shall I?* is aggressive, daring her to say no.

"Yes." She smiles at him. "Please do."

The man walks stiffly away, as though if he bumped into anything he might break and he and his dignity smash all over the floor.

Di snorts. "That'll be fun."

"It's all right for you." Hettie turns on her. "I need the money. I haven't got a man who'll buy me things, have I?"

Di's mouth rounds into a surprised little *o*. "What's got into you, then? Get out on the wrong side of bed, did you?"

Hettie shrugs. She doesn't know why, but she's irritated with Di today. With the Palais. With all of it. The man is back, ticket in hand. She takes it from him, puts it in her pouch, and lets herself out through the small metal gate. And when she smiles at him, it's not just for show, because, really, heaven knows what it must take them, any of them, to come here alone.

She lifts her arms, opens her palms.

This is how it works: You are hired, and you dance. If you're nice to them, and they like the way you move, then they ask you for another, which means another sixpence, and so it goes. The management takes half your pay, so it pays to be nice.

The man's hands are clammy as he pulls her close. He smells of sweat and basements and clothes that need a wash. He's about as far from the man in Dalton's as it's possible to be.

That makes two of them, then.

The band strikes up, and they move out across the floor.

. . . .

By three the queue in front of the office is almost finished, and only five or six men are left. Evelyn sits back in her chair, stifling a yawn. The man at the front of the line is eyeing her, hesitant, moving very slightly from side to side, as though the ground is shifting beneath his feet.

Shell shock.

Private.

"Come in," she says. "Take a seat."

He perches on the chair in front of her.

"Name?"

"Rowan."

She unscrews her pen.

"Surname?"

"Hind."

It's such a lovely name that it stops her in her tracks. *Hind:* gilded and natural all at once. She glances up, finding herself looking more closely than she ordinarily would, searching for a corresponding beauty in his face. He is no beauty, though; too small for his demob suit, left arm in a filthy sling, he has the wizened, old-man look of those who have lived their lives skirting close to the edge. One of the ones who signed up for the grub.

"Rank?"

"Private, miss. As was."

Her pen scratches over the paper. The afternoon sun warms her cheek. Hopefully, by the time she finishes, there will still be enough light to walk home through the park. "And what can I do for you, Mr. . . . Hind?"

"I was just passing," he says. "And then I—I—"

She sits back. She is used to them: the stammerers, the stutterers. She can be patient when she wants to be; she can be kind. Rowan Hind's gaze drops, and he is silent for a moment. Then, "Your finger," he says, catching sight of it.

"Yes?"

"How did it go?" His pale eyes meet hers.

There is something strangely compelling about him, disarming; she decides to tell him the truth. "It was in a factory," she says.

"The war?"

She nods.

"Munitions?" he asks.

"Yes."

"Thought so." He looks pleased. "Canary, weren't you? You still got a bit of the yellow on your face."

"Have I?"

"Did it hurt, then? Must've hurt."

She looks down at the gap where the finger used to be, as the rest of her hand curls around it, a reflex, protective action. "It did," she says. "Though not at first."

At first she laughed. The astonishing sight of it: a finger. Her finger. Until a second before, attached to her hand. The strange, spacious moment before the blood burst out over her apron, her face. She remembers turning to the woman who was working on her left and seeing that her face, too, was spattered in blood. Then back to the machine, still stamping away, the finger inside it, the white tendon, stretched like glue. She remembers someone screaming. Then everything went black. By the time she came around she was bandaged and in an ambulance on the way to the hospital.

In front of her Mr. Hind is nodding away. "I saw that, too. Men lose their arm or leg, first few seconds they don't know their arse from their elbow. If you were a soldier"—he leans forward, conspiratorially—"you'd get a pension for life."

"Yes," she smiles ruefully. "Well."

She can see the man behind Rowan shuffling his feet.

"Was there a complaint?" she says. "Is that why you're here?"

He seems to think about this, then, "No," he says. "It's not that."

She waits for him to elaborate, but he simply sits there, staring at his hands.

"Are you working at the moment?"

"I'm working." He lifts his eyes. "Salesman. Yes."

"And how is that?"

He raises his thumb to his mouth, ·chewing a bit of skin at the side of his nail. "It's terrible," he says.

Of course it is. Do people like him, then, when he knocks at their doors? Traveling salesman? Little Mr. Hind?

"It's not that, though," he says. "It's something else."

"Yes?"

"I want to find my regiment. I want to find my captain. I didn't know where to look. . . . And then I was passing, and I saw the sign. I was in the Seventeenth Middlesex, you see, fighting with Camden men, during the war."

"I see." She takes a scrap of paper from her desk and reaches for her pen. It's not her job, but she can always go to the records office with her worker's pass. Can always bend the rules from time to time. "It shouldn't be too difficult. Providing, of course, that the man in question's still alive. Shall I take your address first?" She unscrews the lid from her pen.

"It's Eleven Grafton Street . . . Poplar." He leans toward her, watching her write.

"And your regiment?"

"Seventeenth Middlesex."

She writes this down. "And which years did you serve?"

"1916 until 1917."

"And 1917 is when you were invalided out?"

"Yes."

"And what was your injury?"

He hesitates. "My arm."

"I can see that." She waits for him to elaborate. "You can't use it?"

"No."

Again, he doesn't say any more. She feels a small flicker of irritation. "And your captain?"

"Yes."

"What was your captain's name?"

His face twitches. "It was Montfort," he says.

At first she thinks she has misheard.

"Captain Montfort." He leans forward, waiting for her to write.

She looks down, to where her pen is held in her hand, pressing into the paper. The ink is running unevenly into the little gray mar-

bled troughs and valleys. She lifts away the nib. "Captain Montfort?"

He nods.

"Well, I'm sorry." She sits back. "I'm afraid I can't help you with
that."

"What? Why?"

"We only deal with pensions here. Pensions and benefits. We
are not a missing persons bureau." She takes a slip from the pile
beside her, turns it onto the blank side, takes out a small, leather-
bound book, opens it, and copies out an address. She does everything slowly and carefully, keeping her pen as steady as she can. "I
imagine the best thing to do would be to contact the army directly.
All of the information is here."

He looks at the piece of paper in her hand as if the letters are
from a foreign alphabet. "But"—he looks up at her—"you said you
could do it. You just said you could help."

"I'm sorry. I was wrong."

He is studying her fixedly. He knows she is lying, she thinks.
She holds his gaze. His head starts to jerk.

"Mr. Hind?"

The jerks are rising in intensity, passing through his body, until
he is moving like a jack-in-the-box and his face is contorted, horrible. But she has seen these fits before. However awful, you can
do nothing but wait. She digs her nails into her palms and looks
away at the stained brown-carpeted floor at her feet.

"All right, old thing?"

She looks up to see that Robin is standing directly in front of
her, his hand on Rowan's shoulder. For a second she thinks he is
speaking to her. Then, "There, there." He speaks quietly, as though
calming an animal, his hand moving slowly up and down the smaller
man's back. "There." He looks enormous beside Rowan, rooted as
an oak. "There we are. That's it. There."

Slowly Rowan's fitting stops, and he regains his self-control, breathing hard. Robin moves a little way away from him, allowing him space, creating a triangle between Rowan, Evelyn, and himself. He thrusts his hands into his pockets. "All right there, old chap?"

Rowan nods, his eyes on the ground. "Yes, sir. Sorry, sir."

"There's nothing to apologize for," says Robin quietly. He looks at Evelyn. "Everything all right?"

"We're fine," she says, curtly. "Thank you."

"That's good, then." He gives her a quick look, then walks back to his desk. She watches him go, blood raging; they all try it, at one time or another. Telling her what to do. She hates nothing more. She has been here for two years; she is the longest-serving member of the staff. She turns back to see that Rowan is staring right at her.

"You," he says. He speaks slowly, as though pushing the words before him through something thicker than air. "You looked just like him, just then."

"And who is that?"

"The man," he says. "The man I want to see."

"Well," she says, passing the piece of paper over the desk toward him. "These are the people who will be able to tell you if—the man you're looking for is still alive."

. . . .

The coffin is loaded into military ambulance number 63638. Along-side it are six barrels of earth, from six different battlefields, one hundred sacks in all. The ambulance sets off on the long straight road that leads north to the coast. A military escort accompanies it: two cars in front and one behind. Four soldiers sit silently in each car, their hats held on their laps.

The land here, though still ravaged, looks more like countryside than the Somme, farther south. Here signs of life are returning to the farms. Here, even after everything, fields still look like fields—like land where something still may grow.

The convoy passes a farmer on his plow. The farmer looks up at the escort and the scarred old ambulance as they pass by. He returned to this farm just last year. He was wounded at Verdun and lost an eye, and was released back home, secretly relieved. An eye seemed a small price to pay for his life. But he left the farm to stay with his father-in-law in Burgundy after the German advance in 1918, after the Germans raced forward in that spring offensive and requisitioned his farmhouse, his cellar, and his lands. After they drank him dry, killed and ate his chickens—stunned by abundance, boys who had been starving behind the lines. After they got so drunk that he and his wife and children were woken by them, shouting in the courtyard, naked, reeling, their helmets held on their crotches, empty bottles of wine rolling around them on the ground. He knew then that it was over. That the Germans were finished. That the advance had been stalled by these drunken, starving boys.

These are some of the pictures he carries of the war. Now he only wants to be left alone. He wants to get through his plowing without disturbing any ordnance that may have been left here. He knows of many farmers who have lost limbs, or worse, trying to make the most of their fields.

He wonders briefly who the approaching cars carry: a foreign dignitary, perhaps? But he doesn't wonder long. He bends back to his work, hunched against the drizzle, against the gray skies, thinking of eating his dinner in front of the fire, sitting alongside his wife.

. . . .

In one fierce, clean movement, Ada slices through the knots, and with a small puff that looks like smoke, the string falls away.

On the top are Michael's letters to her and Jack, two thick piles of them, each held in place with another knotted piece of string. She lifts them out and puts them beside her on the bed. Not yet.

Lying beneath them is a smaller, loose collection of picture postcards. One is a picture of a church. Albert, it says, on the bottom right-hand corner. At the top of the bell tower is a statue of a woman with a baby, the woman holding the child in her outstretched arms, dangling it over the empty air. On the back, her son's handwriting:

The woman is the Virgin Mary.
She's been leaning like this for a couple of years.
They say if she falls then the war will be over.
Pray she falls when we're winning Mum!

It was the first card he sent her, after he arrived in France in 1917, and the day she received it, she had tacked it up on the kitchen wall. It made her uneasy, though; there was something about that woman, dangling over the empty air, holding on so desperately to her child, that reminded her of herself.

She had the same chart on her wall as everyone else she knew; it had come free with the *Daily Mail*, and the town of Albert was right in the middle of the British Zone, marked red on the map. She drew a circle around it. Now she could picture him somewhere at least, could look at the church—see something that he had seen. It sounded like a good English name, too: Albert, easy in the mouth, not like some of the other names on the chart: Ypres, Thiepval, Poperinghe. She wouldn't have had the first clue how to pronounce them.

She shuffles through the contents of the box. More postcards fall out from beneath that first: a picture of a river, and a riverbank, and picnicking people wearing summery clothes. THE SOMME, it says on the bottom. On the back of the postcard Michael had written, "It doesn't look much like this anymore!" She remembers what she did when this postcard came to the door: searched the faces on the riverbank, relieved when the French didn't look very different from the people at home.

The last picture is of the cobbled street of a town. Something is stuck faceup onto the back of it. She peels it carefully away; it is a photograph of Michael.

She remembers now: He sent it to her at the same time as the one that she has in the frame downstairs in the parlor, not long after he arrived. They must have been taken seconds from each other, and by the same photographer, because the same background—a painted wall—shows on each. He is not smiling here, though; his eyes are guarded and his edges are blurred, so that it is difficult to see where the wall ends and his uniform begins. She knows he must have moved as the shutter came down, and that this is the explanation for the way the photograph has turned out, but still, she doesn't like it. It is as though he is already moving into a future in which he doesn't exist.

Underneath are three smaller pieces of light brown card. These postcards have no pictures on them, and each of them reads the same, with printed writing ranged all the way down the left-hand side:

I am quite well.

I have been admitted into hospital

$\left\{ \begin{array}{l} sick \\ wounded \end{array} \right\}$ *and am going on well.*
and hope to be discharged soon.

I am being sent down to the base.

I have received your $\left\{ \begin{array}{l} letter \quad dated \ \underline{\qquad} \\ telegram \ " \qquad \underline{\qquad} \\ parcel \quad " \qquad \underline{\qquad} \end{array} \right.$

Letter follows at first opportunity.

I have received no letter from you

$\left\{ \begin{array}{l} \textit{lately} \\ \textit{for a long time.} \end{array} \right.$

The first two cards are from June 1917, from when he first went into battle. She remembers that they didn't receive a letter for over a week, and then these postcards came, one day after the other, with all of the phrases crossed out except one: *I am quite well.*

How relieved she had been to get these, however little they said.

When they finally printed casualty lists for his company, she fell on the newspaper, running her finger down the list, frantically searching for his name among the injured and killed. It wasn't there. Still, they had to wait a week for a proper letter from him. Meanwhile, she could read and try to understand what it meant: There had been fifty survivors from two hundred men.

And she knew then that, whatever her son had seen, it was something that took him somewhere far beyond her reach.

One more field service card remains in the box. This one is dated September 14, 1917. It came after two weeks of silence. Two weeks in which she had written to him four times. Two weeks in which every morning, when the mail came, she would run into the hall; in which every evening Jack would come into the kitchen, hat twisted in his fist, pretending that he wasn't looking to see if there was a letter propped up against the teapot for him to read. This card, too, read the same:

I am quite well.

It was the last that they heard from him: September 14, 1917. They scoured the papers, but this time there was nothing about his company. Nothing about any action they had been involved in, no clue.

At the bottom of the box is a letter in a small brown envelope. She takes it out and holds it in her hands. For something so heavy, it weighs nothing at all.

It arrived on a Monday in September, a day of late summer sun. She was hanging the sheets on the line. There were women out all the way along, doing the same, their gardens garlanded with flapping white. She hadn't heard the tap of the letter box, and when she came back into the dim hall, she could just make out the shape of a letter lying on the mat. She bent to pick it up and saw a French postmark and Jack's name in an official type. She dropped it on the floor and walked straight back outside.

There was the sun, hitting the whiteness of the sheets on her line, and all the way down the row of gardens, as though all the women of London were surrendering at once. Just in front of her was the rabbit hutch that Jack hadn't got around to fixing yet. She stared at the place where the hexagonal wires were ripped away from the gray unvarnished wood. A fox had come and torn them years ago. Next door's cat was sleeping beside it, lazy in a patch of warmth, its belly falling and rising in the sun.

The next thing she remembers is standing in the kitchen with the shadows lengthening around her, and Jack coming into the room. Holding the letter out toward her. Telling her to sit down.

"Don't open it," she said.

But he did. She watched his face as he read. His eyes as they moved along the page. Stop. Move back to the top. And in those tiny movements she felt her life, her future, contract and collapse.

"It's not true."

He put the letter on the table. Pushed it toward her.

She looked at her husband's hands, at the spray of black hairs on the tops of his fingers.

"You have to read it, Ada."
She took it from him.

```
Dear Mr. Hart,
I am very sorry to have to tell you that your
son Michael died of his wounds on the 17th Sep-
tember.
              Yours,
              —
```

These were the only words, struck into the page. Not even a name, just a signature at the bottom, but blurred, as though it were written in haste, or in rain.

"It's not true," she said, looking up at him. "I'd have known if it was. It's not true."

No further letter came—nothing to say how their son had died. Jack wrote to Michael's company, but they did not receive a reply. Everyone got two letters. Everyone Ada knew who had lost someone. Most got more than that: a letter from someone who had been there at the death, someone who had words of comfort, some small detail to impart.

She was sure there had been a mistake.

For a while afterward, people stopped her in the street to say how sorry they were. How he was a credit to her, as though in his dying he had somehow raised her stock. She just stood there while they talked, until they passed on again. She did not take out the mourning dress, packed in a chest at the end of her bed, folded with mothballs and tissue paper: the dress she wore last for her mother, twenty years ago.

Then, in the winter of 1918–19, when the war was over, the boys began to come home. They were everywhere suddenly, swarming the streets in their demob suits and fifteen-shilling coats.

It was as though some contrary magic had occurred, over in France, as though, far from dying, they had flourished over there in the boggy fields, bred themselves again from the fertile soil. The papers were rife with stories, with miracles: boys who had been hiding behind enemy lines, had walked the whole way home, who hadn't even known that the war had finished, but had turned up in the back garden ragged and filthy and in time for their tea.

That was when she saw him first: at the edge of a group of lads on a street corner, his back turned away from her. She went up to him; the boy turned, but it wasn't him and she hurried away, sweaty, shaking. Then a few days later, there he was, arm in arm with a girl in the park. She started after him, calling his name. It wasn't Michael. It kept happening. She would run after him, only stopping when she saw that it was someone else—someone the same height, with the same tilt of the head, or the same color hair. Or the boy she was following would simply disappear.

Often, restless in the night, she would leave Jack sleeping and climb into her son's bed instead, lying on the narrow mattress in the narrow room, with the football pictures stuck to the wall. She began to see him there. She would wake to find that he was with her, sitting on the bed. She was never surprised. She reached for him, but he put his hand out, as though to stop her. There were shadows moving about nearby.

"Who are they?" she said to him.

"Shhh." He put his finger to his lips and smiled. "Don't worry, Mum, they're all right. They're only dead."

One day, near the end of the long winter of 1918, a doctor came to the house. He gave her an injection, a quick scratch on her arm. When she came around she was back in the bedroom that she shared with Jack, and Jack was in the chair in the corner. The light was clear and cold. He came over and helped her to her feet.

"All right now," he said. It wasn't a question.

On their way downstairs they passed Michael's bedroom. The door was open, the room stripped bare. Only the blank spaces and darker borders showed where his football pictures had been; only the tiny flecks of the flour and water that he had used as a paste. She looked into the room and back to her husband.

"Where are his things?" Her tongue felt too large in her mouth.

"I've put them away." He looked guilty, but bullish, his jaw set tight.

She thought that she hated him then, but that even the hate seemed distant, as if it were happening to someone else—close, but hard to reach, as though trapped behind a pane of glass.

There's a sound downstairs: The back door opening. Jack's tread in the kitchen.

Ada scrabbles the postcards together. The sky outside the windows is dark.

"Ada?"

The meat, left at the butcher. The meal she was going to cook. The day, disappeared. Where has it gone? She pushes the letters down into the box, but the official letter she keeps out, slipping it into the pocket of her apron. She tries to tie the string, but her fingers are clumsy and it is useless and he is already on the stairs. She puts the box back in the wardrobe, closing it as quickly as she can. As Jack opens the door, she turns to him, smoothing down her hair.

"What are you doing?"

"Nothing—I—was . . . cleaning."

"In here?" He looks at her empty hands, back up to her face.

"Yes—I—haven't been in here for months, so . . . I thought I'd check, see if it needed anything." Her heart is going like the clappers.

"Cleaning with what?"

"Nothing, yet. I was—just about to start." She feels herself flush to the roots of her hair.

Jack looks around the room, takes in the bed, the scissors, still lying there. "Looks all right to me."

"Yes," she says. "It does." She edges past him, picks up the scissors, and hurries downstairs, grateful for the cool, dim kitchen. She can hear his footsteps overhead. She listens as he walks across their son's floor. It sounds like he is standing by the window, looking out. The footsteps turn, hesitate. Will he open the wardrobe? See that the box has been disturbed? She hardly dares breathe. But the footsteps cross the floor again, then leave the room and make their way downstairs. She reaches for the sink to hold herself up.

"Dark in here." He comes into the room behind her.

"Yes." She lights a match to the gas. Yellow light laps the walls.

"Is there nothing to eat?"

"I'm sorry. I—forgot."

"You forgot?"

"Sorry," she says, turning to him now. *Twenty-five years.* She waits for him to say something, to mention the date. But he doesn't.

"I'm going to go and get a piece of fish," he says eventually, steadily. "Would you like one, too?"

She nods, wretched.

He gets out his cap and puts it on. "I'll see you later, then."

She watches him go. Sinks to a chair. Thinks of the meat, left on the counter with the butcher's boy. What must he have thought of her, that boy, running away like that? She puts her head in her hands.

Some silly woman, getting old.

Running after ghosts.

Shouting for her dead son in the street.

. . . .

The field ambulance carrying the coffin passes the British and French troops who line the streets of Boulogne. It passes through the gates of the old town, then climbs the steep hill that overlooks the harbor, crossing the bridge that leads to the fortified entrance to the château and then under the great stone arch, drawing up in the courtyard, gravel crunching beneath its tires.

Eight soldiers carry the coffin along the twisting corridors of the old château, past waiting French troops, to the officers' mess in the old library, where a temporary chapelle ardente, *a burning chapel, has been ordained. The room has been decorated with flags and palms, its floor strewn with the yellow, orange, and red of autumn flowers and leaves.*

A guard of French soldiers comes to watch over the body. All are from the Eighth Regiment and all have recently been awarded the Légion d'honneur for their conduct in the war. Candles are lit. The soldiers stand on either side of the coffin with their arms reversed, rifles held against their shoulders. One of them, a thirty-year-old veteran, looks briefly at the coffin before casting his eyes to the ground. The box is raw and rough—not the coffin of one who will be buried in state. He wonders if this understatement is a peculiarly British thing.

The British he knew in the war were crazy, funny men. One, in particular, he will never forget. He met him one night in an estaminet, just behind the lines. The English boy was eating egg and fried potatoes. That was what they all asked for, the Tommies, all the time, in their funny, blunt voices: all they wanted: Egg and chips! Egg and chips! This one was small and stocky. When the French soldier sat down in front of him with his beer and the Tommy looked up, the solider knew, without speaking, what they would do to each other before too long. And they did: at the back of a ruined church, by ancient gravestones, their bellies full of beer and fried food.

Afterward, he remembers, the boy broke down and cried. And he

knew that it was not for what they had done, or not really, but for
everything else. And they held each other, between the crumbled
stones, until the birds started singing and a bleached sun rose over
the remains of the church.

That was in June 1916, just before the Somme.

The French soldier stares at the ground, blazing with color in the
candlelight. He looks at the leaves, at the flowers at his feet.

. . . .

Evelyn packs up her satchel, preoccupied. Robin spoke to her as
he left, and she replied to him, but now that he has gone, she cannot recall anything of what either of them said. She has even forgotten to be angry with him for earlier, for interfering with Rowan
Hind. She switches off the lights and stands there for a moment,
looking out. Through the window, the afternoon sky, which had
looked already black with the lights on, is revealed to be a high,
deepening blue.

Captain Montfort.

She conjures the man's face when he'd said the name. He'd
looked frightened. Plenty of men every day look frightened. Was
that a reason not to help him?

She pulls on her hat and coat and walks down the dark corridor,
stepping onto the street, bringing her keys up to lock the door.

"Evelyn?"

She lets out a yelp and jumps back, dropping the keys, her hand
at her throat. Robin is standing in the gloom of the doorway beside
her.

"For God's sake, you frightened me."

"Sorry. Didn't mean to." He bends toward her keys on the
ground. She realizes that he is going to try to pick them up.

She bends down and swipes them up herself. His face is pale in
the darkness. "Well?" she says eventually. "What is it? Have you

forgotten something? Do you need to get back in?" The light is fading. She wants to get to the park before it closes. She passes the keys through her fingers, making no effort to disguise the irritation in her voice.

"I—I just wanted to ask something."

"What was that?"

He steps forward. "I often go along to dances in the evening and—I wondered if. Well . . ." He straightens himself to his full height, his face looming above her. "Cut a long story and all that, I wondered if you'd like to come along. There's a rather good Dixie band on Thursday night. Armistice Day. Thought I might mark it, you know. Do something different. Not so bleak."

She takes a step away from him. "No," she says. "Thank you, Robin."

"Oh." The air leaves him. "Other plans?"

She waves her hand, something noncommittal.

He turns his hat over in his hands. "Then, some other time, perhaps?"

"Perhaps."

There's a silence. "Well. Can I?" He gestures toward the Underground. "Are you?"

"No. I'm walking home." She stops herself before mentioning the park. She doesn't want him walking along beside her with that leg; going out of his way. It occurs to her that she has no idea where he lives—that she knows next to nothing about him at all.

He nods. "Well, tomorrow, then."

"Tomorrow?"

"I meant, see you then," he says, and turns to go.

She buttons her coat all the way up to her neck. "Robin?"

"Yes?" He turns back toward her, his face expectant.

"In the future, I'll thank you not to interfere."

"I'm sorry?"

"My shell-shock case. Everything was in hand."

"Oh." He takes a pace toward her. "I'm sorry. It's just something that I learned in France. Sometimes it—well, it rather seems to work."

"I'd rather you didn't try out your methods on my time."

There's a silence. Beside them, on the pavement, people thicken in the home-going dusk. "Of course." He nods. "I'm sorry. Till to-morrow then."

She turns and walks away from him, out onto the main road, heading in the opposite direction, happy to put distance between them, to let herself be swallowed by the crowds. She pushes against the tide making for the tube and turns right, heading up Parkway. *Robin?* Asking her to a dance? It's almost funny. Perhaps he was just being kind, taking pity on her. Or, then again, perhaps he had it all planned; the conference of the afflicted: they could shuffle inexpertly around the dance floor together; she could talk about her missing finger, and he could talk about his missing leg. *Dance?* She hasn't danced for years. The thought is almost obscene.

Fewer people are about when she reaches the entrance to the park. The iron gates are open. They are supposed to shut at dusk, but dusk has come an hour earlier since the turning back of the clocks two weeks ago. But there is no sign of the park keeper yet. Once inside the gates, she takes big, greedy gulps of air, eyes hungry for the last of the light, walking fast up the steep rise of the hill, glad to be moving after the day spent sitting down, hands swinging by her sides, feeling the blood rise in her cheeks.

Her heart lifts when she reaches the top, and she sees that her bench is free, and that, apart from a few solitary dog walkers, scattered across the hill beneath, no one else is around. Below, on one of the many paths that lattice the grass, the lamplighter is moving slowly, a trail of small yellow fires in his wake. Low clouds race one another across the gunmetal sky. Despite the cold she pulls off her gloves and puts her palms down flat against the rough wood of the bench.

This is where they sat, here on this seat, she and Fraser, under a burning sky. Three years and four months ago; the seventh of July; three o'clock in the afternoon; the last hour that she spent with him on earth.

He'd written to her at the end of June 1917. He'd been told he was getting ten days at home, the first in months. He was lucky. Lots of leave had been canceled. There was something big coming up. He would have to go to Scotland to visit his family, but, depending on the trains, he would have two days at least at the end.

The thought of London, with all that khaki everywhere, is almost as grim as being here. Can we go somewhere else? Somewhere green? Somewhere neither of us know? I want to sit in a field with you by my side and look at nothing but green.

She was working in an office then, high above the Strand, ticking lists of goods from the docks against government orders, and it was as dull as death. Her nearest neighbor was a large, clammy woman one desk over who came in every day from Horsham and whose chatter consisted mainly of the minor calibrations of the train services that invariably made her late. The day she received Fraser's letter Evelyn went out on her lunch hour and bought a map at Stanford's, wedging it under the shipping orders where no one could see. Then she studied it all through the fetid afternoon, while flies threw themselves against the windowpanes, six floors up.

She searched the map, looking for nothing but green, and picked a village at random, somewhere between London and Hastings, on the main line from Victoria. On the map it was surrounded by fields, and there was a patch of deep blue, a lake or a reservoir, nearby, about the size of her little fingernail. Perhaps, she thought, they'd be able to swim.

When the day came, the weather was stifling. Far from escaping uniforms, the train was stuffed with men and their girls on their way to the sea. Fraser had arrived early in the morning, on the train from Edinburgh, just in time to cross London and meet her.

She had almost walked past him at the station. He caught her arm, and she stopped, stunned. She hardly recognized him. He looked ten years older. Hollow with exhaustion. She saw in a moment that the plan was ludicrous. She wished they'd simply decided to stay at home.

He slept the whole way down, his head lolling and rolling on his neck. Every so often a fractured singsong would break out, and he would wake with a start, and look frightened and confused, and then see her beside him, and squeeze her hand and smile, and go straight back to sleep. She pulled a book from her bag and tried to read, but the print jumbled before her eyes. There was something desperate behind the strained jollity in the smoky carriage, filled with the sour smell of khaki and bodies and heat. The window was stuck shut, and the train kept getting held up for no reason between stops. It made her even more uneasy, being held like that, in the middle of the country; the lushness of the green foliage pressing against the windows seemed shocking, sinister—the summer in full, unconscious bloom.

She shook Fraser awake as they arrived at the little station she had chosen and they bundled off the train, which pulled away in a cloud of smoke and steam, leaving them staring at each other in the silence, strangers suddenly, adrift.

He shook out a cigarette and lit it. "I was dreaming," he said eventually.

"Really? What of? Can I have one, too?"

He passed the cigarette over and lit another for himself. "I'm not sure." He shielded his eyes, looking out over the other side of the tracks to where fields stretched away into the distance. "Something nasty, I think."

The wheat was high. The sun was at its peak. The air was the temperature of blood. He was a tall man but looked shrunken, under the beating sun, diminished, in a way she had never seen before. She had the terrible conviction that something would hap-

pen to them, out here, in the countryside; that she wouldn't be able
to save him if anything did.

"We don't have any water," she said. Useless. How could they
have come away without any water? Or any food? She had had days
to plan this. What had she been thinking of, all those days? Now
they were out here, and they were unprepared, and something terrible was bound to happen to them, and coming here had been the
only thing he had said he wanted to do.

"Well," he said, turning to her with a smile, "at least if I die of
thirst I won't have to go back to France."

As they passed out of the station, he reached for her hand and
they walked together down a hill, past a small terrace of redbrick
cottages whose gardens were foaming with summer flowers. A cat
dozed in the shade of a tree. Somewhere in the distance church
bells chimed the quarter hour. At the bottom of the hill they turned
into a lane where the trees touched, forming a canopy overhead.
Their footsteps were the only sound on the cool earth road.

They were silent, but her mind was racing. It was always like
this: after all those letters—then having his real physical form before you and clamming up.

She sifted things and rejected them. It seemed impossible to
ask anything about France. She thought she should ask about Scotland, after his parents, how it had been to go home, but she couldn't
think of how to begin.

"Shall I get out the map?" she said eventually. "It's in my bag."
She had brought that at least.

When he turned to her, he looked distracted, as if she had inter-
rupted something important. "No," he said, shaking his head. "Let's
just keep on walking like this."

They carried on up the hill. The canopy was less thick now, and
whenever a slight breeze got up, the leaves above them would lift
and the ground dapple with sudden light. After a little while they
came to a gap in the trees, from where they could see out to the

country beyond, and she felt a cold sinking; the fields here were not green at all. They were yellow and bland and full of wheat.

"I—" She broke off. Fraser wasn't looking at her; he had his hand to his eyes. "There," he said, pointing.

She followed his finger to a copse of trees standing on a small rise, and they set off toward it. There was no room to walk together and so they walked single file, she behind. Every so often he would glance to the left or right, as if something might come at them from the wheat. Eventually, they reached the copse and sat down in the scrubby shade of an oak. He sat with his knees up, his elbows resting on them, staring out over the land, which dropped away a little below where they were sitting. He seemed to relax a fraction, now that they had reached the higher ground, and he lit another cigarette. She fished in the pocket of her cardigan for one of her own. In the fields below them, small birds began to swoop and dive. In the heat, her head was beginning to pound. "I'm sorry," she said.

He turned to her. "What for?"

He looked so exhausted that her stomach threatened to cave in.

"For this." She raised her arm vaguely toward the fields. "It's all a bit . . ." She wrinkled her nose.

He stared out. Nodded briefly. "Can we go back?"

"Where?"

"London."

"Already?"

"Yes."

"But why?" She could hear her voice, rising like a child's.

"Because this is wrong."

"I'm sorry," she said again.

"No. It's not your fault. I just— I'm just very tired. Can we please just go back?"

"Am I wrong?" The words were out before she could think of stopping them.

Fraser carried on looking down into the valley, as though there was something there that he couldn't quite make out, as though out in the blue of the distance was something he was struggling to see. "Don't ask me that," he said eventually. "That's not fair."

She could feel herself wanting to cry, feel it forcing its way up in her chest. She took a deep drag on her cigarette to push it down.

That night, back in London, she lay beside him, wide awake, his weight possessing the narrow bed. He had slept all the long way back on the train, and then again as soon as he had lain down in the flat, and slept through the long, hot afternoon, and then, too, as afternoon turned to evening and the sky turned a dusty navy he slept on—but she stayed awake, all through the short night, and when the sky began to lighten she got up and stood by the open window, listening to the birds. When the sun had been up for a while, she heard him stirring in the bed behind her.

"Evie?"

She stayed with her back to him. It was early morning, but already hot. Two children were playing in the street below, their high, thin voices drifting up on the still air.

"Evie?"

She turned to him.

"Come here." He had propped himself up on his elbows. His face was slack, generous with sleep. The pillow had imprinted creases on the side of his cheek. "Come here," he said again. "I'm sorry, Evie, please."

A breeze from the open window touched the back of her neck. She crossed the room toward him. He reached out, but she didn't go to his arms; instead she climbed back onto the bed and brought her legs up and curled around herself, their faces inches apart.

"I'm so sorry," he said again, pushing her hair away from her forehead and tucking it behind her ear. She saw there was a sheen of sweat, gathered in the slight depression above his top lip. She put her finger to that place, and then brought it back to her mouth. It tasted salty; the tang of sleep. He kissed her cheeks then, one after the other, and unbuttoned the shirt of her pajamas and held her there, against his chest. Then he closed his hand around her neck and brought her toward him.

"Is this all right?" he said to her.

"Yes," she said.

Afterward, she lay with her head on his chest. Above her she could hear the crackle of his cigarette paper as he inhaled. The sun was reaching into the room, touching and warming the soles of her feet, and the sounds of the morning traveled up from the street below, the way that sound travels in the summer—percussive, as though the city were a drum, tightened by heat.

They went outside then, to the park, and walked up the hill to this bench. There were two hours to go until he got his train. He closed his eyes and she watched them, flickering beneath the lids, the grooves underneath them a little less black.

"You know," he said, "the men out there. Sometimes I think they're ridiculous."

"Why?"

"Because they believe in things." He opened his eyes slowly and took her hand in his. "Even after everything they've been through. Most of them believe in God. They all believe in a life after death. I walk among them in the evenings and I know that none of them think they're going to be killed. None of them." His fingertip traced the line that curved across her palm. "They tell fortunes."

Something tightened in her. "Do they?" She tried to make her voice light. "And . . . what about you?"

"What do you mean?"

"Have you ever had your fortune told?"

"No," he said, sliding his hand into hers.

She knew he was lying, though.

The land around them was baked hard, the yellow-green of a London summer. The sun was at its height. She could feel him beside her and inside her, too; the memory of him, of the way they had been in the bed, just moments ago, as though it were still happening: his weight, the scrape of his cheek on hers. His mouth.

"Do you think the same?" she said, eventually. "That you won't be killed?"

"That's the thing," he said with a small laugh. "When it comes down to it I know I'm exactly the same as them."

He squeezed her hand, and she felt the life in him race through her.

And they sat, with the July sun overhead, and the smell of summer and the insects and the birds and the air full of buzzing, murmuring life.

"Billy, *Billy.*"

Evelyn opens her eyes. Her hands are freezing. A wind has picked up and is blowing the clouds across the low sky below. A yappy little dog is sniffling around her ankles. Behind her the owner calls out its name, his voice thin and high on the wind. "*Bil-ly.* Come on, Bill, boy. Time to go home."

The little dog scampers away and Evelyn stands, stamping her feet to get some feeling back into them. It is almost dark. She puts her hand to the bench for a moment more, feeling its coarse wood beneath her palm; then she turns her back and sets off down the hill.

Halfway down she stops, pulled up short again at the memory of Rowan Hind.

I want to find my captain.

Captain Montfort.

What did he want with her brother?

She feels a wave of queasy guilt. Pushes it down. There could easily be more than one Captain Montfort. If she helped every lost and hopeless case who ended up in front of her, she would never have any time for herself.

. . . .

When the punters have gone, when Hettie, Di, and the rest of the dancers have stood straight-backed before the eyes of Grayson ("No slouching during the anthem!") while the band play the last resounding chords of "God Save the King"; when the clock has struck twelve, the dancers are finally allowed to go home.

"Time, gentlemen, please!" shouts Simon Randall as the double doors to the dance floor swing shut behind them and they are free from Grayson's gaze. A few of the boys laugh and jostle one another. "If only." "What I wouldn't give for a pint right now."

The girls file wearily back into the dressing room, pull on cardigans, jumpers, and coats, stow dance shoes into bags. There's never much chatter at this time of night.

"How many?" says Di.

"Twenty." Hettie slumps down onto the wooden bench. Nine in the afternoon, eleven in the evening. Not bad for a Monday double shift. "What about you?"

"Twenty-four."

Hettie shrugs. She hardly ever beats Di at this.

"Day off tomorrow," says Di.

Hettie rouses the energy to nod, bending to unbuckle her dance shoes and rub her feet.

Di is fastening her coat, wrapping her scarf around her neck. "Come on, then. Walk down to the market with me?"

"Not tonight." Hettie shakes her head.

"Het?" Di sits down beside her, her pale, pretty face puckered with concern. "You're not cross with me, are you?"

Hettie looks up. How to explain? She feels a bit hollow, a bit empty with all of it. It's since Saturday. It's clear that Di is moving toward her future, while she is standing still. And who knows how long Di will even stay at the Palais for now?

"No." She shakes her head. "I'm—just tired."

"Come round tomorrow?" Di gets to her feet. "We can have a look round the shops."

"All right."

"Bye, then." Di pulls on her hat, and she and the other girls drift away, their voices echoing down the corridor and out into the night. Hettie stays there on the bench for a minute without moving, staring at the dusty tiles on the floor. She's slow tonight. Whatever borrowed luster she may have held from Saturday has faded long ago.

She is the last to leave, turning the lights off behind her and making her way down the darkened corridor to where Graham's light illuminates a small patch of floor. She's about to drag herself past without stopping, but remembers her pay and pops her head around the door of the hatch. Graham is there, back turned, sorting through some papers.

"Night, Graham."

"Hettie!" He turns, smiling, to face her. "Thought I'd missed you! Here you go." He rummages in his pocket, passing a lozenge through the hatch. "See you home," he says with a wink.

The sight of it turns her stomach. "No, thanks." She pushes it back over toward him. "You keep it. I couldn't. Not tonight. Have you got my envelope, please?"

He turns to the wooden pigeonholes in front of him. "Let's have a see, Burns. Here we go." He pulls it down and passes it across.

"Thanks, Graham."

She fingers the slim brown envelope. There will be three ten-shilling notes inside. Half of them expected on the kitchen table in half an hour.

She moves to go, but Graham puts up a finger. "Hang on a sec. There was something else."

He rummages in his pocket and takes out a piece of paper, folded in half. "Came for you earlier on," he says, pushing it through the hatch.

She stares at the folded paper without touching it. Her first thought is danger. Or death. Of her father. The swiftness with which awful things strike.

"Nice-sounding man," he says with another wink.

"Who?" She looks up at him.

He shrugs, and she opens it.

Thinking of blowing your cover.
Blackmail imminent.
Shall we meet to discuss terms?
Dalton's? Tuesday? Ten o'clock?

"Who was it?" She leans toward him, hands shaking. "Did they come here?"

Graham shakes his head. "Nah. Phoned it through, didn't they."

She looks back down at the page.

Thinking of blowing your cover.

Di? Playing a joke?

But Di didn't see him. Di didn't meet him. Di didn't hear how he talked.

Blackmail imminent.

This is how he talked.

"Very posh. Very polite. Asked if there was a Hettie there, and if I could pass this message on." His face creases with worry. "Hope I haven't upset you, love."

"No," she says, shaking her head, smiling. "You didn't upset me. Not at all." And she leans in and kisses him on his leathery, pipe-smelling cheek. "Thanks, Graham!"

"Blimey." He grins. "I'll try and rustle up another of those for tomorrow, then!"

"Night-night."

"Ta-ra, lovely."

Hettie almost skips down the corridor, through the door to the outside, to where the sky is high above her, and there are no clouds, only stars, scattered as though thrown from a generous hand.

Thinking of blowing your cover.

No one she knows talks like this.

And it is there, in the night air; she can taste it: the future, come for her, *finally*, fizzing like sherbet on her tongue.

. . . .

By the time Evelyn reaches home, she is frozen. She just about manages her key in the lock. The flat is silent and empty around her. She hauls herself up the stairs, disappointed. Doreen must be out again, with her man. They hardly see each other anymore. They just leave curt little messages—*Char?? 10 shillings. Your share!* Or *Milk?? Two bottles?? Disappeared.*

She lies down on her bed, hands plunged in the pockets of her old coat, too tired to light a fire, too cold to move. For a long while she just stays there, the branches of the tree outside casting strange shadows across the ceiling, the wavering yellow of the streetlamp the only light in the room. Listening to the sounds of the night as they rise and pass away: the chain in the bathroom of the flat next door; a couple walking quickly up the street, their voices low, until the woman laughs, sudden and bright; and then a motor cab, stopping only long enough to drop someone off, then turning in the street.

She rolls onto her side and props her head on her hand. She sees Rowan Hind again, almost as though he is in the room with her: his small face, his jerking body. His hanging, useless arm.

Captain Montfort.

Was it really her brother he wanted to see?

What could a private want with a captain, after all this time?

She hauls herself over to the fireplace and rakes over the coals, blowing on her hands to warm them, then twists paper in swift, tight rolls and packs them into the grate. There's a small stack of twigs by the scuttle, and she piles a few on top. As the fire catches, she takes out a cigarette and lights it, hugging her knees to her, staring into the flames.

It came in a short, simple letter from his father. Because they were unmarried, she had been told nothing, since she wasn't his next of kin.

But Fraser had told him something of her and had left them her address in case of this. They were very sorry not to have met her. They were very sorry that this was the first time that they had spoken. Perhaps they might meet her one day?

Two weeks. Two weeks in which she had believed the world still held him in it, in which she had been sending off letters, sitting in the stuffy office with the woman from Horsham, with the thought of him keeping her steady somehow as she moved about her life.

How was that possible? Why had some instinct not stopped her in her tracks?

So this is how it feels.

It felt like nothing, though; it felt numb, as though she had performed some trick—had stepped out of herself and was looking from outside. She read the letter again, trying to concentrate on every little detail.

At first, since there was no body—

She looked up. Tried to think about this. *No body.*

She looked back to the page.

At first, since there was no body, there had seemed to be hope.

But then two reports came from his company: He was seen, moving forward, and then a shell exploded right beside him. When the shell cleared he had disappeared.

Disappeared? What did that even mean? How was it possible to disappear? She had the strangest compulsion to laugh. She started to, and then the laugh stopped. She waited for something to take its place, but nothing came.

To walk forward.

To disappear.

To have no body anymore.

One instant there, the next blown to the four winds.

They were sorry, they wrote, *that there was no body. That there would be no burial place. But in time, they hoped, there would be somewhere to go.*

They were so polite. As though it were their fault that their son had vanished from the face of the earth.

She looked up at the things around her: the umbrella stand with the broken umbrella in it, the table that was scarred from when she and Doreen had carried it and bashed it on the doorway in the communal hall. Everything seemed like itself and not like itself at the same time; and she saw now, absolutely, what he had meant. Nothing here was real.

She had to make herself real.

The next day she went to the munitions factory and she asked for a job. They told her she could start on the shell casings on Monday. They gave her a uniform on the spot.

Day 3

Outside, the rain lands quietly, the slurry of dead leaves breaking its fall. Ada lies awake, thinking about her son. About wherever he lies in France and whether it's raining there.

Jack stirs beside her, and she closes her eyes, pretending to sleep as he stands and scratches and yawns. She can hear every tiny movement, every little grunt and groan as he pulls on socks, buttons his fly, tightens and pops his braces. When he has gone she turns onto her back and stares up at the ceiling, watching as the light fills the room.

Downstairs, Jack gathers himself for work. She hears his footsteps halt briefly, as though he is debating whether to call to wake her up. He doesn't. The door bangs shut behind him.

So, it's easier for them not to speak to each other, then.

It's always easier not to speak.

She gets out of bed and dresses, goes over to the wooden chest that stands at one end of the room, opens one of the drawers, and takes out the letter from beneath the pile of linen where she hid it last night. She slides it into the pocket of her cardigan. She will need it later; there is someone she needs to see.

. . . .

The office telephone was installed a couple of years ago, but it is supposed to be for emergencies only and is hardly ever used. Evelyn goes over to it and picks up the receiver. Most of the morning it has been drizzling, but it is raining now in earnest, fat greasy streaks racing one another to the bottom of the glass. Outside, the men hunker down under greatcoats and pieces of tarpaulin, their smoke a damp pall above their heads.

"Grim," says Robin, looking out.

"Yes. Well." They have been more awkward than ever with each other this morning, neither mentioning their exchange of last night. She puts the receiver to her ear and waits for the operator.

"Hello, caller?"

"Can you put me through to London 8142?"

The telephone rings and rings, and she listens to its hollow tone. She can feel her breath against the receiver, her blood swooshing like a distant tide; then, after what seems like a long time, the phone is picked up.

"Ed?"

"Eves?" Her brother sounds confused, thick with sleep. "Sorry, I was—just a bit tied up."

"How are you?" Her voice sounds stilted; she's no good at talking into these things.

"Fine. Just a bit of a cold but—fine."

"I was wondering"—she taps her fingers on the pale wood of her desk—"if you'd like to meet for lunch?"

To her right she hears Robin shift slightly in his seat.

"Today?" Her brother sounds surprised.

"Yes." She tries to make her voice bright. "Why not?" She hears him light a cigarette, cough. His voice is stronger when he speaks again. "Fine. Whereabouts?"

"I haven't got long, just an hour; there's a Lyons round the corner from the—"

"A *tea shop*?"

She could have predicted this. "All right. What about that little
French place, just between you and the park? La Fourchette. See
you there? Ten past one?"

"All right. See you there. Eves?"

"Yes."

"You all right, old thing?"

"Of course. I just—thought it would be nice."

"Right—well, see you then."

She puts the receiver back into its cradle and stands, her hand
resting on the mouthpiece. Behind her Robin clears his throat. She
looks over toward him. He gives her a halfhearted smile.

"Lunch date?"

"Oh no, it's—" She feels herself color.

"Sorry." He puts up a hand. "Too curious."

"Just my brother."

Outside, a man taps on the window, his breath clouding before
him, then gestures to the clock above Evelyn's head. It is high time
that she opened the door.

. . . .

"But who *is* he?"

They are sitting on Di's bed. Despite the fact that it's almost
lunchtime, and the day is doing its best to make its presence felt
behind the thin curtains, Di is still in her nightie, her black bob
mussed from sleep, smoking, leaning forward, peering down at
Hettie's note.

"I told you," says Hettie. "I met him at Dalton's. I danced with
him there."

"How many dances?"

"One."

"When?"

"Early on."

"Where was I, then?" Di looks suspicious.

"You were busy, with Humphrey."

"And where was Gus?"

"At the bar."

Di's eyes widen. She looks astonished that Hettie could be capable of such a thing. "But . . . why didn't you *tell* me?" she says, in a small, wounded voice.

"I don't know." Hettie shrugs. "I just—didn't have the chance."

Di stands up, goes over to her chest of drawers, rummages around on top of it, and brings over an old sardine can, balancing it on the yellow counterpane between them. "So . . . who is he, then?" she says again, tipping her ash into the remains of the oil.

"I don't know."

Di lets out her smoke in an incredulous little puff. "You don't *know*?"

"No." Hettie pushes the piece of paper away from her with a sigh. "You're right. I suppose I shouldn't go."

"I didn't say that, did I? Give it here. Let's have a see." Di picks it up and reads it haltingly. "'Thinking of blowing your cover.'" She looks up, a delicate eyebrow raised. "But what does that even *mean*?"

"He said . . ." Hettie plaits the tasseled edge of the bedspread. "That he thought I was an anarchist."

"An *anarchist*? What? Like in the papers? Like with the bombs?"

"He was joking. Or—at least I think he was."

"Oh. Well." Di hands the paper back to Hettie. "He sounds like a crackpot to me."

"He probably is."

"Is he handsome?"

Hettie nods. "But sort of different." She thinks of his face: his gray eyes, and then the way they cracked open when he smiled, as though it were all a mask, and someone else entirely was hiding underneath.

"*Different?*" Di looks unimpressed. "Is he rich?"

"I don't know. Well, he might be, but—"

"But what?"

"Oh, I don't know." It's impossible to explain. Hettie looks back down at the piece of paper in her hands.

Dalton's? Tuesday? Ten o'clock?

"I'm going to go."

"*Whaaat?*"

"I liked him. I'm going to go."

"You might well have *liked* him . . ." says Di, eyes like plates, "but what if he's one of those . . . *perverts?* Or a *white slave trader?*"

Hettie smiles.

"Or what if"—Di leans over the bed toward Hettie, speaking in a low voice—"he wants to take you to Limehouse and make you *smoke opium?*"

They both saw *Broken Blossoms*—saw it three times and could have seen it more—over in the big cinema on the Broadway, sitting there among the sucked oranges and the cracked peanut shells, swooning while Lillian Gish fell in love with the Chinaman and smoked opium and was battered by her father and died.

"He's not going to take me to Limehouse," says Hettie.

"How do you know?"

She reaches for Di's cigarette. "I don't."

I want to blow things up, too.

"I'm going," she says again, taking a deep, satisfying drag.

"You're mad!" Di squeals, shaking her head.

She may be. She may be mad. But she feels suddenly, gloriously free.

"Di?" she says.

"What?"

"Can I borrow something to wear?"

Di frowns.

"Please? I've only got my old dress. And it stinks."

"Why don't you wash it, then?"

"Di. *Please?*"

Di looks disgruntled, her bottom lip thrust out in a pout. "I thought we were going to the pictures tonight. *Mark of Zorro's* on in town."

This is not usually how it works. Not this way around. Di is the smaller one, the prettier one, the one the future wants. Di is the one who knows how to carve out her life—the one *things happen to*. Hettie can see her, wrestling with the turn that things have taken, trying to be nice.

"All right," she says eventually, grudgingly. "What do you want to borrow, then?"

But she knows. Hettie knows she knows. There is only one dress. She can see it, hanging up on the rail beside the bed, its dark beauty winking in the hazy, filtered morning light. Hettie can feel her need for it, twisting the pit of her stomach. "Can I . . . the black one?"

"The *black* one?" Di groans. "Oh, God."

"Please?"

"Oh, all right." She throws herself on her back on the bed, blowing a resigned smoke cloud up into the air.

"Really?" Hettie scrambles to her feet.

"Please." Di puts her hand over her eyes. "Don't ask me twice."

Hettie crosses the room and lifts the dress toward her. It is beautiful. Heavier even than she imagined, and she can feel it now, that skirt falling against her legs, moving against her as she dances with him around the floor.

"How are you going to get to Dalton's, then?"

Hettie turns around, the dress clutched against her. "I'll take the tube. I'm meeting him there at ten."

The words batter the air like typewriter keys.

`I'm meeting him there at ten.`

Incredible. Indelible. No way to take them back.

"You better look after it," says Di, sitting up and pointing, "or I'll have your guts for garters."

"I will. I promise I will." Hettie goes over to where her friend sits, leans down, and hugs her. "*Thanks, Di.*"

"Hmm."

Hettie folds the dress, stowing it carefully in her bag. "There's— something else," she says, straightening up.

Di raises an eyebrow.

"Something else I wanted to ask . . ."

. . . .

The restaurant is smaller than Evelyn remembered it, only five tables, each covered with the same simple cloths, a lit red candle at each. Only one of the tables is taken—an elegant woman and balding man, heads bent over their food. They look up as she comes in, and she can feel the small ripple as they register her presence— a woman here alone. She shakes out her umbrella and puts it in the stand by the door as the waiter comes to take her coat. A prix fixe menu is chalked up on the blackboard: steak and potatoes, tarte tatin.

She takes a seat facing the window and orders a carafe of wine. When it comes, she drinks half a glass quickly, staring out through the rain-spattered window to the street beyond. She lights a ciga- rette. The couple at the next table look across at her, and she feels their hot disapproval in the air. She puts her cigarette out, and then is furious with herself for doing so. When she lights it again it tastes foul.

The door opens, and Ed is there, holding a sodden newspaper above his head. He comes toward her, laughing. "Didn't look out of the window properly. Had no idea it was raining so bloody hard." Her brother looks pale. He's dressed carelessly in a jacket and badly knotted tie, as though he rolled out of bed and got ready in the dark. The dining couple look up. She sees the woman sit taller in her seat, lengthen her neck.

Ed, as usual, seems happily oblivious to the effect he causes. He always has been. At those awful country balls they were forced to attend when they were younger, the twittering girls would queue up for him, but he was always just as happy dancing with her. And, because she hated those occasions—the small talk, the inept dancing, the chaperones, the marriage market of it all—Evelyn was always profoundly grateful for that. He was the best dancer of the lot.

She twists her watch face around. It's already twenty past one. "I'm hungry. Shall we order now?"

"You order." He waves his hand as he sits. "I don't mind."

"Fine." She calls the waiter over and orders the steak for them both.

He leans over, takes a sip of her wine, and makes a face.

"Oh, come on, it's not that bad."

He lights up a cigarette. "So you say."

"So," she can't resist, "still in bed at eleven then?"

"Late night."

"Easy life."

"Whereas you, old thing, are a connoisseur of the rocky road." He picks up his glass. "This wine, for instance. Can we even *call* it wine?" He beckons to the waiter. "Can I see the wine list, please?"

The list is brought. His eyes flicker down the page. "I'll have the red burgundy," he says. "Ninety-four."

"Let me see." She snatches the menu back. "That's two pounds a bottle!"

"So?"

"So, I've got to get back to the office, Ed."

"Come *on*." He grins, leaning forward. "When do we ever do this?"

Not often enough. And whose fault is that?

The new bottle arrives, along with two fresh glasses. Ed indicates that she should taste. The waiter pours a little into her glass and she drinks, closing her eyes for a brief second. It is delicious. Of course it is. It costs two pounds. She nods to him, and the waiter pours a full glass for them both and moves away.

Evelyn takes another generous sip. It goes down so easily. Outside, rain is bouncing off the pavement and the soft hoods of the parked motorcars, battering the sodden geraniums in the flowerpots on either side of the door. She sits back in her seat. She is glad to see him, she thinks, her handsome brother. Glad to drink his two-pound bottle of wine. She could just stay here, in the warm cocoon of his ease, and drink this bottle down. Not go back into the rain to the dreary office, with dreary Robin and the rest of the dreary men.

"So?" His eyes look amused. "What's all this in aid of, then? Do I detect subterfuge?"

"Subterfuge?" She colors. "Not at all. I just—" She puts down her glass. "We don't do this enough anymore."

He raises his glass to her. "I'll drink to that."

Their glasses clink.

"I meant to ask you, actually," he says.

"What's that?"

"Are you going to come on Thursday?"

"Where to?"

"Anthony's invitation?"

She must look blank, because he shakes his head, smiling. "The

flat on Whitehall? For the ceremony? *The Unknown Warrior?* Do
you read the papers at all?"

"Oh." She wrinkles her nose. "I haven't thought about it much,
to tell you the truth."

"I thought we might go down together." He leans forward.
"Make up for Sunday. Leaving you at Paddington. Dereliction of
duty and all that."

"I don't know, Ed."

It makes her feel queasy somehow. A public burial, all the pomp
and state.

"Don't you think it's all a bit . . ."

"What?"

"Hypocritical? As though it could make a difference. Make people forget."

"I'm not sure it's to make people forget, Eves. Surely it's remembrance, if it's anything at all."

She shrugs. "Perhaps."

"Well, think about it. We could make a day of it. Go on somewhere afterward. I'd love to go with you, if you'd like."

She is pleased, despite herself. "All right," she says. "Thanks.
That might be nice."

The steaks arrive. Thin, peppered, cooked in cream, and steaming, with buttered potatoes on the side. She loads her fork, looks
up, and notices her brother isn't eating. "Aren't you hungry?"

He shrugs. "I might eat in a bit." He opens his cigarette case.
"Do you mind?"

"Not at all."

He smokes, and she eats, in companionable silence.

"So," he says, when she has nearly finished. "Come on, then.
What's this really all about?"

She has a last mouthful of steak and cream, then puts her fork
down on her plate. "I had a man," she says, "come to the office
yesterday."

"Yes?"

"I think he was looking for you."

"For me?"

"I think so, yes." She takes a piece of bread from the basket and crumbles it onto her plate. "His name was Rowan Hind."

Her brother's hand has stopped, quite still, the smoke from his cigarette traveling straight up into the air. She can hear the chink of glasses from the waiter behind her, the scrape of the forks of the diners to her left.

"Rowan Hind?"

"Yes." She puts the bread and cream in her mouth, chews, swallows.

He takes a sip of wine. There's a small groove in the middle of his brow. "What did he look like?"

"It's quite an unusual name."

"Yes, it is." He nods. "And I'm sure I'll remember. Remind me. Any distinguishing features?"

She leans back in her seat. "Not really." She takes a cigarette for herself. When she thinks about it, the most distinguishing thing about him was his utter ordinariness. "He was small. Hungry-looking. He'd been a private. Invalided out in '17."

"And what was the injury?"

"Lost the use of his arm." She lights up. "Though it was still there, in a sling. And nerves, I think, as well."

"Right." He nods. "Well. And why had he come to you?"

"To find you."

He looks astonished. "But that's ridiculous. How in hell did he know—?"

"He didn't. He had no idea I was your sister. It was chance that brought him to me."

"And did you tell him who you were?" He leans closer.

"Of course not. It would have been unethical."

She looks at her brother's face, at the vein beating at his temple, the skin stretched tight across his skull. "But I gave him the address of the records office. If they take pity on him then they might tell him where you live."

"Unlikely."

"Why?"

He sits back in his chair, takes a big swig of wine, and looks down at his steak; a thin skin has formed where the butter in the sauce has congealed. "Excuse me a minute." His napkin drops from his lap to the floor as he stands. She leans down to pick it up, and puts it beside his place.

"Have you finished?" The waiter is at her elbow.

"Yes, thank you."

"Would you like some dessert?"

"Thank you, no. I think we'll just have the bill."

She drums her fingers on the tablecloth and drinks down her glass of wine. There's still most of the bottle left. She pours herself another large glass. Behind her, she hears the sound of a lavatory flushing and a door shutting, and then Ed reappears, standing to her left, just behind her chair. "I should be getting back."

"I've asked for the bill," she says, twisting around, her tone conciliatory. "Sit down till then."

He sits. His leg is jiggling under the table, making the glasses judder and ring as though a tube train were passing underneath.

"Ed? Are you all right?"

"Fine." He cannot look her in the eye.

"It's just odd, isn't it?" She leans forward. "Why would a private be looking for you? After all this time?"

"How should I know?" he snaps. "Come on, Eves. You know what people are like. They get ideas. Fixed in their heads. They can't move on. Surely you of all people know that?"

That stings.

"What's that supposed to mean?"

He opens his hands. "Take it how you want."

"No. Tell me. What? What do you mean?"

He leans toward her. "Listen, Eves. Don't take this the wrong way, but you should try to get a bit of air round things. It might stop you brooding quite so much."

She can feel the familiar acid of anger seeping through her, turning the afternoon, curdling her steak and wine and cream. "Is that what I'm doing, then? Brooding? Forgive me. I wasn't aware."

He takes another swig of wine and then looks around for the waiter, his face clenched, impatient. He looks just like their father, suddenly. In a flash she sees him, in fifteen years, the same assurance, the complacency, the set of the jaw.

"What's the man doing? For *Christ's* sakes."

"Ed—"

"What?" He flings her a look.

"You're saying you have no recollection of a Rowan Hind?"

"I didn't say that. I've told you. The name. That's all. Do you know how many men I had under my command?"

She doesn't. "A hundred?"

He looks scornful. "Two hundred and fifty. There or thereabouts. You think I remember every little private that lost his mind?"

"I didn't say he lost his mind."

She feels something then, a chill, settle in the air between them.

Her brother pauses. "Eves," he says very quietly, "what exactly did you want to achieve by my coming here?"

"I—" She closes her mouth. She doesn't honestly know: information of some sort, but what?

"Leave it."

"What was that?"

"I said leave it. You're meddling."

"*Meddling?*"

"Yes. Eves. That *job*. It's depressing. For God's sake, it's not good for you. It's not as if you even *need* to work."

"No. Well. We don't all want to stay in bed till midday. Remind me again—what, other than order decent wines, is it that you actually *do*?"

His leg is jiggling again. He puts his hands on the table, as if to still it, but it doesn't work. "I'll pretend you didn't say that," he says. "Shall I?" The air between them feels tinder dry, as though it needs only a spark to set it alight.

She turns to see the waiter at her shoulder, the saucer and the bill in his hand. She goes to open her bag, but Ed is already up. He throws down some notes and leans across the table, his lips brushing lightly against her cheek. "I'll see you soon, Eves. I hope you'll be feeling better by then."

He is out the door by the time she has got to her feet.

. . . .

The shop is small and intimate, tucked away down a side street at the back of Shepherd's Bush. It smells of shaving foam and leather and men. It took a bit of persuasion, but eventually Hettie got it out of Di:

It doesn't look like much from the outside. You'd never know it was the place. It looks more like a barber's. Which is what it is.

Ignore the men—they'll stare at you, but don't take any notice. Just ask for Giovanni. Say I sent you. He's the best.

The decision was easy in the end.

It wasn't even easy; it was already made.

And now here she is, sitting in a cracked leather chair, in the middle of a busy barber's, with what looks like a white tablecloth tucked into her dress and an old Italian man wielding a pair of scissors behind her head.

"How much?" he says again. It sounds like *Howa mucha?*

Hettie can see two men standing, staring at her through the window. But she doesn't care. *She doesn't care.*

"All of it," she says.

He walks around her, a full half circle, lifting hanks of hair and letting them fall. "All. Of. It," he repeats to himself as he walks, then comes to a stop. "You have beautiful hair," he says, his eyes finding hers. "But it looks terrible. You look like a horse."

"I know," says Hettie. "That's why I want it cut."

"Not a horse." He corrects himself. "Little horse."

He lifts a handful and holds up his scissors. The blades flash in the afternoon sun.

"This will be a pleasure," he says.

Snip!

He holds the first hank in his hand. A trophy. A severed pony's tail. For a moment, she is horrified. For a moment, she expects there to be blood.

Snip!

She sees her mother.

Snip!

Your father! Your father loved your hair.

Snip!

She sees her dad, the lines on his face. The way they softened when he smiled.

Snip!

Sorry, Dad.

Snip!

I'm so sorry that you died.

Snip!

Filthy little flapper.

Snip!

Snip!

I'm thinking of blowing your cover.

Snip!

Snip!

Snip!

Do you like blowing things up?
Snip!
The future is coming.
Snip!
It's getting closer.
Snip!
It
Snip!
Is
Snip!
Almost
Snip!
Here!
The shock of the air. Her neck revealed.
The man steps back. "Beau-ti-ful," he says.
"Killing," Hettie whispers, as her eyes meet his in the glass.

. . . .

I hope you'll be feeling better by then.

It rattles round and round in Evelyn's head. How *dare* he? As
though something were wrong with her, as though she were *ill*, and
that is why she has dared to question him—question any of them.
As if all of it, the whole bloody war, were nothing more than an
extended gentlemen's club.

The rain is still falling, and the pavement is hazardous, clogged
with pedestrians and umbrellas. She clashes with a man ahead who
is moving slowly and she stumbles, catching herself against his
heel. She has to grab an iron railing to steady herself.

"Watch where you're going, can't you?" He is old but upright,
the bearing of a military man, his ringing voice cutting through
even a wet afternoon like this. Evelyn stands, swaying, staring after
him. There are too many men like this: They are everywhere, and

she is sick of them, of their florid intactness; it is the old who have inherited the earth. "Oh, go to hell," she spits.

The man opens his mouth as though to bark a response, and then closes it again. He turns first, impeccably upright, and walks stiffly away. Evelyn is immediately ashamed. She grips the spikes at the top of the railing. The world around her is hazy. Now that she has stopped she is starting to realize just how unsteady she is. How much wine did she drink in the end? Nearly the entire bottle on her own. She's in her cups, all right. She'll have to gather herself before she gets back to work. She shakes her watch from her cuff and stares blearily at its face. She's already late but can't arrive like this. Her flat's not far from here; there's a shortcut she can take if she turns right now. She could go home for a minute and sort herself out. It's tempting, and it's much better to be late than drunk. She pushes herself away from the railing and turns onto a side road, moving fast, almost running, skirting the puddles, lifting her umbrella high.

The flat has the blank, slightly surprised feeling of a weekday afternoon. The air is still, a little stale. Several days' worth of dirty dishes are piled in the sink. Her bedroom curtains are drawn. She can't remember the last time she opened them. She does so now, and a movement in the flat opposite catches her eye. Someone is over there, in the shadows; she can't quite see them in the depths of their room. She stands there for a moment longer, looking out, but the view blurs in the rain.

She turns back and winces. Her bedroom is atrocious in the daylight. A pit. Why has their char not been? Then she remembers. She is away, visiting her mother; Dorset, Devon, something like that. Doreen left a note about it last week. She takes off her wet coat and blouse and leaves them on the bed, then goes to the bathroom and runs cold water into the sink. She lifts her face and stares at herself in the glass.

Her brother was lying.

Liar, Edward Montfort. *Liar.*

She splashes freezing water onto her skin and gasps.

He knew exactly who Rowan Hind was; she could see it all over his face.

So what has he got to hide?

She splashes the water again and again until the top of her camisole is wet through. She pulls that off, too. Then she brushes her teeth thoroughly, dries herself off with a towel, and goes back into her room.

In the flat across the road the shadows move. Evelyn jumps. She had forgotten that she had opened the curtains. She is naked from the waist up. The rain has lifted now, and the view is clear. The shadows thicken, then part and reveal themselves to be a man—a man in a wheelchair staring out over the street toward her.

As she stands there, watching him, he wheels himself closer to the glass. She can see the pale line of his skin, his hooded eyes, and the shadows beneath. He is younger than her; from where she stands he seems no more than twenty. He has a beautiful face, and he is looking straight at her—straight into her eyes.

She can feel the skin around her nipples contract.

Her cigarettes are lying on the corner of the bed. She can just see her case and lighter from here. Carefully, and without turning, without taking her eyes from the boy's face, she bends and picks them up.

She lights one, inhales, and lets out the smoke, letting the lighter fall. It lands on the bed beside her with a soft thud. The boy unbuttons his trousers. She watches as he reaches his hands inside. She can feel the air across her skin; hear her breath, low in the room. She takes another deep pull at her cigarette. The boy's hand begins moving slowly up and down. He doesn't take his eyes from her face. She opens her legs slightly, feels the friction of her knickers against her skin: the swollen pulse of herself. She pulls again at her cigarette. They stay there, eyes locked together as he moves faster, faster. Her breath catches in her throat. When she sees him slump she lets out her breath in a sigh.

His head is bowed. He stays like that for a long moment and then, without looking up, wheels himself from the light.

She puts her arm across her chest and pulls the curtain, plunging the room into sudden darkness. She sits on the edge of her bed and puts her head into her hands. For a moment, she feels as though she might weep.

But she doesn't. She stands. Pulls herself together, takes another camisole from her wardrobe, and pulls a jersey on over the top.

She is over an hour and a half late when she finally arrives back at the office. By some miracle the queue is not so bad, and only ten or fifteen men wait outside.

Robin doesn't notice her as she slips into her seat. She feels the exact moment when he does, though, a few seconds later. She can feel him shift, feel a slight buzzing in the air between them. It is odd, the buzzing, but she doesn't look up to meet his gaze.

. . . .

"Ada!" Ivy stands in the doorway. Her broad cheeks are rosy and there's a fine film of sweat glistening on her skin. "This is a nice surprise. Kettle's just boiled. I'll make us both some tea."

Ada touches the envelope in her pocket, and then follows Ivy down the dark hall to the kitchen, where something sticky is simmering on the stove. The windows are covered with mist and the table is a jumbled mass of branches, the smell of cut wood mingling with the sugary steam. "Something smells good."

"Rose hips." Ivy lifts a bowlful of the shucked fruit. "You know me. I always make a bit of a syrup for the winter colds. I'll bring you some over when I've done."

"That'd be nice."

"Sit down and I'll get the tea on, shall I?"

Ada sits at the scrubbed table, watching Ivy as she bustles about the room, lifting the lid off the teapot, peering in, shaking in a few more leaves, and then pouring the steaming water inside. Ivy is heavier than she ever used to be and moves more slowly now. They have known each other for years: Ivy was living here when Ada moved onto the street. Ivy is older, by three years or so; she already had her two girls then. They were pregnant together with their boys, though, Ada with Michael, and Ivy with Joseph, her third. Ivy was lovely back then, always throwing her head back and laughing at the smallest thing. She lost her son in the summer of 1916. She didn't laugh for a long while after that.

Ivy carries the pot over and arranges cups and saucers and pours.

"Feels like ages since I've seen you." She smiles, and Ada, as always, is taken aback. Ivy got given new teeth, just at the end of the war; her daughters saved up and bought them for her; she had the old ones pulled out and new ones fitted, bottom and top. They look funny, as though they were made for someone else. They don't fit too well either; they clack and whistle when she talks. "Jack doing all right, is he? Much coming out from that allotment still?"

"There's still a few things coming out."

"That's good." Ivy takes a seat. "I'm glad you popped over, actually; I've been wanting to ask you something for a while."

"What's that?"

"About whether you're going to go to town, for the burial. The Unknown Warrior. You know."

So far, she and Jack have avoided this subject. Ada knows without asking that he will not want to go.

"I was reading in the papers," says Ivy. "They're going to put up barriers in the streets. They're expecting thousands."

"Is there going to be space for everyone, then?"

"That's the point, isn't it? For everyone to go—for all of us to pay our respects."

"I suppose so."

"I thought I'd be going with my girls, but neither of them want to." Ivy looks saddened briefly, and then brightens. "But then I thought, we could walk there together . . . if you like?"

"I'm—not sure. Can I have a think about it?"

"Of course. You take your time."

Ada touches the letter in her pocket, puts down her cup. "Can I ask you something, Ivy?"

"What's that?"

"It's something about your Joe."

"What about him?"

"You got a letter, didn't you? Telling you how it happened? After he died?"

"Yes, I did."

"And then did you get another one? Telling you about his grave?"

Ivy nods.

"Can I see it?"

There's a moment in which Ada worries she has said too much. Then, "Of course," says Ivy. "If you really want to. I'll fetch it for you now."

She goes into the parlor and Ada can hear her moving about. In the darkened garden, beyond the window, a sudden breeze picks up, tossing a spray of small leaves into the air. *The Unknown Warrior.* It sounds so grand. She knows the meaning behind this burial: the one to stand for all of the many bodies that have not come home, but why didn't they just call him a soldier? Just like everyone else?

"You read it." Ivy is back, standing in the doorway, "I'm sorry, I can't." She puts two brown envelopes onto the table in front of Ada. "I'd better start clearing these anyway." She lifts an armful of the branches and takes them over to the counter, where she begins snapping them in two.

Ada slides the first of the letters from its envelope.

```
I am directed to inform you that a report has
been received which states that the late Private
Joseph White is buried about 2000 yards North
West of Gueudecourt, South West of Bapaume.
    The grave has been registered in this office,
and is marked by a durable wooden cross with an
inscription bearing full particulars.
                I am,
                Your obedient servant,
                Captain,

                Staff Captain for Brigadier-
                General, Director, Graves
                Registration and Enquiries.
```

The other letter is longer, in a denser type. There's a stamp on the top dated March 20, 1920. She squints at the page. It is difficult to read in the failing light.

```
I beg to inform you that in accordance with the
agreement with the French and Belgian Govern-
ments to remove all scattered graves and small
cemeteries which were situated in places unsuit-
able for permanent retention, it has been found
necessary to exhume the bodies buried in certain
areas. The body of Private White has therefore
```

```
been removed and re-buried in Grass Lane Burial
Ground, Gueudecourt, South of Bapaume.

    I am to add that the necessity for this re-
moval is much regretted, but was unavoidable for
the reasons given above. You may rest assured
that the work of re-burial has been carried out
carefully and reverently, special arrangements
having been made for the appropriate religious
services to be held.
        I am,
                    Your obedient servant,
                        Major D.A.A.G.
                        For Major-General,
                        D.G.G.R. & E.
```

"They don't half put in lots of big words," says Ada, folding it back.

Ivy slides the pan off the stove, shaking her head. "It's all a load of old balsam though, isn't it? They're just making it easier for themselves. They're just lumping them all together so as it's easier to count them up. I don't like to think of it. Why couldn't they have just left him in peace? And that bit at the bottom—that bit about religious services. They never even asked me what religion he was. He might have been a flaming Hindu for all they knew. He was an atheist, though, wasn't he? Like his dad."

"They didn't even ask?"

Ivy sucks her teeth. "No. And you seen the other bit there?" She brings a candle over to the table. There's a second piece of paper tacked onto the back, which contains only this information:

```
Name Joseph White
Regiment 10th London.
```

```
Location of Grave. A.I.F. Burial Ground (Grass
Lane) Gueudecourt. Plot 7. Row D. Grave 4.
Nearest Station Bapaume
Nearest Town "
Nearest Enquiry Bureau. Albert.
```

"I know that place." Ada points, feeling a thrill of recognition. "That was on the card that Michael sent back. Albert. It's the place with the church, with the woman and the child."

"That's right," says Ivy. "I've seen pictures of that, too."

"Here." She takes her own letter out of her pocket. "Would you have a look at this for me?"

Ivy eyes the envelope. "Sorry, Ada. I don't know if I can."

"Please?"

Ivy relents. Taking the thin letter from its brown envelope, she reads it quickly, then nods and pushes it away. "I got one of them, too, at the beginning. That's what they always send, don't they?"

"I know," says Ada. "But I never got anything else. Nothing about how he died. Nothing about where he was buried. None of this." She gestures to the letters on the table.

Ivy starts. "Why didn't you say something at the time?"

"I kept thinking he was coming back, didn't I? That they got it wrong."

"Didn't you ever try to write to anyone?"

"Jack wrote to the company. They wrote back and said that he had to write to the war office. So he wrote to them. Then he heard nothing back."

Ivy sucks the moisture from her teeth. "God, it makes me boil. After all those boys did, and they just don't care. Here, take a look at this." She goes over to a drawer, comes back with a folded piece of newsprint, and puts it down on the table. "You seen this? They're doing tours now, so as you can look at the graves."

"I've seen."

"You seen how much they're charging then?" Her finger hovers over an advert in a bold box at the bottom of the page,

**All-inclusive tour. Graves and battlefields. Led by
sympathetic veteran. £6—food and transport included.**

Ivy shakes her head. "They asked me for an inscription, for the gravestone. That was sixpence a letter on its own. You'd think they'd pay for that, wouldn't you? An *inscription* at the least. Then I sat down with my Bill and I counted up how long I'd have to save. Twelve pounds for both of us to go on a tour. What's that, then? I've got fifteen shillings a week to manage this house on. If I save two shillings a week it'll take over four years. They didn't think about that, did they? When they decided not to bring them home?" She is shaking with anger. "It's all right for those who can, isn't it? Like every bleeding thing else."

A light, acrid smell is coming from the range.

"Hang on, let me have a look at this." She goes over to the stove. Outside, the wind picks up, rattling the windows. Ada plaits her fingers in her lap.

"Ada?" Ivy sounds calmer now. "You remember my cousin May? Lives out Islington way? Lost both her boys? You met her last summer—Ellie's wedding."

Ada looks to where she stands, slowly stirring the contents of her pan. "That's right. I remember." May was a small birdlike woman, sadness struck through her.

"Well, she got a letter about her boys just the other day."

"Oh?"

"Said they were going to be on a memorial. A big one in France, where people would be able to go and pay their respects, with the names of her boys on it along with all the rest. It was in one of those places with a funny name. Began with a *T,* I think."

Ada nods. She cannot really conceive of this. Of how this might look. Of how a memorial could possibly help.

"They didn't find anything of her boys, you know." Ivy speaks quietly. "Not one little bit."

There's a silence.

"You've not had a letter like that then, Ada?"

"No."

"It might be coming, though."

"It might." Ada puts down her cup and picks up her own letter, turning it in her hands. "Ivy?"

"What's that?"

"What about that woman? The one you saw."

"Which one?"

"The one who said she could speak with the dead."

Ivy puts the lid back on the pan, turns, and wipes her hands on her apron. "What about her?"

"Could she do it, do you think? Did it work?"

Ivy crosses her arms in front of her chest. "What's this all about, Ada? What's brought all this on? What you got to go digging around for now?"

Ada rubs the side of a knuckle with her thumb. "A boy came to the door," she says, speaking quickly. "Selling some rubbish. I don't know why, but I invited him in." Something occurs to her, and she looks up. "Did anyone come here? Sunday morning? Did you have anyone knock on the front door? Selling dishcloths and that?"

Ivy thinks and shakes her head. "No, and I was in all day."

"He came into the kitchen. I didn't want to buy anything, but he was cold, so I let him have a smoke. And then, then he—he said Michael's name." She looks up. "And I know this is daft, but when he spoke, this boy, it was as though he was looking at him. As though he could see him in the room."

Ivy comes to sit in the chair beside her. "What do you mean? Like a ghost?"

"I suppose . . . yes."

"But Ada," says Ivy gently. "You know there's no such thing."

"I know that—but then, yesterday . . . I saw him in the street."

"Who?"

"Michael. And I followed him all the way to the house, but when I got home—he had disappeared."

"Oh, Ada darling." Ivy reaches out, and for a brief moment they sit there, clasped together, until Ada pulls her hands away. She hasn't finished. Not yet.

"Then yesterday, I went and got out all his letters. I haven't looked at them for two years. And I kept thinking, *Why?* Why didn't anyone tell us what happened? And why did that funny boy come to see me? He didn't come to see you, did he? He can't just have been selling cloths."

"You never know."

"No." She shakes her head, fierce now. "He came to see me. I know it. I know he knew something about Michael. And then I thought, He's never coming back. And I'll never know. And then I kept thinking of her, that woman you saw. And I couldn't get her out of my head. Where was she? That woman? Where'd she live?"

Ivy's face closes. She pulls her hands away and stands, shaking her head. "I don't like to talk about it. The dead are the dead. Best just leave them be."

There's a knocking at the window. The two women freeze. There's a shape out there, a humped black mass, but with the candle so close it's impossible to see just who or what it is. Ivy stands and goes over to the glass. "It's Ellie," she says, and Ada can hear the relief in her voice as she opens the door. There's a blast of cold air as Ellie, Ivy's daughter, a smart, tidy girl, bustles into the room, baby on her hip.

"All right, Mum?" Ellie peers into the dusk. "Ada? Hello! You all right? I was just at Sal's. Thought I'd pop by to see how you're getting on."

"We were just having a cuppa."

"You need a bit more light in here."

"I should be going." Ada stands.

"Don't go on account of me." Ellie looks from one to the other of them.

Ada rustles up a smile. "I've got to get the dinner on anyway. Jack'll be back soon."

Ellie nods, losing interest, and wanders over to the stove, showing the baby the syrup bubbling in the pan. "What's this then, Johnny, eh? What's this?"

"Ivy," Ada says. "Please. Just give me her address."

"I've told you." Ivy's voice is low, warning. "It was four years ago, anyway. A lot can happen in four years."

"I know that. I just—"

Ivy leaves her side. She goes over to stand with her daughter and grandson at the stove. "Ada's going, John," she says to the little boy. "Say ta-ta."

Ellie looks up. "Granny says say good-bye to Ada." She lifts the arm of her son, who submits, gurgling, his mouth stretched wide, his cheeks bright red in the warmth of the stove, as she waggles his arm up and down. "Ta-ta, Ada. Johnny, say ta-ta."

. . . .

Two British undertakers walk through the winding, vaulted corridors of the château, their footsteps echoing on the flagged floors.

Their names are Mr. Sowerbutts and Mr. Noades. They arrived in France yesterday, on the evening boat train. In the pocket of his suit, Mr. Sowerbutts carries a letter of introduction from Sir Lionel Earle, permanent secretary of His Majesty's Office of Works. Six British soldiers follow them, carrying the heavy, empty coffin that the undertakers have brought with them from London. The coffin has been hewn from an oak tree that grew at Hampton Court Palace. Messrs.

Sowerbutts and Noades oversaw the construction themselves. It took two weeks, in which the oak was finished, planed, sanded, and polished to the undertakers' exacting standards. Iron girders were strapped around the wood, and rings were riveted to the girders. A Crusader's sword, given by the king, was grafted onto the lid, and the following was inscribed there in Gothic script:

𝔄 𝔅𝔯𝔦𝔱𝔦𝔰𝔥 𝔚𝔞𝔯𝔯𝔦𝔬𝔯 𝔚𝔥𝔬 𝔉𝔢𝔩𝔩 𝔦𝔫 𝔱𝔥𝔢 𝔊𝔯𝔢𝔞𝔱 𝔚𝔞𝔯 1914–1918

𝔉𝔬𝔯 𝔎𝔦𝔫𝔤 𝔞𝔫𝔡 ℭ𝔬𝔲𝔫𝔱𝔯𝔶.

At the threshold of the chapel, Mr. Sowerbutts and Mr. Noades pause. They stare in astonishment at the floor, strewn as it is with curling flowers and leaves. The colors are extraordinary. There is something faintly disturbing, faintly pagan almost, about the scene.

The French guards salute, their boots ricocheting like a fusillade as they leave.

Mr. Noades gestures to the British soldiers behind him to set the oak coffin down. Mr. Sowerbutts grips the bag that he has brought with him from England. He eyes the plain wooden coffin waiting for them in the center of the room.

The two men were told that they might ask for anything they needed for this day's work, but they are perfectionists. They consider themselves, with good reason, the very best; they prefer to work with their own tools.

They have been told nothing of where exactly this body has come from, nothing of how long it has been in the earth. They know only that it has been taken from the fields of northern France. They are curious. They know that the fields there are made from thick, muddy clay. But how high was the clay content? How wet was the soil?

Mr. Noades joins his colleague on the other side of the plain wooden coffin.

"Ready?"

He nods. There's a pause, and then the two men unscrew the lid and lift it.

A close, musty smell escapes from the box. Not particularly unpleasant. Well past putrefaction and decay. The body is still inside the burlap sack it was wrapped in two days before. Mr. Noades takes his shearing scissors and cuts open the material from bottom to top. Both men lean forward, breath held.

Inside is a small, hunched skeleton. Small remnants of skin cling to the bones of its skull. There is a patch up near the right cheek. It looks like parchment. Another covers the chin, and a tiny bit more remains on the scalp. Muddied khaki still adheres in places to the bones; the jacket is fairly intact, though most of the trousers is missing, except around the groin, where the skeleton appears to have been bent over itself in the ground.

Five years, thinks Mr. Sowerbutts.

Four and a half, thinks Mr. Noades. Depending, of course, on the wetness of the soil.

Autumn 1915, thinks Mr. Sowerbutts.

Spring 1916, thinks Mr. Noades.

Gently, they lift the remains of the man in the sack and arrange them in the oak coffin. They can do very little in the way of traditional preparation. They simply spread the bones with care, so that the skeleton is lying on its back, arms by its sides.

The men carry out their work silently.

Soon, these men know, the whole of the country will have their eyes on this coffin. The very power of this coffin will depend upon every person that looks on it imagining that the body inside belongs to them.

It is strange, even approximately, to know when this man fell.

And though they have been desperately curious, all the way here, there is something diminishing, somehow, about deciding on a year, about pinning this down.

Nevertheless, as they work, each of them crosses off men they knew who served: one who was taller than this, or one who died later than this one in the war.

When the body is ready, the undertakers seal the heavy lid.

Without saying anything, each knows they will not speak of this—not of the sight of this body, ever, to anyone. No matter who may ask.

. . . .

Evelyn doesn't look up from her desk until the last man has been dealt with. Then she sits back in her chair and stretches. Five o'clock.

Robin is standing over by his desk, buckling up his bag with his back to her. "Shall I lock up?" He speaks quietly, without turning around.

"If you would. I just have to finish something off here."

She takes the round of keys from her bag and puts them on the edge of her desk. She doesn't look up as he crosses the room toward her, but she sees his hand reach in and lift them, the fine light hairs on the tops of his fingers. While his back is turned, she rifles through the papers on her desk. She cannot find what she is looking for—must have filed it yesterday.

"Well, good-bye, then." He is standing beside her.

"Wait." Evelyn looks up. "Listen, Robin, I'm most dreadfully sorry for leaving you like that this afternoon."

"It's fine."

"No, it's not. It was my lunch. It overran."

"Lunch with your brother?"

"Yes."

His eyes flicker to her jersey. She remembers that she has changed—is wearing different clothes—and feels the blood race to her cheeks. There's no way of making this seem better than it looks. She will only be digging herself a deeper hole.

"Here." He holds out the keys in his palm. "For you."

She puts them on the desk. "Wait, Robin." For some reason she doesn't want to be left here on her own tonight, not even for a minute or two. "Would you wait, just for one moment, please?"

"If you like." He sounds surprised.

"I won't be long, I promise." She goes over to the ranged boxes on the wall, following them down until she reaches the letter *H* and then searching through the drawer until she finds what she is looking for: a small green slip with Rowan Hind's name at the top. She copies his address into her notebook, *11 Grafton St. . . . Poplar,* then looks up. Robin's tall silhouette is over by the window, hands in his pockets, staring out. Rain falls from a stooped gray sky. It is almost dark already. Evelyn feels the same strange beginnings of panic she felt a moment earlier; Doreen will most likely be out again, and she will be going home to an empty flat. "Ready," she says, after a moment.

He still has his back toward her, looking out the windows.

"That rain looks foul."

"Yes," he says. "It does."

"I'm not sure I'm up to braving it just yet." She gives a small laugh. "I might make a cup of tea."

"Fine." He nods. "See you tomorrow, then." He makes to go.

"Would you care to join me?"

He halts beside her desk. "For the tea?"

"Yes."

"Er, no, thank you. I don't much go in for consolation prizes."

"Oh, God. I didn't mean it like—" She stands up too quickly and her head is pounding. Her drunkenness of earlier on has shrunk to a thick, tight band across her scalp. "Actually"—she shakes her head, pressing her fingers against the desk—"I'm not

going to have a cup of tea at all. I'm going to go for a proper drink.
How about that instead?"

He starts to speak, but then she raises her hand.

"You know what? Don't bother. Do what you like. I'm sorry that
I asked."

She puts on her coat and gathers her things. But Robin hasn't
moved. When she looks up at him he is smiling—a strange sort of
smile she hasn't seen before. "Actually," he says, "I was going to say
that a proper drink is just what I feel I need."

The pub is on the corner, a few doors down from the office: one of
those brown-hued workingmen's pubs where women are rarely
seen. Usually she would avoid it, but it's raining hard, and she has
no idea how far Robin can easily walk.

Inside it's fairly quiet, just a few men, drinking on their own,
hunkered down over their pints. She makes sure that she is the first
to reach the bar. "I'll have a gin and orange please, and . . ." She
turns to Robin.

"A pint should do it," he says, giving a brief nod to the barman.

"Gin and orange and a pint then, please."

Robin looks across to the rain-spattered windows. "Filthy day."

The memory of herself, half-naked, drunk, and standing by a
window floods Evelyn. "Yes," she says, drumming her fingers
against the wood of the bar. "It is."

The barman puts their drinks down, and Robin reaches into his
pocket.

"No!" She puts her hand on his sleeve, and then pulls it immediately away. "I mean, let me. I wanted to make it up to you, for this
afternoon."

His eyebrows shoot up, but he half-steps away from the bar and
opens his hands in mock defeat.

"Got a live one there," says the barman to Robin, who smiles.

Evelyn takes out her purse and pays with a stony glare. They turn with their drinks, and stand, awkward. Which table? Over in the corner is too intimate, by the door too drafty. She makes for an empty table in the middle of a row, slipping into the seat on the side closest to the wall. As Robin settles himself into the chair in front of her, she sees that his leg sticks out slightly: out and to the side.

I often go along to dances in the evening.

How the hell does he manage then, with that leg?

"So," she says.

"So." He looks at her. And there is something different in it. Challenging. It's the same look that he gave her in the office before.

"Was it dreadful, then?" She sips her drink.

"I'm sorry?" He looks momentarily confused.

"This afternoon."

"Oh, no, it was fine. Though I should probably pretend it wasn't." He smiles, lifting his glass. "This is interesting. I've never had a woman buy me a drink before."

She raises an eyebrow as she lights her cigarette. "I'm sure it tastes the same."

He makes a great show of holding the liquid to the light. He takes an exploratory sip. "Yes," he says. "Everything seems to be in order."

Despite herself, she smiles. She can feel the gin from her own drink hit her blood, and the band around her head eases a merciful notch.

"Listen, I don't suppose I could have one of those, could I?" He points to her cigarettes.

"Thought you didn't smoke."

"Just sometimes, when I'm having a drink. Used to smoke like a chimney, like the rest of you, but I got a bit of poison, you know, bit of gas in the lungs."

She pushes them across the table toward him.

He lights up, takes a small puff, and then puts the cigarette down in the ashtray, where it plumes blue smoke into the silence between them.

"So," she says, eventually, "how are you finding the job?"

"How am I finding the job?" He sits back in his chair. "Well . . . it's . . . many things." He turns his glass in his hands. "Harder than I thought, in some ways; simpler in others. Mainly I'm just happy to be in employment. It's not the easiest with—this." He gestures to his leg.

Evelyn rests her eyes on it briefly. For a moment she wonders what it looks like. The plastic instead of flesh. How it must have been, getting used to that.

"And it beats selling magazines door-to-door or matches in the street." He leans forward, his fist around his glass. "I saw a man the other day. He had a barrel organ, and there were photographs on the side of all his children."

"How many?"

"I counted nine."

She lets out a low whistle.

"And beside all of that, a list of his service record."

"Whereabouts?"

"The Somme, and others. The duration, from what I could tell."

"God." She picks up a beer mat and tears it in half. "They make me furious. It's as though we're walking around a pit, all of us. One of those awful bomb craters in the middle of the city, only a million men are inside it and no one is looking. People are just walking past, whistling, pretending not to see."

"I don't know about not seeing," he says quietly.

"Well, all right." She looks up at him. "Perhaps not that. But I just boil with fury that they should be there in the first place— reduced to begging in the street. It's the older ones that always get me most; they stand there, in their best suits, and their hats, and

they look so *patient* and they all have such—such *dignity* and we
all just . . ." She trails off, shaking her head.

"Then why do you work for them?"

"Excuse me?"

That same look of challenge is on his face. "The people that put
them there. If it isn't the pensions service, then who is it? Surely if
there were a fairer distribution, then . . ."

"You're confusing the messenger with the message."

"Perhaps. But you could always do something else."

"Perhaps I could." She leans back, opens her hands. "What do
you suggest?"

He shrugs. "There must be many office jobs out there."

"You know as well as I do that's not true. Especially for women.
Not now."

Are they arguing? She's not sure, but it feels like it; her blood
is up.

"How long have you been there, then?" His tone is softer, conciliatory.

"Two years."

"And before that?"

"Before the office, or before the war?"

"Both. You can start at the beginning, if you like."

She gives a brief laugh. "We'd be here all night."

"Well"—he looks down at her empty glass and his half-full
one—"we could certainly have another drink."

"Yes." She smiles. "I suppose we could."

He drains his glass, gets up, and goes over to the bar. His cigarette is still smoldering gently in the ashtray. She leans over, takes
a couple of last drags, and crushes it out. She watches as he comes
back with the drinks. It is difficult to tell from watching him walk
that he has a false leg; he moves surprisingly well.

"How long have you had the leg for?" she says as he nears the
table, then immediately regrets it; but he doesn't flinch.

"Three years." He puts the drinks down. "Though it took a while before I had one that fit. But hang on." He lifts a finger. "We're not finished yet. You were going to tell me what you did before this."

"Munitions."

He raises an eyebrow—seems surprised. "And how was that? Hard?"

"Hard enough." She wonders if he will comment on her finger now.

"And before that?"

"I . . . well." She puts her finger and thumb from her good hand into her drink and squeezes the little slice of orange. It bobs on the surface, bumping against the ice when she lets it go. *Before that I fell in love.* "I moved up to London. Shared a flat. Did this and that. Thought I had plenty of time to decide, and then the war came and . . ." She looks up at him. He is watching her so intently that she has to look away. "By the time it was finished I was here." She picks up the last half of her beer mat and rips it in half again. "Well," she says. "Your turn now. You've been very clever so far at making me talk."

"I'm not sure you've really told me very much at all." He smiles. "But, all right, then. Perhaps I could pretend to smoke another of your cigarettes?"

She pushes them across the table toward him.

He lights one up, but this time keeps it in his hand. "I was in university when the war broke out. I'd gone there late. Somehow I thought it would be the thing to travel first."

"Whereabouts?"

"India, Nepal, the Levant."

"How was that?"

"Have you ever visited?"

She shakes her head.

"You should go."

She looks up at him. Surprised. *Should I?*

"I lived on not very much and I spent rather a lot of my time away from people and things. And—it was rather wonderful."

"What did you do?"

"A lot of walking, mostly. Some climbing, too. Northern India and Nepal. I had a thought that I'd like to be attached to the colonial government, but when I was out there I decided that"—he smiles—"well, it was clear that wasn't what I wanted to do. I thought I should do something constructive. So I took up my place at Cambridge and went to study classics." He gives a short laugh. "God only knows why."

"And was it? Constructive?"

He shakes his head. "I was already older than most of the other men. Only by three years or so, but I felt ancient. The only thing that I wanted was to get back out into the world again. So the minute war broke out I hassled for a commission. I wanted to get to Jerusalem. Thought there was a good chance a third front would open up there. And so I pushed for that." He grimaces suddenly. "Does that sound terribly cynical?"

She shakes her head. "Did you get there?"

"No. Strings were pulled, but the wrong ones, and I ended up on the Western Front."

"Unlucky."

"Perhaps."

"Where were you?"

"Ypres first. That's where I got the gas. They sent me home for a few months after that. The leg happened in '16."

"And—how?" She doesn't quite know how to ask.

He looks down at the cigarette in his hand, as though surprised to see it still there. He takes a swift, shallow drag. "I remember nothing at all of the shell. When I woke in the hospital and they told me the leg had gone I didn't believe them at first. I could still feel it. I can still feel it now, sometimes. It's—strange. And then"—

a line appears in his brow—"all I could think of was those men. Standing at street corners with a crutch, and a tin. The fact of never climbing again. Perhaps not being able to walk. And I think I wanted to die."

He says it matter-of-factly. She likes him the more for it.

"Then—that changed, too, and I felt . . . I'm not proud of it, but I felt relief."

"Yes." She leans forward.

"And then, when the relief had faded, I was overwhelmed with—"

"With guilt."

He looks up at her.

"I'm sorry," she says, drawing back, coloring. "Putting words into your mouth."

"No." He shakes his head. "You're right."

But it is as if some delicate membrane has broken, and sound floods her ears. The pub is busy, the air thick with smoke, men talking loudly at the tables on either side.

"I should be going," says Robin, draining the last of his drink.

She has a fleeting vision of him, at home. Living alone? What is his home like? Suddenly she doesn't want him to go. "Where do you live?" she says.

He looks surprised. "Hampstead," he says with a smile. "The cheaper bit. Further from the Heath."

She nods, unable to think of anything more to say.

They pull on their coats. He stands back to let her pass, and they walk side by side toward the door. Night has fallen properly now on the street outside. The air carries the scent of leaves and evening fires.

"Well," he says, smiling and putting on his hat. "Thank you for the drink."

"It was a pleasure." As she buttons her coat to her chin, she feels again that same hollow, racing panic that she had in the office.

Is it a terror of being alone? How did it begin—this fear? It is her brother's fault, she thinks; it is the things he said this afternoon. "Robin?"

"Yes?" He turns to her.

"That—Dixie band that you mentioned. Thursday, wasn't it? Are you still going to hear them play?" She can't believe she's saying it. She can't believe the words are actually coming out of her mouth. "Or have you—found someone to go with you yet?"

"Yes, I am." He looks surprised, pleased. "And no. I haven't, no."

"Well, would you—I wonder? Perhaps I could come, after all?"

. . . .

Ada weaves in and out through the scrubby stand of plane trees in the park. She skirts the cricket pitch, the grass roped off for the winter now, and when she reaches the crumbling brick of the far north wall, turns around and makes her way back again, in and out, in and out, her thoughts thrumming with her footsteps.

Ivy is selfish, *selfish*. There with her pieces of paper, with her maps of graveyards. These are the things of riches; Ivy is rich. It may well cost pounds to visit France, but if she knew that there was a patch of land that held the body of her son, she wouldn't complain about *money*. She would save everything she had until she could go and visit it. Sit by that piece of grass. Put her hands to it.

It is the lack of a body.

If she had had that, at least.

When her father died, Ada was eight. She stood at the entrance to the downstairs room into which they'd moved him, staring in at where he lay on his back. He was a large man but looked small on the table, as though death had taken more than his life from him. Her mother asked Ada to boil a pail of water, fetch a washcloth, and bring it to the room. "You can go now," she said, touching her gently on the top of her head and closing the door. But Ada stayed and listened, her ear pressed up against the wood. She could hear the dipping of the cloth in water, the small sounds of washing, and her mother, sobbing quietly. When she came back out, her mother's face was calm, as though it, too, had been washed clean. Even then, Ada could see there was sense in that.

Not like this, though; not this . . . *absence*. No body and no grave.

A gust threatens to take her hat, and she clamps it down onto her head, as damp, sticky leaves whirl and eddy in the air. There are odd figures scattered in the dusk: dog walkers, people coming home from work. Jack may be among them. She turns back, heading for the north end of the grass where there are only the trees.

If she had had Michael's body at home, then she would have washed it. However injured, however broken, she would have washed him, gently, as she did for him when he was a baby, when he was a boy. And if not that—if that last rite is to be denied to her, and to all of them, all the mothers, wives, sisters, lovers—then to know where the body lies in the ground at least.

It is the least that they are due.

The wind whips her hair across her face.

Why did Ivy's daughters not get her a ticket to France instead of those stupid, ill-fitting teeth? Why will they not go with her to the burial on Thursday, if that is what she wants? Those silly, preening girls.

She is being unfair. She knows she is. She knows she should leave it. That Ivy is right. That Jack is right, that she should stop picking, stop scratching at this wound that she cannot let heal. But he will not let her. Her son will not let her. It is as though he is pulling at her, tugging at her sleeve, as he used to when he was a little boy.

She comes to a stop, the only figure on this patch of grass, where the trees are purple against the sky. The first lights are coming on in the houses alongside the park. Shapes are moving at the windows, the women at work in their kitchens, preparing the evening meal for their families, for their children, for their men. It is odd, standing here, looking from the outside, at the rhythms and routines of life. It seems suddenly so clear. Some contract has been broken. Something has been ruptured. How have they all agreed to carry on?

She should go inside. She should make some food for their dinner, or there will be nothing to eat for the second night in a row. But at the thought of it, of her and Jack facing each other, silent across the kitchen table, she could scream.

Why doesn't one of them do something about it? Just stand up and shout into the silence, "That's it! I'm not doing it anymore!" Say the unsayable, release the charges, let the explosions blast it all away.

But then what? Where would she go? Nowhere. There is nowhere else to go at all.

She makes her way out of the darkened park, turning left down her road, feeling life claim her with each step. In the kitchen she wipes her face with her sleeve, takes a couple of dirty potatoes from the pantry and begins scrubbing them, hard. There's a knock at the front door. She ignores it. Whoever it is knocks again, louder this time, and she is forced to give up and go out into the hall.

It is Ivy, wind-blustered, standing on the step. "Can I come in?"

"Why?"

"I'm sorry, Ada."

"All right. You don't need to come in to tell me that." She goes to close the door.

Ivy puts a hand out to stop her. "She lived up in Walthamstow. An ordinary house. Ordinary street. Can I come in, Ada? Please?"

They go into the kitchen. Ada crosses her arms over her chest.

"Go on, then. What did she do? How did she do it?"

"I'm not sure." Ivy hovers, nervous. "She—just—asked me to

take something along: a photograph of Joe and then . . . something that had meant something to him. I didn't know what to take. I scratched about for ages trying to think. In the end I took an old bit of cloth he'd had when he was little. He used to drag it around with him for years."

"I remember that."

"You remember?" Ivy's face softens. "If I ever washed it he would cry and cry. I didn't have the heart to take it off him. Anyway, I'd kept a bit of it all this time. Had it in the Bible for years." She gives a rueful laugh. "Never took it down to read it, so that was all right. I felt a bit daft, I can tell you, sitting there in her parlor, bringing it out of the bag."

"And what did she do with it?"

"I think she just—sat with it there in her hands. Held it for a bit. And then . . . she started to say things."

"What sort of things?"

But it is as though whatever energy Ivy has mustered for this has gone, and she is sagged, finished now. "Oh, goodness, Ada. I don't know. I can hardly remember, honestly. Here." She steps forward, handing over a piece of paper.

Ada takes it; there's an address written on it in a small, careful hand.

At the door, Ivy turns back. "I will say one thing, though," she says. "After I went, I got a letter the next week, telling me they'd found Joe's body. Telling me where he was."

Ada looks up, her pulse racing.

"They'd identified him from the tags around his neck."

She nods. "Thank you."

"Here." Ivy crosses the room and pulls Ada toward her, pressing her against her chest in an awkward hug. Ada can smell the wet wool of her cardigan, the soft cleanness of her friend's skin. Ivy steps back, gripping her hands. "Come with me on Thursday. It'll be good for you. For all of us. Might put a few things to rest."

"I'm sorry, Ivy." She pulls away. "I'm just—not sure I can."

"Well." Ivy nods. "You take care of yourself, won't you?"

"Yes." Ada fingers the thin piece of paper in her hands. "I will."

. . . .

Even with her old tam-o'-shanter on, Hettie's head feels different: the skin more alive, as though her nerve ends are exposed. And under her coat she can feel the dress, the weight of it somehow reassuring and terrifying all at the same time. She can't quite believe she is here, could almost imagine it is a different street altogether, were it not for that strange blue bulb and the bronze plaque beside the door.

She hopes she has timed it right.

She didn't go home after her visit to the barber's but went straight to Di's instead, who squealed and flung open the curtains and made her turn around and show herself from every angle and finally pronounced her hair *utterly killing*, then helped her bandage her breasts so they looked as flat as they ever have in her life. Di had to go to work then, and Hettie sat and waited in her flat, smoking too many of Di's cigarettes, her hand constantly straying to the newly shaved V at the nape of her neck, stroking it one way and then the other, standing up every five minutes to check her reflection in the mirror, to adjust the dress, until nine o'clock came, and she slipped her old coat on and pulled her old hat over her hair, and went to the tube.

But when she emerged at Leicester Square it was a quarter to ten—way too early, since she and Di had agreed she had to be late: *You don't want to wait in the club on your own, do you? You know what people will think of that!*

So she walked a few steps down from the tube, self-conscious in the crowds of chattering people coming out of theaters, milling on the pavements, and eventually ducked into a small café, where she sat nursing a cup of tea while the sad-eyed waiter wiped smeared fingerprints from the glass shelves and stacked cake stands in the sink. At twenty past ten he turned to her. "Sorry, love," he said, folding his cloth with a weary motion of his hands. "Now I really have to get home."

She carried her empty cup and saucer to him and caught sight of herself in the mirror behind the glass counter. She looked terrified.

"Are you all right? You look ever so pale."

She swallowed. "I'm fine."

But she felt anything but fine leaving the lights of the Charing Cross Road behind and coming down this street alone. Even though it was earlier than last time, the street was still deserted, the only sign of life that eerie blue bulb above the door.

And now here she is.

She takes a breath, lifts her hand, and knocks. The hatch is opened; the same oblong of light appears. "Yes?"

She clears her throat, trying to steady her voice. "I'm here to meet Ed."

A pause, and then, "Ed who?"

Oh, God. She hasn't thought of this. Why hasn't she thought of this?

But the door opens nonetheless and she edges around it to stand in front of a different doorman this time, older, suspicious, with a thin, ratty face. "How old are you, then?" He looks her up and down.

"I'm—twenty-two."

The man snorts. "If you're twenty-two, I'm forty, love."

Hettie thinks longingly of Graham, smiling from his cubbyhole. She'd even eat one of his meat lozenges to see him now.

"You can't go in there unless you're with a member. We get a lot of girls . . ." He leans forward. "Trying their luck."

She tightens her belt, knowing what he might think she is. Had thought to guard against this. But it looks as though she's gone and mistimed it after all, and the night is over before it has even begun.

Then she has an idea. "Can I see?" she asks. "In the book?"

He looks unconvinced, but slides it in front of her.

She can feel him watching her as she traces the line of signatures with her fingertip. No Ed, or Edward, or any other name that might fit. Damp springs into her palms. Was that even his real name? She looks back up at him. "I'm sorry. Do you mind telling me the time?"

He looks at his wristwatch. "It's half past ten." He turns the book back around to face him. "Sorry, love, looks like you're out of luck."

The door opens behind her, and she turns, her heart in her throat—but it is just a couple, the woman wrapped in fur and laughing, red lips wide as a cat's. The man leans down to sign them in, and then they are gone again, disappearing with a clatter of heels down the stairs.

"You still here?" The doorman shakes his head. "Listen, love. Do yourself a favor. Go home."

She steps forward, hands in fists. "Is there any chance he could have come in here earlier?" She's not quite sure what is making her so bold.

The man straightens out his mustache with his fingers. "Well, you're nothing if not determined, I'll give you that. What's so special about this Ed, then?"

She doesn't answer, but he searches her face, and whatever he sees there softens his own.

"All right," he sighs. "Let's have a look." He licks his finger, turning back the pages of the book. "Right, then. This is for this afternoon. But don't tell anyone I've let you or I'll lose my bleeding job."

She leans forward, following the list of names, and halfway down the page she sees it—*Edward Montfort*. Time In: *Three p.m.*—and underneath the column where the Time Out is marked: nothing. "That must be him." She pushes the book back toward him, her heart battering against her ribs.

The man peers at the signature. "Well, looks like he's been in here all day." He straightens up, concerned. "You sure it's wise to go and meet him, miss?"

She can't go home. Not now. Not after all this.

"Go on," he says, jerking his head behind him. "You can send him up to tell me you're all right. That's if he can make it out on his own two feet."

There's the same dank smell on the stairs she remembers from before, but what was exciting on Saturday with Di is threatening now, seedy. What on earth was she so sure of earlier? She could be at home, resting, on her only night off this week, instead of here, walking down these stairs . . . toward—

Crackpot.

    Limehouse.

        White slave trader.

          You

            silly,

              silly

                girl.

No roar greets her when she opens the door. No heat and sound and fug. The club is half-empty. A different band is going through the motions on the stage; there's no Negro singer this time, only a pasty white man with an unconvincing drawl, and a few desultory couples marking time on the floor. There's no sign of Ed at any of the sparsely populated tables, and suddenly, with a fist of fear around her heart, Hettie cannot even remember his face. She stands at the door, hands still thrust in her pockets, and is ready to turn around and leave when a clutch of people between her and the bar shift and disperse, and suddenly there he is, sitting alone at a table in the corner, not far from the band, slightly slumped, his left hand wrapped around a glass, almost as though it is holding him up.

She steps toward him, then hesitates, caught in the middle of the floor.

He looks so sad.

Just then he glances up and sees her, and his face changes in an instant, as he lifts his hand and pushes himself to his feet. "My anarchist!" he says, stepping out from behind his table. "You came!"

He isn't wearing an evening suit. His shirt is creased, and he looks tired. But it is him all right. And now that he is in front of her she cannot speak.

"Have you come here to cause trouble, then?" he says with half a smile.

"I—" She shakes her head; her mouth is dry. "I don't think so, no."

"Pity." He straightens up and drains his drink. "Could do with some trouble. Dead in here tonight."

She follows his gaze. He's right. Even the band look bored.

He leans his weight on the table. "Shall we get some air? I've been here for *hours* . . ." he says, shaking his head. "Waiting for you."

"But—you said—in your note—you said to come at ten."

"Did I?" He picks up his coat and pulls it on with a distracted air. "Well, then . . . I was wrong."

The ground shifts beneath her.

Wrong about the time?

Or wrong to ask me to come?

They walk up the stairs, and she can feel him, close behind her, leaning on the rail. She avoids the doorman's gaze, but Ed salutes him and calls him "Sergeant" as they leave, and then they are alone together, standing in the dark on the street outside. There's a silence, the fizz of a match. A ghostly voice, half-singing—"While you've a Lucifer . . ."—and then his face, distorted, lit from below. "Want one?" The sound of a cigarette clamped between his teeth.

"No, thank you."

He is drunk. Of course he is. He has been in there all afternoon, and now he is drunk.

Her heart stumbles. She should go.

He shakes out his match, and it falls to the ground with a tiny clatter. "Nice night," he says, as the end of his cigarette flares red.

Hettie looks up at the sky. It *is* a nice night, though she hadn't noticed before; the air is clean and damp with the memory of recent rain. High ragged clouds frame the moon.

"Fancy a walk? Could do with a walk. Been cooped up in there for *hours,* waiting for you."

She's not dressed for a walk. She's dressed for dancing. She'll be cold, and the dress and her new hair—her whole new self—will go to waste.

"Hate that horrible club."

"All right," she says, eventually, because really, what else is there to say? And it is safer, probably, in a way, to be outside.

They leave the dark side street and head back onto the Charing Cross Road, which is still alive with the lights of restaurants and theaters. Ed walks quickly, as though he is in a hurry, and she has to take long strides to keep up, but when they reach the entrance to the tube he stops and turns to her. "Listen," he says, "I can't be bothered with all of this. Can you?"

It is as though he has slapped her. "I'm sorry." She shakes her head. "I don't know what you mean."

"All of the *preliminaries.* All of the *nonsense* you have to get through. I mean . . . really. Can you?"

"I don't understand."

He steps toward her. "The stuff that keeps us *separate.* Don't you think for *once,* we should all just . . . tell the truth? Say what we bloody well *mean?*"

She is silent, heart pounding.

"Sorry," he says, throwing his cigarette away and watching it go. "I've just had a bit of an . . . odd day." He runs his hands through his hair and lights another cigarette immediately. "Can I ask you something?" he says. "Can we make a pact? Just for tonight? Not to say anything to each other that isn't honest? Can we do that? Please?"

"Yes."

"All right." He nods. "So, I'm going to say something first. And then it's your turn."

Hettie feels as though she is on one of those rides at the funfair that you long to get on—and then give you the familiar queasy fear in your stomach as they start to spin, and you wonder why you wanted to get on them after all.

"You remind me of someone I once met," he says. "And ever since I saw you, that night at the club, I've wanted to kiss you."

She is spinning.

"Can I kiss you now?" he says. "Please? Because I can't think of a better time."

He steps toward her and she closes her eyes as he tilts her mouth to his. He tastes of whiskey. It is a lovely, gentle kiss.

"Thank you," he says quietly, as he pulls away.

When she opens her eyes he is staring at her, but his expression is softer, as though something has left him. "Now you say something," he says. "Something true. I only want to hear true things."

She's not sure she's ready to speak yet, with this mouth that has been kissed by this man. Really, what she wants is to be kissed again. She tries to think, but her thoughts are all jumbled, and "I— don't know," she says, shaking her head. "I'm not sure."

"*That*," he says, stepping back, pointing.

"What?"

"That thing you stopped yourself from saying. Just then. That thing. Tell me *that*."

Hettie swallows. "All right. . . . I was going to say that I liked what you said, about blowing things up."

"Oh, God." Ed shakes his head. "You must think I'm barmy."

She thinks of Fred, thinning himself to nothingness, sitting in their father's chair, of the terrible sounds that leak from him at night. Of her mother, furious and alone, turning in and in and in. "No—" she says. "In fact, I think—I want to blow things up, too."

He throws his head back and laughs. "Thank you for that." Then he claps his hands, looking around him. "Bloody cold out here, isn't it?"

She hadn't noticed, but it is. The streets are thinner now, too. The crowds appear to have gone home.

"I need a drink. Fancy a drink? I know somewhere not so far from here." He smiles, sheepish suddenly. "Well, it's my flat, actually, if we're being honest. Which we are. How would you like to have a drink at my flat?"

When she hesitates, he holds his hands up. It is the same odd gesture he made in the club on Saturday night. As though he were unarmed.

"I promise you," he says. "I'm a very honorable man."

The floor stretches to dark-paneled walls, smelling of polish and old, expensive wood.

He *is* rich, then.

Hettie stands on the limit of the parquet, as though on the edge of a deep, chill lake. His flat is vast. Five of her mother's Hammersmith living rooms could fit easily inside.

Ed makes his way about the room, turning on lights. "Hope you don't mind. Been in that damn foxhole all afternoon." He looks over to her. "Come and stand over here. Give me a minute and I'll warm the place up."

He seems different now that he is inside: steadier, less drunk.

She steps over to the fire, where he has bent, adding coal from a scuttle in the hearth. Beside the fireplace, a door to another room is open. She can just see the corner of a bed.

A man. A girl. A bed.

"Right," he says when the fire is finally roused. He moves to a low table where glass-stoppered bottles catch the light. "I've got . . . whiskey, gin, and . . . *vodka!*" He lifts a bottle filled with clear liquid and turns to her. "Ever tried vodka before?"

"No." She's never heard of it, but doesn't like to say.

"All anarchists should know their vodka. Know what they're doing, those Russians. Let's have a vodka, then." Humming, he turns back to the cabinet, takes out two glasses, and pours.

Hettie holds her hands to the fire. On the mantelpiece stand two photographs. One is of Ed, serious in uniform. The other picture is very different: Here he is younger, his hair longer, wearing a cricket sweater. Beside him is a beautiful young woman, looking straight at the camera and laughing. Hettie feels a small contraction in her chest.

"My sister." Ed comes up behind her, gesturing with his glass.

"Oh." Her chest releases as he hands her the drink: clear liquid, ice.

"Probably about the last time I saw her smile." He takes a swig, rocking on his heels, staring at the photograph. "She's bloody miserable. All the time. You got any?"

"Any what?"

"Brothers? Sisters?"

"Oh. One brother." She tries a sip of her vodka. It is cold and clean.

"And is he bloody miserable, too?"

She laughs. "Actually, yes, I think he is."

He lights a cigarette and offers one to her. "Did he serve, then?"

"Yes." She leans in to his light.

"Whereabouts?"

"In France."

"Know where?"

She racks her brains but cannot remember if he has ever told her. Even during the war, they never spoke about France. She feels terrible suddenly. She ought to know this, oughtn't she? But Ed just nods.

"Here." He puts down his drink. "You look as if you're about to run away. Let me help you with your coat."

He takes it from her and puts it over the edge of a chair. And now, finally, when she had almost forgotten she was wearing it, the dress is revealed. The fabric shushes as it falls back into place. The sequins catch and glitter in the low light, and she can feel her skin flush in the heat; acres of it, it seems, are suddenly exposed.

"Goodness," he says.

She pulls off her hat and holds it in front of her dress. When she finally looks up at him, his expression is confounded.

"You cut your hair," he says.

"Yes."

"Why'd you do that?" His voice is oddly flat.

"Because"—she puts her hand to the tapering point at the back of her neck—"I wanted to. I've been wanting to for ages, and I . . ." She trails off. Behind her the fire crackles and spits.

There's a pause, and then "It looks nice," he says, in that same dull tone.

You're lying.

"That's not true," she says, heart thudding.

"I'm sorry?"

For a moment she sees something in him, anger? A quick flash and then it is gone.

"You said—before," she says. "You said we wouldn't say anything that wasn't true."

"Very good." He points his cigarette at her. "You're right. I did. But you're wrong. It is true. You look beautiful. I'm just—"

"You're just what?" It is as though he is twisting her insides.

"Nothing." He turns away, throwing his cigarette onto the fire. "Don't pay any attention to me."

She laughs. It sounds harsh, and hurt.

"Here." He rummages in his pockets and takes out a small round cardboard box. "I've got some of this. Know what it is?" His tone is coaxing, soft.

She has no idea.

"It's snow," he says. When she still doesn't respond, he walks away, over to a sofa in front of a low wooden table. "Come and sit by me."

She stays where she is, watching as he pours a small mound of white powder onto the chessboard and rakes out two long lines.

"This'll liven me up a bit. Make me better company, I promise." He brings a small silver tube from his pocket. "Here." He holds it out toward her. "You should try first."

She has a vague memory of a story. Something from the papers. Two years ago; a girl. An actress. Found dead in her bedroom in the West End.

"Go on. You might like it. You never know."

She crosses the floor toward him. "Can you die from it?"

Ed looks amused. "I suppose you could, if you took enough. But people die all the time, don't they? Of all sorts of silly things."

Who is allowed to think like this? To say things like this? To take things so lightly?

Not her.

Not her mother, or her father or her brother, or the people at the Palais. Not anyone she knows. Not even Di. They are all too busy holding themselves in, not stepping on the cracks, not looking left or right in case the world collapses around their ears.

She sits on the edge of the sofa. "How do I do it, then?"

"You sniff."

"Sniff?"

"Here, I'll show you." He leans down and, passing the tube up one of the lines, he sniffs, and the powder disappears. Then he touches his nostril with his thumb. "You have to keep going," he says. "Keep it continuous."

Hettie takes the tube from him, her heart racing. She bends over the table, puts one finger over the other nostril, and does the same. It hits her hard, burning the back of her throat. "Gosh." She comes back up, her eyes stinging, half of her share still there on the board.

"Have some vodka." Ed pushes her glass toward her, bending down and finishing the rest off.

She does as he suggests. The combination is pepperish and strong.

He sits back up. "It's like the bloody *grave* in here. We should have some music!" He jumps to his feet and goes over to a cabinet in the corner of the room. For the first time she sees he has a beautiful Victrola, the kind that she and Di dream of, all dark wood and glossy gold handles. "What do you like?" he says, winding it up.

"Um—"

"Wait! I forgot. I got something for you yesterday." He takes a record from the cupboard beneath. *"The Original Dixies!"* he says, straightening up, holding it up like a trophy.

"No . . . ? *Really?*"

"They made a record when they were over here, when they were resident at the Palais. Didn't you know?"

She crosses the floor, and he puts the sleeve in her hands. The Dixies are all there on the cover, Nick LaRocca in the middle, grinning, trumpet in hand. It is like seeing an old friend. And suddenly she feels better about everything; suddenly the night is full of promise again. "That's killing!" she says, grinning up at him, passing the record back.

"It certainly is." He slides it from its sleeve, balances the disc on his middle finger, and, bending forward, winds the Victrola a couple more times.

The green baize spins. He puts the glossy disc on top and lowers the arm. There's a burst of static on shellac, and then the unmistakable sound of Nick LaRocca's tumbling trumpet fills the room.

Hettie laughs out loud. She can't help it. Something is jumping through her, asking for release. That powder. That drink. She's going to have to move.

"Give me a hand," says Ed. "Quickly, help me move this." They lift the low table, carry it to the side of the room, and then get down on their hands and knees and roll the carpet away. Now the floor stretches, polished, gleaming, and they come to face each other, and they dance: wildly, crazily, and the small part of Hettie that is aware knows, as she dances, that this is what the people at Dalton's felt; that this is what she has been searching for, that this is what it feels like to be free, beyond yourself, to move as though you just don't care. When the number is over they stand, still holding on to each other, laughing, catching their breath.

"Damned fast," says Ed, shaking his head.

"They played it even faster live."

He gazes at her, a smile on his lips. "There aren't many, you know. Not many girls are interested in music. Not many know jazz."

I could introduce you to ten, at the Palais alone.

"I love it," she says.

The record scratches into the silence between them.

"You really are most awfully lovely, you know. Do you know?" He leans toward her again, and this time, when they kiss, it is different; it is charged and hard and full of intent.

"Come here," he says, pulling away from her, taking her wrist. "Will you come in here with me?"

Day 4

Tangled in her blankets, Evelyn struggles to sit. She is hot and terribly thirsty. She soon sees why: Last night she must have gone to sleep in her clothes. She is lying crossways over the mattress, and her pillow has somehow migrated south to the space between her legs. She sits and curses, pulling her cardigan off over her head, leaving only her jersey and her knickers on, stumbles to her feet and out into the corridor. Doreen's door is ajar. She pauses outside and listens. Silence. She didn't hear her come home last night; she must have spent the night with the man.

They'll be getting married before long; she can see it now.

In the unlit kitchen the taps whine in protest before giving up and shuddering forth water. She fills a glass and drinks it greedily down, takes the kettle from the stove, fills it, and puts it on the range, then pulls the curtains aside so she can see the sky. There's an almost full moon ahead, shaded very lightly away at the top, hanging over the clustered chimney stacks that march east toward Camden Town. She stares out at it, arms wrapped around her chest, hazy from sleep. Behind her comes the quiet *shhh* of the kettle as it rouses the water inside.

Is the moon waxing or waning? She used to know such things. At the beginning of the war, when Fraser was still alive, she would often wake at this time, late in the night but long before the morning, at two or three o'clock, her nightdress stuck to her body with sweat. It was difficult then, in the blackout, to have a light after dark, and she couldn't distract herself by reading, so the only thing that eased the feeling would be to come in here, put a kettle on the stove, open the curtains, and look out at the sky. Distance contracted in the small hours before dawn, and if the night was a clear one she would look for the moon.

I am becoming pagan, Fraser wrote, that first winter. *Here, in this muddy brown monotony, where blood's the only colored thing. There is no God here, only the moon and the sky.*

And so I have made a pact with the moon. On clear nights she will bring me to you.

There's a soft call from the street below. Evelyn watches the milk cart travel around the corner, coming to a halt beneath the gaslight on the other side of the road. The dray horse stamps as its breath streams white into the air. Her eyes light on the window of the terrace opposite, the one belonging to the man in the wheelchair. Looking at it now, blank, unreadable, its curtains shut tight, it's as though she imagined that alcohol fug of yesterday afternoon.

On clear nights she will bring me to you.

She cringes at the thought of it; as though, in its pure bone whiteness, the moon can see into every cranny of her tawdry self.

What has she become?

The man in the wheelchair. Robin, last night: *Perhaps I could come, after all?*

She leans against the side of the counter and breathes out. She misses him. Fraser. Here in the shrunken hours of the night. She misses him still so much. Who is there to share her thoughts with? They wither inside her. She cannot even write them to him as she used to; can't take a cup of tea back to bed and sit with a candle in the blackout and think of him—trying to imagine where he is, what he sees. She cannot imagine where he is, because he is nowhere, he is nothing. All of the many tiny things that he was: the way he turned his head toward her, the slow breaking of his smile, the laughter in him, the roll of his voice; the way that he eased her, eased her—these are all gone. These are all dead. All of the life that was in him, all of the life that they could have spent together. Gone.

Her heart thuds dully into the silence. Her broken heart, still beating on.

And she is alive. For what? She has endured. Is enduring. *Killing time.* Like all of them; the pathetic women with their adverts in the papers, the palpable desperation behind the cheer:

Spinster, 38. Loving disposition. Anxious to correspond.

Spinster.

Spinster.

Old maid.

She has become one of them. Slowly and then all at once. Those women other women pity. The lucky ones, with rings on their fingers and prams in the street. They cross the street to avoid her. They can smell it on her. Bad luck.

What next for her? For any of them?

Robin? Is he what is next?

Perhaps I could come, after all?

And would it be so bad? After all?

She shakes her head. She will not go. It is ridiculous. Weak. Her life has made her weak.

Behind her, the kettle whistles and jiggers on the stove. She pulls it off the flame, makes her tea, and then carries it into the bedroom and climbs back into bed.

When she worked at the munitions factory, she no longer woke in the night. She was too tired. They made her a machinist first. There was a grim satisfaction to it: punching holes in metal over and over again. Five holes in each sheet. Twenty-odd sheets an hour. She got up from twenty-four to thirty in her first week, working on a large bench with fifteen other women from eight till five o'clock. It was tiring, but she made sure that she never leaned against the bench, never ran the risk of being thought soft. At ten o'clock they all marched downstairs to drink a glass of milk. They stood in two long lines: one formed of the machinists, like her, and the other with women from different parts of the sheds. On her first day she noticed that they had bright yellow skin on their faces, their arms, and their hands.

"Canaries," whispered the woman in the queue behind her. "Some of them haven't got long left."

Evelyn turned to her. "How do you know?"

"They're sick, aren't they? That's why they look like that."

The canaries sat at different benches on the other side of the room.

At the end of her second week she skipped lunch and went to the office of the overseer. "I'd like to move sheds," she said. "I'd like to work with the TNT."

The man stared at her over his glasses. He had a mild, distant face. He looked as if he might have been a schoolteacher before the war.

"Women like you don't work on shells," he said.

"I'm sorry?"

"Women like you don't work on shells."

"What do you mean, women like me?"

The man took off his glasses; without them his eyes were pouched, tiny things. He rubbed at them. One side of his right eye was pink and irritated. He sighed. "Miss?"

"Montfort."

"Miss Montfort. The TNT sheds are a wholly different place from the rest of the factory."

"I understand."

"Do you?"

"Yes. That's why I'd like to work there."

He eyed her. "Why are you here, Miss Montfort?"

"Why is anyone here?"

"Money, Miss Montfort. Money."

"Then money is why I am here."

He stared at her. He looked unconvinced.

"I should like," she said crisply, "to work with the TNT."

"All right," he said, putting his glasses back on his nose, dismissing her with a wave of his hand. "As you wish."

The girl she shared her bench with looked all of fifteen. On her first morning she passed Evelyn a stump of something. The girl had a round child's face and plump lips. "Cordite," she said. She spoke with a lisp. "We're not supposed to eat it. But it's ever so sweet and nice."

Evelyn touched it to her lips. It was true. It was sweet.

"If you suck it," said the girl, "it's nice."

The TNT buildings were on the far side of the factories. To get to them you had to pass through other sheds, full of older women: barefoot, thin, bent over their pots of molten lead, ladling the scaly liquid out; they looked liked Gypsies, or witches, with their long hair unbound.

When daylight savings time began, and the world was plunged even further into blackness, Evelyn volunteered for the night shifts. To sleep in the day at least had novelty to it. So she lived her life in the dark. Coming on to the night shift in the blackout, the women would call to one another, holding each other's hands to walk from the railway station to their buildings, forming long, snaking chains.

She was given the job of examiner, which meant she had to test the gauge of the calico bags filled with the TNT. She would handle up to a hundred bags a day. After two weeks her hair had turned a bright ginger hue. If she were ever out in the daytime, people would stare at her in the street. They would nod, as though they were acknowledging some unspoken debt, but were frightened nonetheless.

The yellowness spread to her skin—first her face, then all over the rest. She watched her hands turn with creeping fascination. Her eyes were tinged with bronze. She hardly recognized herself in her mirror. After her bath, the water was the color of blood. But she felt a strange, creeping power from this subterranean life. She felt she was getting closer to something real. She felt she might be turning into a witch.

Then she started to become sick. She noticed a peculiar taste in her mouth after meals. She was sick, often, and the vomiting would relieve the taste. Her urine was the color of strong tea. She began to lose weight. Her temperature rose. A rash broke out all over her body. When she fainted at work they took her out of the sheds and sent her home. The doctor came and examined her in bed. When he had finished, he made a few short notes on the pad in his hand. She listened to his pen, scratching into the silence, as she stared at the faded flower pattern that was papered to the wall.

"Miss Montfort," he said. The *s*'s in *Miss* sounded sibilant; they lingered in the air.

"Yes?"

"Are you aware that you're pregnant?"

She turned to him.

"No?" He shook his head, closed his pad, and put it back into his bag. "You need to stay in bed. To recover from the TNT poisoning." His voice softened. "I doubt very much that you will keep your child."

She did as the doctor ordered, and stayed in bed for a week. She told no one, not even Doreen. It was easy not to, since everyone already thought she was ill. She slept late—long strange sleeps, full of dreams—and when she woke, in the late mornings, she put her hands to her belly and thought of the tiny life that was gathering itself there. She thought back to that last morning she and Fraser spent together: the heat of the day, the tang of the salt held in his lip. A small, clear voice in her rejoiced. Whatever the consequences, it made sense, somehow, of everything that had gone before.

But after a week she began to bleed, first brown and scant, then red and bright. A week later the bleeding was finished. The small scrap of life had left her, a tiny addition to the crowded ranks of the dead.

When she was well again she went back to the factory and asked for a job. They put her back in the machine shed where she had started out. Two weeks later, she had her accident and lost her finger.

When the bandages came off she almost smiled. It was eloquent, with its smooth, rounded stump. The proof of absence. The real thing.

She rubs the nub of her finger now with her thumb. In the darkness she can just see the outline of her satchel, hanging from the back of her bedroom door. Rowan Hind's address is on a piece of notebook paper inside. Today is Wednesday. The office will close at twelve as it always does, and she will have the afternoon free. Tomorrow, Thursday, Armistice Day, is a national holiday, so if she wants to catch Rowan Hind then she should go to Poplar after work today; there will be no chance on Thursday, the streets will be thronged and he will most likely not be at home.

She brings her knees up and clasps her arms around them.

So she said she would go with her brother, to the burial of this Unknown Warrior; to stand on Anthony's balcony with Lottie and the rest of them and listen as they bray at *the show*.

How pleased she is for the scraps that Ed throws her way.

They get ideas. Fixed in their heads. They can't move on.

You're meddling, Eves.

Her little brother. Dismissing her. He used to look up to her once. To listen when she talked.

She won't go. She hates it, anyway, this *Armistice Day;* this new tradition already dripping with oily reverence; another opportunity for those with blood on their hands to play fancy dress in their murderers' suits and drag their horses and their gun carriages behind them as they parade the London streets. As if there is no other way to honor the dead.

Someone should do the world a favor. They should take one of those great guns that they wheel out for the occasion and turn it around; they should train it on the massed dignitaries at the Cenotaph, in the abbey, on the king and Lloyd George and Haig and the whole lot of them, should shoot them while they sit there, their old heads bent in prayer. Praying for the souls of the dead. Hypocrites; stinking hypocrites all.

. . . .

She can't see much between the legs. There are lots of different sorts of legs, though: brown trousers, black trousers, checked, and blue and black women's stockings. There's a strong, fusty smell, like her granny's house, only stronger.

The little girl gives a tug on her father's hand.

"What's that?" His big face looms high above her.

"Can I come up again, Dad?"

"All right, chicken." He smiles. "Come on." And he lifts her, hoisting her high onto his shoulders, in one clean movement of his strong arms. She puts her hands on his head, the way he taught her to, steadying herself, and now she can breathe again, and see. She can see her family far below, her two older sisters and her mother on the other side of her dad, surrounded by all of the other hundreds of people, who are standing up here together on top of the cliffs. She

can see the high, white cliffs, which are not white today, but gray, and the gray sky, and the gray-green sea. And then below, down in Dover where they have come from, the town where they live, she can see even more people. She tried to count them, earlier on, but had to stop, because it made her feel hot and dizzy. Her dad said there are thousands and thousands. The reason there are so many is that all the children have been given the day off school. And all the dads have been given the day off work.

The little girl scans the horizon.

She knows they are waiting for a ship—a ship that has a soldier on it. But they have been up here forever already and there has been no sign.

Then, at the blurry line where the sea meets the sky, she sees something. The little girl squints. Looks away. Looks again. It is definitely there: a dark shape in the fog. "Daddy," she says, excitedly, kicking her heels against her father's chest. "Look!"

Her father straightens up and gives a low cry. A murmur moves through the crowd; the girl stretches to watch as it ripples through the people below.

Now lights appear—ship's lights—and then . . . a ship, many ships, a large, dark ship and six smaller ones on either side. Below, her older sisters jump up and down, clamoring to be lifted so they can see, too. But her father ignores them, and she stays up there on her father's shoulders as the ships come closer, her heart beating a frantic rhythm on her chest. He pats her on the shins. "Good girl," he murmurs. "Good girl." And she could just about burst with pride, because she was the first, she was the first one to see.

. . . .

Poplar is even farther than Evelyn thought.

She left the office at half past twelve; she hasn't had any lunch and it's already nearly two. She's sitting on the bottom of the omnibus, squeezed in between the window and a large, damp-smelling woman; and the whole bus is crammed full of people, in the aisles, standing all the way up the stairs. She rubs her sleeve against the glass and peers out but recognizes nothing; she traveled into uncharted territory hours ago.

The scars of war are more obvious out here: entire houses missing in the middle of terraces, the gaps given over to tumbled rubble and wild grass. Earlier, the bus stopped by a half-ruined house and she could see into the upstairs bedroom, see the red-flowered wallpaper that the last unlucky occupants chose, weather-faded now, streaked with water and rust. When the bus lurched on again she was glad; it seemed too sad a thing, too intimate to be seen.

The conductor passes, and she leans over the woman and touches his sleeve. "Excuse me?"

"Yes, miss?"

"I'm looking for Poplar High Street. . . . Are we nearly there?"

"Next stop."

She leans back in her seat. Poplar. It sounds so bucolic; Pissarro was the one who painted poplars, wasn't he? There was a letter that Fraser sent her, an early one, describing a route march that he had taken.

Just like something out of Pissarro, a long, straight road with poplars on either side. You could never have imagined what was going on twenty miles north.

"Excuse me." She squeezes past the woman beside her and, as the bus starts to slow, jumps off the back. The cold air is welcome after the packed, fetid bus. To her left is a straggling row of down-at-the-heels shops and costermongers, several of them with black-clad queues of women alongside who eye her as she passes by. The barrows are half-full of unpromising-looking vegetables: graying potatoes, carrots, gritty turnips, and swedes. From her right, on the other side of the road, comes the clank and trundle of distant, heavy machinery, and across roofs and scrubland she can see the tilting cranes of the docks.

She heads along a wide main street in which rubbish and dead leaves fill the gutters. On either side of the road a few bored-looking men sit sprawled on benches, smoking. She avoids their gaze—knows the look, sees it every day, the stare of unemployment, of anger and apathy: a combustible mix. Farther up the hill she passes two cafés with a steady stream of dockers pouring out of each. A couple of the men turn their heads and shout halfheartedly after her. She puts her head down and pulls her collar up.

Grafton Street is two streets farther on: two rows of low terraces facing each other across a narrow strip of earth. There are no pavements and no trees, only a tangled knot of children whose noisy, scrappy game has full possession of the road. She looks for numbers on the doors, but sees none. When she turns, having covered the houses on one side, she sees the children have left off whatever they were playing and are standing, staring her way. Some of them are older than she first thought; they look to be all ages, from toddlers to nine or ten.

"Excuse me." She takes a couple of steps closer to them, cursing her accent. "I'm looking for the Hinds. I know they live at number eleven, but I'm not sure from which end I'm supposed to count."

The knot of children contracts like a dirty brown sea anemone and a small girl is given a push from behind. Despite the cold, she's not wearing any shoes. She crosses the dirt with small, wary steps toward where Evelyn stands.

"Number eleven?" Evelyn holds out the paper and points to the numerals.

The girl stares blankly at it.

"Hind?" She bends so that her face is close to the girl's. "Rowan Hind?"

"That's my dad," the girl whispers, and flinches away; and then she is gone, running, a pale streak disappearing around the back of the terrace.

Damn. Evelyn straightens up. She should have said something to reassure the kid; she must have thought her father was in trouble and ran back to warn him. He'll probably hide—probably never come out now.

The rest of the children are still staring at her, as watchful as cats. She has the sudden, silly impulse to do something stupid, to pull a face or do a dance on the spot. But she does neither. Instead she folds the piece of paper, puts it back in her bag, and walks slowly away, toward the sounds of the distant docks. As she walks, she racks her brain. She could knock on doors, asking for the Hinds, but then that would only arouse more suspicion. Who knows what type of person they think she is? Someone come to cause trouble, no doubt.

And wouldn't they be right?

She shakes her head. Damn. Damn. *Damn.*

A door to one of the terraces opens to her right. A pretty woman stands framed within it. Evelyn can just make out the little girl hiding behind her skirts.

"Mrs. Hind?"

The woman is pregnant, close to her time, and tired. Pale eyes. Thin, fair hair tied loosely at her neck.

"Who wants to know?"

Evelyn crosses to her door, holding out her hand with a confidence she doesn't feel. "My name's Evelyn Montfort. I—work in a pensions office in Camden Town." She tries a smile but feels it fall to the ground somewhere between their feet. "Your husband came to see me, two days ago. He was looking for help. I said that I couldn't help him. But now I—find that I can."

The woman is silent. Behind her Evelyn can see an uncarpeted hallway and the little girl, staring out.

"Is he there? Is he at home?"

The woman shakes her head. "He's at work."

"I see."

"He's a salesman," she says, with a pale hint of pride. "Door-to-door."

She nods. "Of course. It was silly of me to come so early."

The woman's eyes dart over Evelyn's face. "Is he in trouble? He's not in any trouble, is he?"

"He's not in trouble, no," she says softly, coming closer to the door. "Look. I realize that this must seem very strange, me coming out here like this, but I would very much like to talk to your husband. Do you think you could tell me what time he finishes work?"

"Four." The woman narrows her eyes. "There or thereabouts."

"Then if it's all right, I'll come back at four?"

There's a silence.

"Mrs. Hind?"

The woman nods, briefly, and goes to shut the door.

When she reaches the end of the road, Evelyn turns, expecting to see the children still watching, but their fleeting interest has passed. They have knitted inward, and are playing again whatever noisy game they were playing before.

. . . .

Two hours after it weighed anchor, the ship begins to move. It leaves the destroyers behind and starts to steam slowly to the eastern entrance of Dover Port, skirting the high, reared cliffs.

A young naval officer stands at the stern of the ship. The coffin is in front of him, covered with wreaths, with more wreaths piled high around it. The young officer had to help carry those wreaths aboard. Some of them took four men to lift. He wonders if it is a peculiarly French thing. They seem to go in for their flowers, all right.

He stands, legs spread, arms held behind his back. He can see the massed crowds, now, clustered deep around the port. High up on the cliffs, faces are fixed on the ship. On the ramparts of the castle, he can see the cannons readying to fire.

The cannon fire echoes and booms around the still harbor, causing the water to lift in tiny, shivering waves. A nineteen-gun salute. A field marshal's welcome.

After the guns comes silence. An astonishing silence, clean and bare. Then the ship's horn sounds briefly, once, and the young man moves to man his rope.

. . . .

Hettie turns over in bed.

Rock-a-bye your baby
With a Dixie melody

The music is coming from somewhere nearby. Someone is singing along underneath. For a moment, in the darkness, she wonders if it is her brother, thinking hazily that Fred must have gone and bought himself a gramophone, but when she stretches her leg out, something feels immediately wrong, since the bed she is in is enormous. Then she sits up, hugging her arms around her, breathing hard. She is still wearing Di's dress; its sequins have pressed themselves into her arm. It comes back to her then in a sort of sick, horrified rush.

It didn't happen.

None of it. None of it happened in the way she had hoped.

At first—when they came in here, it had seemed as though it would. And when his mouth was on her neck, and they were lying, side by side, it was happening, and she was ready for it—and then—

Then there was space, and air; he had rolled away from her and was lying on the other side of the bed.

"Sorry," he said, his voice muffled by his hands.

"What?"

"I just—" He started muttering then, just on the edge of hearing, something about losing something, about something being lost. Hettie watched, horrified, until after a moment he stopped and lifted his head. "Stay," he said. "You can stay here till the tubes start running."

"No." She shook her head violently. "I'll go."

"Please!" He held his hands out as though to press her down into the bed. "Please just . . . stay. I want you to stay here. You'll be safe. I promise. Just—" He ran his hands through his hair, tugging at it. "Just stay." He moved away from her, over to the door. "You're safe," he said again.

Then he turned off the light and shut the door, and she lay there, heart hammering in the dark, wanting to run but unable to move, listening to him walking around, talking to himself outside. After what seemed like hours, he was finally quiet, and then she must have fallen asleep herself, because she doesn't remember anything more.

The music has stopped now. Hettie slips out of bed, crossing the carpet to where a crack of light comes through the curtains. She pulls them apart, leaning forward, her fingertips pressed against the cold glass. The house she is in is part of a line of cream terraces, and she is high up, on the fifth floor or so. Part of a park, the branches of the trees almost leafless, stretches away up a hill to the right of where she stands. The day is cold-looking, and from the light, which looks to be failing, it must be afternoon, at least. Then she has slept through the day. She has to be at work at half past seven. She has to go home.

She finds the bathroom, uses the lavatory as quietly as she can, then picks up her shoes and pads to the door. She does all of this mechanically and quickly, because if she thinks too much then she might cry.

Behind the door the living room stretches, curtains drawn, the only light a corner lamp. The table is still shoved over to one side, the carpet rolled away. She can see the powder box on the chessboard. The Victrola hisses and scratches in the corner of the room.

Tsss *du* tsss *du* tsss *du*.

A large wingback chair is in front of her, and beyond that she can see her coat and hat still draped over the back of the sofa. She sets off toward them.

"Morning."

She jumps and whirls around; Ed is leaning around the side of the chair, frowning. "I hope you weren't planning to go without saying good-bye?"

She grips her shoes and shakes her head.

"That's good." He nods. "Sleep well?"

She stares at him. He is smiling now, acting as though nothing strange happened last night at all. "I'm—not sure," she manages. "Why. Did—you?"

He takes his time thinking about her question. His white shirt is untucked and unbuttoned. He has taken his collar off, and the collar and his tie are lying on the floor. There's a decanter of whiskey on the table beside him and a half-empty glass in his hand. "I'm not sure I've slept at all," he says finally. "Although . . . I may have nodded off for a minute just then. There was music on, I think. It's finished now." He lifts his glass toward her. "Like a drink? I think I might have another now you're here." He is speaking very precisely, as though it is an effort for him to do so, but the edges of his words are slurred.

She can feel a twisting in her stomach. She doesn't want another drink—doesn't want to be here in this dark room, with this man she cannot read. She is tired and on the edge of tears and wants to go home. "Do you know the time?"

"Time?" He shakes his head. "Don't bother about *time*. Time's a useless, *useless* thing."

A flash of anger passes through her. "I have to be at work soon."

"All right." Ed stretches his neck around the wing of his chair. "It's half past three," he says, as a clock on a side table whirrs and clicks out the half hour. "Early still," he says, shaking his glass with a blurry smile. "Come and have a drink."

"I have to go." She bends down, pulls on her shoes, and starts to buckle them.

"Whiskey?"

"No, thank you."

"Vodka?"

She shakes her head, straightening back up.

His face creases in thought. "Tea?"

Silence. The Victrola hisses. They regard each other across the space.

"Tea," he says decisively. "Just the thing for the afternoon."

He pushes himself up out of his chair, and makes his unsteady way over to a door, on the other side of which is a small kitchen. "Come on," he says, turning to her at the door. "Come and keep me company."

And there is something in the way he says it, something so help-less suddenly, that she relents and follows him, standing in the door while he fills the kettle, hugging herself against the cold.

He doesn't open the blind, just puts a little electric light on and roots through tins, opening them and smelling them. It's as though he's never made a cup of tea in his life. After a moment he straight-ens up and turns to her, seeming to read her thoughts. "I usually have help," he says, "with things like this."

"Oh. Yes." *Of course.*

"But . . ." He turns back and starts rooting around in the cupboards again. "I gave my man the morning off. *Aha.* He lights on the right tin, shakes leaves from it into the pot, then takes a knife and holds it up. "Not entirely sure where he keeps the teaspoons," he says, apologetically, before dunking the knife and using it to stir. "Come on, then. Shall we take it next door?"

He carries the pot and a cup and saucer carefully over to the table in the living room. "Sit down," he says. He sits opposite her, frowning as though weighing something up. "Think I'll leave it awhile," he says after a minute, pointing in the direction of the teapot. "And then I'll pour."

She puts her hands under her thighs. Her arms are covered with gooseflesh. Last night's fire is an ashy pile in the grate. She thinks about putting her coat on. Under normal circumstances that would be impolite. But the normal rules of behavior seem no longer to apply, so she reaches for it, sliding it over her lap.

Ed smiles hazily in her direction. "We need music, don't we? Hang on." He stands again, weaving his way over to the Victrola and bending forward to wind it up. The scratching stops and the singing returns—the same song that woke her. He joins in softly, his back to her, swaying to and fro.

> *Rock-a-bye your baby*
> *With a Dixie melody*
> *When you croon, croon a tune*
> *From the heart of Dixie.*

"You know this one?" He turns to her.

"No."

"It's an old one. A lullaby."

He lifts his arms up and starts moving with a ghostly partner around the floor. "Come on," he says after a bit.

Hettie stays where she is.

"Come *on.* You're no fun."

Fun?

Was what happened last night fun, then?

She stands defiantly and walks over to him. He puts his hands on her shoulders, leaning his weight on her, and they move a little, side to side.

"This is nice," he says, his eyes almost closed. He reeks of drink. When he tries to turn, he catches himself on the low table and begins to sway, like a tree half-felled, and she has to move to save herself as he falls onto the floor.

"*Fuck.*" He puts his hands up to cover his eyes.

"I'm sorry." She kneels beside him. "Are you hurt?"

"'S all right. 'S not your fault. Shouldn't be so—goddamn *tight.*" He lies there for a moment without moving. "*God,*" he says. "I'm just—so bloody *drunk.*" He closes his eyes. "Think I must be tired, too," he says. "Hard to tell."

Over on the Victrola the singing warbles to a stop and the scratching comes back. Hettie eyes the door. Ed opens his eyes and smiles up at her. "Would you mind awfully giving me a hand to my feet?"

She puts her hands out and he takes them, nearly toppling her over as he pulls himself up. "That's better." He pats himself down. "Nothing broken." He is still swaying a bit. "Shall we sit down?" he says. "I think I need to sit."

He makes it to the sofa, where he sits heavily, shading his eyes to look at her, closing one of them as though he is in sudden, blinding sun. "That's better," he says. "Two of you, then. Come and sit beside me."

"I have to go," she says.

"Please?"

She sits on the very edge of the sofa, the bit nearest to the door. She feels him lean closer to her, but she doesn't look at him.

"Did I tell you you remind me of someone?"

She threads her fingers together in her lap. "Yes. You did." She can feel his eyes on her face.

"And did I tell you who it was?"

"No."

There's a silence, then, "How old are you?" he says.

"Nineteen."

"Nine*teen*?"

She turns to his gaze, which is steadier all of a sudden, tender, and she is caught in it. It is as though some of his drunkenness has left him in his fall. And her stomach plunges, because he is still here, this man she met at Dalton's, this man who is unlike anyone she has ever known. "Why?" she says. "How old are you?"

"Twenty-seven." He shakes his head. "Twenty-eight soon. *Ancient history.*" He fishes a cigarette case out of his pocket, taps one out, and puts it in his mouth. "You remember," he says, leaning forward to light it. "Last night. How we were going to speak to each other. How we were going to tell each other the truth?"

"Yes."

"Well, I didn't. I'm a liar."

His eyes find hers. Her heart thuds.

"And I want to tell you now."

"I should leave—" she says.

"Not yet. There's time. Just stay. For a minute. Please." He gives a small smile. "You look frightened."

"I'm not frightened."

"You've no reason to be. You're perfectly safe. I can't do any of that stuff, even if I wanted to."

"What do you mean?"

"All that," he says, waving with his hand. "Down there."

She swallows.

"That's it," he says. "*That's* the truth." He sits back, opening his hands. "There it is." Then he looks back up, his hands still open, as though offering her something. It is as though he wants her to do something, with this thing he has said. Take it from him somehow.

She doesn't want it.

She wants him to stop.

But he doesn't stop. He carries on speaking.

"Happened in France first," he says. "One of those girls behind the line."

Hettie brings her arms around herself.

"Country girls. Their fathers would open the houses for the men."

For a second she wonders if she has heard him right. "Their *fathers?*"

He nods, looks up at her. "They'd do it to make money. They were desperate by then. Starving. Their farms had been destroyed. You'd pay more for it, you see, if it was in a house. But they were always clean. You were less likely to get the clap."

She cannot imagine it. She heard the stories, in the beginning, about German soldiers, and Belgian women, and the rapes, but this is different somehow. Her father would never have done a thing like that. He would have protected her. Wouldn't he?

But the idea has a creeping fascination—a war in London; coming to Hammersmith; soldiers in the street.

Some fathers would. Some fathers might.

How hungry would she have to be to do it herself?

"What happened?" she says. "In the houses, I mean, how did it work?"

He shrugs. "Usually . . . you'd queue up—"

"How many—people—men—how many would there be in the queue?"

"Depended. Army-sanctioned whores . . . they'd be doing it for days at a time. There'd be forty, fifty, sixty men waiting their turn. They didn't last too long though, the women, they were usually on their last legs. This house was for officers, and the girls were fresh.

I only had to wait two or three until my turn." He grows quiet. "She was young."

"How old?"

"About your age. Perhaps a bit younger." He stares ahead of him. "I went in and I washed myself. They always had a little sink in the corner for that. Then, when I turned to her, she was looking at me. Mostly they didn't, you see. And she had such a lovely face. In the midst of all of that—awfulness." His face contracts. "She was so . . . fresh. And then she lay back, and I lay on top of her and"—he gestures with his hand: a flat line—"nothing." He gives a brief, rueful laugh. "I couldn't touch her." He looks up at Hettie. "She had hair like yours. Long and brown and unbroken. And that's what I thought, when I saw you in that terrible club; I'd been about to go home, but then I saw you standing there. And I thought, Maybe I can get it back. That thing I lost. Maybe you can help me get it back."

He is not making sense.

"You cut your hair," he says, and there is something terrible, imploring, in his face. "Why did you do it? *Why?*"

Hettie shakes her head. She can feel anger now, rising in her. She is angry with him. With all of them. All of the men, waiting their turn. For those young girls. And those women. *On their last legs.* What happened to them, after that? Where did they end up?

"Why does it matter?" she says. "Why does it matter if I cut my hair?"

"Because you can never go back," he says.

"Hair grows."

"I know it does," he says sadly. "But you can never go back." And he bends forward, putting his head in his hands.

She can hear him, breathing hard.

She should touch him, she thinks. This is her job here. She should reach out and touch his arm. Say something to make him come back to himself. Rouse him to his manhood somehow. She thinks this, but she is angry, and this anger is a fierce, clear thing, and she does not.

"I didn't want to hear that story," she says.

He looks up at her. "Oh, God," he says, and his face drains of blood. "I'm so sorry. It's just—there was something—I lost. And I—haven't tried to be with anyone since."

"I want to go home." She stands up, pulling on her coat. "I have to go to work and I want to go home."

"Of course. That was dreadful of me. All of it. God," he says, shaking his head. "What an utter fool."

And then he hits himself, punches himself hard in the temple. He hits himself so hard that her hand flies up to her mouth. He sits there for a moment, as though stunned. Then lifts his hand again.

"No!" She puts her hand out to stop him and catches his wrist. "Please! Don't."

He stills, nodding slowly, as though acknowledging something, and brings his hand onto his lap. He flexes his fingers out. "Sorry," he says quietly. "I don't know quite what happened there."

After a moment, he stands up. He straightens his trousers. All of his drunkenness seems to have drained quite away. He simply looks exhausted now. He pats his pockets and takes out some money. He looks at it, seeming to think about it. "Have you enough money to get home?"

"Yes. I'll get the tube. It'll be running now."

"Right-o." He puts the money back in his pocket, and she is glad. "Your hat," he says, picking it up and passing it to her. Their knuckles graze briefly as she takes it from him. Then he walks to the door, and they step out onto the green-tiled landing. He presses the button for the lift.

He looks down the lift shaft, as though it is fascinating all of a sudden, as though study of lift shafts is his favorite thing in the world. It seems to take an awfully long time traveling up. They stand side by side, not speaking. When it arrives, he pulls back the cover. "Forgive me," he says, quietly, "for being such a terrible bore."

"You weren't," she says.

He shakes his head. "You're very kind," he says, with a tiny, rueful smile, "but I know that's not true."

Hettie steps into the lift, and he pulls the grille across.

As the lift starts to jerk and crank its way down, she catches a last glimpse, through the grille of the door, of the latticed, broken jigsaw of his face.

. . . .

This is not how Ada had imagined it. She had imagined somewhere different: a dark room with a round table, like somewhere from the pictures, or from the comedy sketches—the ones of people talking to the dead. There have been plenty of those these last few years. But this room is ordinary and light: the back room of a house in a street as ordinary as Ivy had said it would be. And the woman sitting opposite her is ordinary-looking, too, in a way. There is something about her, though, difficult to grasp. It is hard to tell her age, for a start; she could be forty-five or so, the same age as Ada, but she could be ten years older. Her skin is smooth and unlined. She seems to have all her teeth.

The woman was reluctant when Ada knocked on her door. She could tell that, when she asked for a Mrs. Kempton, holding out the piece of paper she was carrying, explaining that a friend had recommended her—a friend who had come to see her during the war. The woman looked up and down the street and then, "All right," she'd said, she supposed she'd better come in. "But I don't really do this anymore."

She showed her down a hallway smelling of recently cooked

meat, past an open door through which Ada glimpsed a parlor with a piano against one wall, then into this room at the back of the house, with just one table in it and no other furniture, no pictures, looking out over a small garden, in which a rosebush stands, still heavy with the last of its blooms.

"Have you brought something of his with you?" the woman asks now.

Ada's heartbeat increases. They haven't even spoken of money yet. How much will this woman ask for when they are done?

She takes the lumpy one-eyed rabbit from her bag. It took a long time for her to decide what to bring. It is a toy she stitched for Michael one Christmas, when he was a baby, and which he didn't let go of for the next few years. She puts it on the table, where it sits, sorry-looking and saggy; the felt rubbed bare in patches, its one brown eye staring back.

The woman turns the worn rabbit in her hands. In the silence, Ada can hear a clock ticking somewhere in the house. "Have you nothing else?" the woman says eventually. "Nothing else of his?"

Her mouth feels dry. "Is that wrong, then?"

"Not wrong, no." The woman puts it back on the table. Her hands are pale, her fingers long. "I just wonder if we may need something a little more recent than this. Have you a photograph at all?"

The most recent one Ada could find was the one from the box, the one that was blurred, and she had hoped not to have to get it out, but she takes it from her bag and puts it in the woman's outstretched palm.

"I'm sorry." She begins to sweat; it inches its way between her skin and her stays, a long slow curl.

"Why?" The woman looks up. Her gaze is even.

"It's not a very good photograph."

The woman holds it for a moment more and then nods briefly

before putting it down on the table. Then she stands and draws the curtains, which are green but thin, so now green light filters into the room. "I hope you don't mind the curtains drawn," she says. "But we don't want to be disturbed."

Ada wonders who or what would disturb them, around the back of this quiet house. The woman comes to sit, and there's silence again as she touches the rabbit and then the photograph in turn.

Even though none of this is funny, Ada is filled with the urge to laugh.

The woman opens her eyes. "I'm not one for the séance," she says. Her voice has changed; it is light and clear.

Ada jolts.

"None of those tricks or performances for me." The woman takes her hands away and puts them in her lap. "I've been trying to listen," she says.

"Listen to what?"

"To your son."

A sour thin chill passes down Ada's spine, and in its wake comes a wave of nausea. She closes her eyes and waits for the feeling to pass.

"Are you all right?"

Ada opens her eyes again and focuses on the woman's smooth face. "I think so."

"I should have said," says the woman, "if at any point you feel that you want this to stop, then you must say." She spreads her hands on the tablecloth. "I've been trying to listen," she says again, frowning, "but it's hard."

"How do you mean?"

"He is dead. Your son. Without a doubt. I cannot feel him here."

The room tilts.

"Are you all right?"

Ada comes back to herself. Nods.

"Good," says the woman, evenly. "Your son is dead. But you didn't come here to learn that." She speaks almost briskly, in a matter-of-fact way.

Didn't I?

Ada finds that she is glad of the briskness.

Perhaps I didn't, after all.

"Tell me about him." The woman puts her finger on the photograph. "Can you tell me when this was taken?" She pushes it across the table.

Ada glances briefly toward it. "I'm not sure."

"Why do you carry it if you don't want to look at it?"

"I don't like it."

"Why not?"

She makes herself look. "His face is blurred."

"Yes, it is." The woman looks up. "If you don't like it, then why do you carry this particular photograph?"

"I don't."

The woman raises her eyebrow.

Ada shifts in her chair; she feels like this is a test she is failing— has already failed. "I have one in the frame, in the parlor, but I didn't think I should bring that one on the bus."

The woman's face softens. "I'll tell you what," she says. "I think that you should put this away." She hands the photograph back. "And I wouldn't look at it again if it makes you feel like that."

Ada takes it and puts it back in her bag, feels relief course through her.

"Why don't you describe him to me instead?"

"Pardon?"

The woman's gaze is steady. "Why don't you describe him to me? I'm sure you could describe him better than any photograph would."

This feels like another test, a worse one.

"Don't worry," says the woman softly. "There's nothing to get right. Just see what comes into your mind."

She tries to think, but her mind is blank—or rather, not blank, but fizzing and thick. She shakes her head to try to clear it. She cannot see him. Cannot conjure his face. She cannot do this and the photograph is blurred and her son is dead. She stands up, putting her hands on the table. They do not look like her own. Her blood is like a tide. Then the woman is beside her, her cool hand on hers. The tide passes. There is silence behind it.

"Let me get you some water."

Ada sits. She can hear noises from the kitchen, water being poured from a jug. The woman returns, placing a glass down on the table before her. "Would you like to stop?"

"No." She is thirsty, suddenly, terribly thirsty. She drinks the water down. "I want to go on." She puts the empty glass on the table between them. "No one," she says. "Not one person. Not in three years. Not my husband even, has ever asked me to talk about my son."

The woman nods. "Tell me."

Ada closes her eyes. "He was—ordinary. An ordinary boy." She remembers something then, something she hasn't thought of in a long time. "He was funny. He told daft jokes."

"What was his favorite?"

"He told a joke about—" She grimaces. "Terrible jokes."

"Tell me one."

"He used to tell a joke about India . . . about Indian food. And India-gestion."

The woman smiles. So does Ada. "He told that one over and over again. Terrible." She shakes her head. "He'd play out with his football—all hours—till I had to drag him in. He went along to the games with his dad, you see, ever since he was small. He liked swimming in the canal. In the summertime. I always told him not to, but he wouldn't listen. I always knew when he'd been doing it, though."

"How?"

"He smelt funny." She wrinkles her nose. "He couldn't hide it. I used to worry he'd get sick. But he never did."

The woman nods again. "Did he want to go to war?"

The question is simple, but shocking somehow, in its directness.

"At first." Ada nods. "When all the lads from his team joined up. But he was too young then. He went after his birthday in 1917." She pauses. "But by then it felt . . . different."

"How?"

"Well, it felt—like they were all—like it was hopeless, didn't it? Like they were all just going to their deaths. And I think he knew."

"Why do you say that?"

"There was something that he said to me. 'There's nothing safe,' he said. 'There's no such thing.' I couldn't get that out of my head. I still can't. And I think—I could have stopped it, somehow."

"How could you have stopped it?" The woman leans forward in her seat.

"I could have hid him." She looks up. Her heart is beating so hard and so fast that she believes that the woman must be able to hear it, see it, through her stays, through her dress.

"How?" says the woman, equally softly. "How could you have done that?"

"My husband." Her voice is thick, but she clears her throat. "He works at a factory. He knew someone in the union who was doing it. They did it for one or two of them at the same time." She has never told this to anyone before. Cannot believe she is saying it now. "He wanted to, Jack. But I said no." She shakes her head. "I said he had to go."

"Jack is your husband?"

"Yes."

"He would have risked an awful lot to do that."

"I know."

"So would you."

She can feel a tightening, her heart, her throat. Pressure building. It is difficult to swallow. She speaks quickly, the words tumbling out. "I thought that if he went, if he hid, and they found him, then he could be worse off. That they would have sent him over anyway. You read about those men that they found like that. And anyway"— she shakes her head—"he wouldn't have gone. Michael. He'd never have done it. But I keep thinking now, What if I'd let Jack try? We might still have him today."

The only sound is the quiet hissing of the gas.

"Do you feel guilty?"

She looks up. For the first time she feels scornful of this woman. What use is she, if she can't tell the obvious? If she can't read what's right in front of her face? And what is she doing here, in this empty room, talking to this stranger of the most intimate of things? "Of course I do."

"Guilt is a very powerful attractor."

"What do you mean by that?"

"Do you see him?"

"Who?"

"Your son."

She feels a prickling on her scalp, as if insects were running in among her hair. "Yes."

"Is that why you're here?"

The insects start to sting and bite. "Yes."

"Tell me about it." The woman holds her gaze.

She shifts in her seat. "I see him, in the street."

"Go on."

"At first it was all the time. Then not for years, and then this week . . . I saw him again."

The woman's face is still. "And does he speak to you? When you see him?"

She shakes her head.

"Do you ever see his face?"

"No. He's always looking away."

The woman nods and lets out a breath. It is as if none of this surprises her. "I want to tell you something," she says. "I don't know if it will help." She pushes with her hands against the table and stands. "But then there's not much that does help, is there?" she says. "In the end.

"I see so many women here," she says, "and they are holding, all of them. Holding on to their sons or their lovers or their husbands, or their fathers, just as surely as they are holding on to the photographs that they keep or the fragments of childhood they bring with them and put on the table here." She gestures with her hand. "They're all different but all the same. All of them are afraid to let them go. And if we feel guilt, we find it even harder to release the dead. We keep them close to us; we guard them jealously. They were *ours*. We want them to remain ours." There's a silence. "But they are not ours," she says. "And in a sense, they never were. They belong to themselves, only. Just as we belong to ourselves. And this is terrible in some ways, and in others . . . it might set us free."

Ada is silent, absorbing this, then, "Where do you think they are?" she says.

"Who?"

"All those dead boys. Where are they? They're not in heaven, are they? They can't be—old people. Ill people. Babies, and then—all of these young men. One minute they're young, they're alive, the next they're dead. In hours they're all dead. Where did they go?"

"Were you ever a believer?"

"I used to think I was."

The woman's face changes; it looks older suddenly, the shape of it less sure. "I don't know where they are," she says. "I can listen, with the objects that people give me; I can try to hear. And sometimes . . . some of them seem . . . calm. I can feel that. And I can pass that on. And that helps, I think. Some of them are harder."

Ada licks her lips. They are cracked, dry. "And what about Michael?" she says. "What about my son?"

The woman frowns, comes back over to the table and puts her hands on it. For a moment more she stands there. Then she shakes her head, as though to clear it. "I think," she says, "that you must learn to let him go."

Ada is silent.

"Tell me," the woman says. "Your husband. Jack, you said his name was?"

"Yes."

"He is well, is he?"

It is an odd question. "Yes, I think he is," says Ada.

"Can I give you some advice?"

She nods, warily.

"Look at your husband," says the woman. "See what you find there. He's living. He's alive. He wants to be seen."

. . . .

At a quarter to four the woman starts stacking chairs onto tables. Evelyn is the only customer left in the place, over in the far corner of the café, by the greasy window, the remains of her third cup of tea and a bacon sandwich by her side. She closes her book and pulls on her coat. "Thank you," she calls to the woman as she leaves. The woman lifts a vague hand in good-bye.

It is getting dark already on the brown street outside, the buildings thickening, growing bulky with it. Yet the sky ahead is still high and light blue, as if it might be readying to detach itself, leaving the earth to its darkness, floating free. For a moment she feels it again, that tipping panic that seems to grip her so often now, and she has to lean against the wall to catch her breath.

It is two minutes past four when she knocks on Rowan Hind's door. There is only empty silence from within. The temperature has plummeted with the going down of the light. She feels hopeless, suddenly, parasitic. What in the name of God is she doing all the way out here, hounding people in their homes?

Spinster.

Meddling spinster.

The door opens and the little girl stands there, wearing an apron now, and with a scrappy piece of blue ribbon tying her hair. One leg twists around the other. She still has no shoes on her feet. "My dad's not back yet."

"I see. I don't suppose I could wait inside, could I? Just until he is?"

The little girl turns and pads into the violet darkness at the end of the hall, from where there come hushed voices. Then she comes back. "She says you've to wait in here." She pushes open the door of a room to her right, and Evelyn follows her into a little parlor. There's an armchair in the corner: a lumpy-looking two-seater along the wall. It looks as though there hasn't been a fire in the grate for years. They stand for a moment, she and the little girl, facing each other in the half-light.

"Well." Evelyn's breath clouds before her face. "I don't suppose you have a candle, do you?"

"I'll have to get a match."

"Wait. I've got some here, look." She takes a box from her pocket.

The little girl brings the stub of a candle over from the mantelpiece, holding it out in front of her. Evelyn bends to light it. "That's better," she says, when the wavering light has taken hold. "Now I can see your lovely ribbon." She smiles. "It's a very pretty color."

The girl doesn't take her eyes from Evelyn's face.

"What's your name?"

"Dora."

She has a low, cracked voice, the way some children do.

"Pleased to meet you, Dora. I'm Evelyn." She holds out her hand.

Dora looks at the hand, then back up to her face. There's the bang of a door and low murmuring in the kitchen. Evelyn recognizes the voice of Rowan Hind.

"That's my dad," says Dora.

Evelyn straightens up.

"Why have you come to see him?" She presses her lips together; they are white with concern.

"Don't worry, I promise, it's not about anything bad."

The little girl gazes at her, seeming to consider the possible truth of this. Then, "I'll go and see if he'll come," she says, passing the candle to Evelyn to hold.

Evelyn walks over to the mantelpiece and puts the candle down. She sits on the edge of an armchair. Stands again. Crosses the room to the window, half of which is covered with a piece of sagging yellowed lace. No lamps light the street outside; it is almost completely dark. She longs for a cigarette.

Behind her the door opens and Rowan Hind is standing in the doorway. "Mr. Hind." She steps forward, her hand outstretched. "My name's Evelyn Montfort. I work in the pensions office in Camden Town. You came to see me on Monday." Her words collide with one another in her haste to get them out.

His head is moving slightly from side to side, the same involuntary movement she remembers from the other day. It was pitiful then, amid the late afternoon tedium of the office, but now, when she cannot properly see his face, it makes her afraid. "I remember," he says. "I'm not daft. I remember you."

She clasps her hands together and presses her thumb into the opposite palm. "That's good, then. I didn't want—"

"Munitions."

"That's right."

"No finger." He points to her hand.

"Yes."

"What are you doing in my house?"

There's so much hostility in his voice that she steps backward again, catching her heel awkwardly on the grate, and for a brief, awful moment, she feels as though she will fall, but then catches the mantel, steadying herself just in time.

"Careful," he says.

"I'm sorry," she says, straightening herself. "I came because you were looking for someone. For a Captain Montfort. Is that right?"

He says nothing.

"Was it an Edward Montfort? Captain Edward Montfort?"

Something about her words changes the temperature in the room.

"He's my brother," she says. "I can help you, if you tell me why you want to find him."

He turns and closes the door behind him. "Why?" he says.

"Why what?"

His face is pinched, suspicious. "Why would you come all the way out here?"

"Because, I thought this was what you wanted. And—I was sorry that I lied."

He stares at her.

"I didn't have to come."

The minute it is out she realizes how untrue it is. And how petulant it sounds. She had to come. She couldn't not.

He pulls a bent cigarette from his inner pocket, straightens it out, and puts his head in his right hand, his first two fingers rubbing at the space between his eyes.

"Have you been working today?" Evelyn asks quietly.

"Yes."

"Did you have any luck?"

He shakes his head and goes to sit on the sofa. "Nothing. Too bloody cold."

"You'd have thought they'd have let you in, if it's cold."

"Well, doesn't work like that, does it?" He lights the cigarette, pulling a stray piece of tobacco away from his lip.

"Do you mind if I smoke, too?"

He shrugs. "Do what you like."

She lights one of her own. "What did he do?" she says.

"Who?"

"My brother."

His head is still down, but he is listening, she can tell: she can see the tension in his body; it's almost palpable reaching toward her. He lets out a small, involuntary sound, and then begins to shiver. At first she thinks it is the cold, but then, when it carries on, she sees that it is the same shivering she remembers from the office that had preceded his fit. There's a small knock at the door. She jumps, but it is only Rowan's daughter again, carrying a tray set with a teapot and two cups, a sugar bowl, and a milk jug. The girl carries it carefully, an expression of grave concentration on her face, setting it down on the small table before the empty grate.

Evelyn can see Rowan on the sofa, away from the candle, wrestling with himself, can see the shaking threatening to take him over: the fight within him, his foot rapping out a jangled rhythm on the floor. She feels a corresponding panic rise in her own body. Her eyes flicker to the little girl. She should protect her somehow, from what is about to happen—cover her eyes. But the girl is already turning toward her father. "Dad?" She leaves the tray and goes to him. "Daddy?" He is shaking badly now, but she clambers into his lap and wraps both her arms around his neck. She sits like that, with her arms tight around him, until her father is still.

As she stares at the two of them, twined together, Evelyn is filled with a hot, stinging envy; she wants to be in that chair with that little girl's warmth in her lap, those thin arms wrapped around her neck. She sits down in a chair with her cold arms and her empty lap and thinks of Robin, his hand on Rowan's back, stroking him, calming him, and of her sharpness with him afterward. Reginald Yates, that awful man, was right: She really is a bitch. She really is a sadistic bitch.

When Rowan is finally still, his daughter reaches a hand up to his cheek and holds it there for a moment, before slipping off his lap. She pours tea and milk into the cups and hands one of them to Evelyn.

It is difficult, somehow, to look at the child.

When the girl has gone, she places her cup and saucer on the floor. "I'm very sorry to have troubled you, Mr. Hind. I'll leave you now." She stands and pulls on her gloves. It was a mistake to come. She has disturbed these people, and she is glad to go.

"Stay," says Rowan, and his voice is different, calmer now. "Drink your tea. It's rude to leave when you've been given a cup of tea." He looks at her then, square in the face, and his gaze is steady and bold.

She does as he says, taking a seat back in the chair.

"Your brother," he says.

"Yes?"

"What's he ever done to you?"

"He . . ."

He made me feel small. Like a small, stupid spinster. He's able to be happy. He's able to forget the war.

"He lied to me," she says.

Rowan nods, seems satisfied with that. "All right," he says. "I'll tell you. I'll tell you what you want to know." He lights a cigarette and points it at her. "But I want you to remember you asked for it."

She is silent.

"Say it," he says.

"Say what?"

"Say you asked for it. I want to hear you say it."

"I asked for it," says Evelyn.

"All right," he says, and then he begins to speak.

"I had a pal. We met in a rest camp, behind the lines. They called it rest, but it wasn't really; they had you doing all sorts of jobs. The only rest you got was when it went dark and you could get into your bed. They'd brought a load of other men to the company, but I didn't really notice. I was keeping myself to myself.

"One day me and this other lad were put together, loading coils of wire and taking them further up the line and dropping them off. We had to chat a bit, and I could hear straightaway he was from near me. Turned out he was from Hackney. Few miles north of here.

"By then all the regiments were split up. It wasn't like before, with pals from all the same places serving together. Too many had gone by then for that. By that time you'd get a Yorkshireman with a London man with a man from Wales. They'd shift them around after an action, all the ones that were left and able to fight. It wasn't often you'd meet anyone from near where you were."

"What was his name?" Evelyn shifts forward in her chair.

"Michael," he says. "Michael Hart. He was from a company that had lost nearly all their men. They'd been in something pretty bad, and only forty or so of them were left."

"Out of how many?"

"Few hundred." He shrugs. "So they put them into ours. They would never talk about it. What happened. But we'd heard about it all right. They'd all been drowned in the mud."

"Drowned?"

He nods slowly, looking up at her. "You wouldn't believe it unless you'd seen it."

There's a silence as she tries to take this in. She cannot. Her mind balks at it. "What was he like?" she says. "Michael?"

He sits back and scratches his neck, considering this. "I'll tell you something," he says. "When we finished work, in that camp, most would sit around and smoke and play cards a bit. But he'd never play. He said he didn't want to know how much luck he had left."

"Why? What did he mean?"

"You'd play some gambling game or other. Bet pennies. But if you did well you'd get jumpy. You didn't want to think you'd had your luck. I expect, since he'd got through that last bit alive, he thought he might have had his luck. So he thought it was best not to play. Said he didn't want to know."

"I see." And she does; it makes a kind of sense.

The end of Rowan's cigarette glows red. "He didn't talk much to anyone. None of them from the new lot did. But we were behind the lines for a good few weeks or so. Every night they had you on working parties going up to the front line."

"What did that mean?"

"All manner of everything: You'd have to carry up ammunition, sandbags, trench mortars, barbed wire. That was the worst. You'd carry it on a stick, two of you, and you'd more than likely cut yourself to ribbons before you got where you were going. You'd walk two or three miles like that, trying not to fall into the mud. But whatever we had to sign up for—me and Michael—we'd do it together.

"He got a cake once. His mum sent it him. A big fruitcake." He looks up at her, half-smiles, gestures for size with his hands. "He shared it about. It was tasty. I remember wondering how she'd got it so tasty. She must have saved up her sugar for weeks. He used to get letters from her, too, regular. I never got any letters from my ma."

"Why not?"

He looks scornful. "Couldn't write her name, could she?"

"Oh," she says. *Of course.*

"After a few weeks, they started giving us more food. Double rations. That's when we knew we were going to have to move up the lines again. Everyone always got twitchy when you got more food. You wanted it, but you didn't want it, if you know what I mean. No one knew where you'd be going, but you'd be taking bets on where it would be. The only thing anyone wanted by then was a cushy one, a nice quiet bit of line.

"Captain Montfort came out in the morning. Said we were moving out at dawn tomorrow. He looked jumpy. I had a feeling straightaway. I just knew it was going to be bad."

The sound of her brother's name in this man's mouth makes her flinch. *Captain Montfort.* She leans forward. "Was he good?" she says.

He looks up at her.

"A—good captain, I mean?"

He shrugs. "He was. He was all right. Till the end."

"The end?"

"Yes."

He says no more on this, and she can tell he won't be pushed. She is filled with a strange feeling, half-defensive, half-guilty; she finds she wants her brother to have been good at his job.

"I turned to Michael," says Rowan, "to say something, but he'd gone white as anything.

"We were staying in billets in a farmhouse, and when the sun went down you weren't allowed a fire. You weren't allowed to do anything but get into your bed. We were lying in our bunks in the dark but I was wide awake. Then there's a sound over where Michael was—

"'You awake?' I says.

"'Yes,' he says.

"'I've got a bit of a bad feeling.'

"'Yes,' he says. 'Me, too.'

"'Will you promise me something?' I say.

"'What's that?'

"'Will you tell my wife if anything happens to me?'.

"'Course,' he says.

"'Tell her what happened. Proper. I don't want her getting the bollocks they write home. I want her to know the truth.'"

"And what did he say to that?" Evelyn says, lighting another cigarette.

"He said he'd do it. He promised. Then he says, 'Can you do the same for me? I haven't got a wife, but you could go and find my mum.'

"'What's your mum's name?'

"'Ada,' he says.

"I made a joke. I said I'd thank her for the cake. He laughed. The next day, I wrote down her address."

He leans forward, putting his hands to his head and speaking to the ground.

"I made sure that I learned it, in case I lost the paper. So I could still come and find her. For years after he died I had that bloody address in my head."

"You didn't go to see her, then?"

"No."

"Why not?"

He shakes his head. "Couldn't tell her, could I? I was a coward."

"Couldn't tell her what?" she says.

He doesn't answer. Then he speaks again. "One day, a couple of weeks ago, I was working the streets, selling my brushes and soaps and *crap,* and when I looked up I realized that I was on his street. The street he'd written down for me. And I was standing right outside his door. And as I'm standing there, the door opens and his mum comes out and she walks straight past me."

"She didn't see you?"

He shakes his head. "She had her own thoughts about her. She walked straight past me down the hill. But before she turned I got a look at her face. And she looks just like him, same dark hair, except smaller, and sort of tidy-looking, and I thought, That's the woman sent him the cake I ate. That's the woman sent him all those letters. And then I start to shiver, right there in the street, and I'm looking right and left and I'm thinking, Someone knows I didn't keep my promise. Someone wants me to tell her now. Three years passed and I'm standing here." He looks up at Evelyn, his face fierce, as if daring her to contradict him. "I knew it was him that had brought me there. To his house."

She swallows. "And what did you do then?"

"I went back. Last Sunday it was. I took my bag along with me and made out I was selling something. It was a Sunday, but she didn't say anything, his ma. She let me in anyway.

"First thing, I get in there and already I know I'm not going to see this through. And I'm standing there in the kitchen and staring at her and I'm thinking, You look sad. And I know why. I know why you're so bleeding sad." He pauses a moment, and then meets her eyes. "Have you ever seen a ghost?"

"No," Evelyn lies.

His foot is tapping, tapping on the floor.

She takes a swift drag of her cigarette. Then, "Once," she says.

"Tell me," he says. "What did you see?"

"I can't." She shakes her head. "I'm sorry."

"*Tell me.* I'm telling you." His voice is raised now. "You *tell me.*"

She releases her breath. She has never told anyone this. Not a single soul. "Once . . ." she says, slowly, "when I woke, in the night, I saw a little girl. She was standing in the corner of my room. She looked lonely. I wanted to go to her. I wanted to comfort her, so I got up, out of my bed, and as I went toward her, I knew—" She stumbles. "I knew that she was mine. My daughter. And that she needed me to hold her. And I wanted to, so much. But when I got close enough to reach her, she turned away from me. She walked into the wall." She is shaking. *Don't cry. Don't bloody cry.*

"Were you scared?"

She returns his gaze. "Yes," she says. "I was."

He leans toward her. "I saw one, too," he says. "That day. Michael. He was standing there, in his mum's kitchen, clear as you are now."

Her heart is at her temple, at her throat.

"Pointing his finger straight at me, and his mouth's going, but I can't hear. It's like in the pictures, when there's no words to tell you what they're saying but you just know they've got a murderous rage on them anyway. And all I can think is I've got to get out of there. I try to leave. But she's guessed by then, his mum. She's trying to keep me in the house."

"How? How did she guess?"

He opens his palms. "I don't know. But she said his name. She said 'Michael.'"

Evelyn can hear the sound of pans in the room next door, and the hushed, twining voices of the mother and child.

"And I'm thinking that all I have to do is tell her the truth. Because you can bet she doesn't know it. She doesn't know any of it. You can bet your brother didn't write the truth in his letter to her."

"What do you mean?"

"I killed him," he says. "I killed her son." He rocks backward and forward, cradling his useless arm. "And it was your brother made me do it."

For a moment it is as though time has stopped. Then a sound comes from her, a strangled laugh. "That's ridiculous. He—Ed—he would never do a thing like that."

"How do you know?"

"He's a—good man."

"Really? How are you so sure about that?"

She closes her eyes briefly. She shakes her head. What can she say?

He always loved me. He used to look up to me. He was my ally. He made me feel like the braver, better part of himself.

I just know.

Rowan's voice is raised now; he is almost shouting. "Why are you here, then, if you're so sure about that?"

She shakes her head. "I'm sorry, I suppose—I'm not."

She doesn't want to hear this. Whatever it is he has to tell. And yet she knows she must—that they have unleashed something, the pair of them, and now they cannot move until it is done.

Rowan lights another cigarette, sits hunched over himself, spitting his words into the space between them.

"The minute we got close to the line I knew that my feeling was right: It was going to be bad. We went up through Albert. All of the houses were boarded up. It was like the plague had been through there. There was an angel, hanging off the church, holding a child in her hands. It looked like a woman on the front of a sinking ship.

"They had us waiting by that church for hours. There was something up with Michael. He was shaking. I sat down beside him. 'All right, chum?' I said. He looked at me. He started to say something. I think he was trying to talk about what had happened to them all, before. That they'd come through here before they went to the front. He wasn't all there, though. He wasn't making much sense.

"No one liked it if you talked. No one liked it if you got windy around them. So we're all sitting there, and people start hearing him chattering and start going, 'Shut him up, can't you.' You can tell they're getting rattled. And I says to him, 'It's not the time. We've got to go on. You know that. I'm sorry, but I can't listen to you. We've got to go on.' He was quiet again, after that. I thought he was all right. They brought us some tea from one of those field kitchens and we had a bit of grub, too, and a smoke. He was quiet. We waited till it was late, and when it got dark we went up toward the line. There was no moon, and that was good in a way, because moons were bad."

"Why?" she says. "Why were they bad?"

He looks up at her, scornful. "Because the other side could see you, then, couldn't they? Full moons were the worst."

I have made a pact with the moon. On clear nights she will bring me to you.

Evelyn shivers. *Stupid.* Of course.

"After we'd been marching for a long time, it must have been about two, three in the morning, we could smell that we were getting close."

"How?"

"Because it stank. Like hell. And the mud started up. We were marching on duckboards. If you fell off, then you'd drown. You could hear men, horses, stuck in there, crying out. You just had to walk past. You had to hold on to the man in front of you and keep going. You couldn't go very fast. But when we got closer you could feel the men who were leaving the bit of line we were going to take over."

"How?"

"They were coming toward us, pushing past in the dark. They were moving as fast as they could. You could just tell they couldn't get away from there quick enough. We'd have to crouch down, so as we didn't fall in when they went past us, and we'd whisper to them, in the dark, asking them what it was like. You wanted to know what it was like where you were going. And they just said, 'Cushy, mate, cushy.'" He pauses, gives a short, hard laugh. "But that was what they always said.

"You couldn't see anyone's face in the darkness, but sometimes the Germans would send up one of those Very lights, like big red fireworks. They'd send them up from time to time so they could get a good bit of a look at us. Michael was marching right behind me. I happened to turn around just as one went up, and I saw his face. He was standing, staring, and there was a hand, just in front of him, sticking out of the trench wall. I'd brushed past it myself, but I hadn't seen what it was."

"How?" Evelyn leans forward. "How did it get there?"

"They'd do that, with the trenches. If it was a bad bit, that they'd been fighting over for a long time, and they had to dig themselves in again, they had to cut through the corpses. They had no choice. But it tips him, and he starts to make this sound. It's low but he doesn't stop. Sort of like, '*Oh—oh oh oh oh oh.*'"

Even here, even sitting in this room, it sounds awful. Even here, she wants him to stop.

"Everyone's whispering at him to shut up. But he carries on. It's as if he can't hear them. '*Oh oh oh oh oh.*' Captain Montfort comes pushing back from the front of the line and grabs him and tells him that if he doesn't stop he'll slice his fucking neck open and that'll shut him up for good. And that does it. That shuts him up. We start walking again. But I can hear him shaking. It's like the words have gone inside him. I can hear his pack, shaking against his back.

"When we get into the line they're shelling it like all hell. We report for duty. The sergeant's giving out work details. Michael's sitting all slumped over; he looks like he's not all there. I try to think of something to say to him, to calm him down a bit, but I can't. Sergeant tells me to take a message into Captain Montfort's dugout. He's screaming down the telephone at someone. *What the fuck this and what the fuck that.* The bastards who were there before us had all gone in a hurry and no one had left anything there at all. No information, nothing. They'd all just run away.

"'Hind,' he says. 'There's a load of bodies out behind the support trench. Take five men and some shovels and go and bury the poor fuckers. And Hart,' he says. 'Take fucking Hart. I don't want him screaming the place down.'

"And I'm thinking, At least if we're out of the line for a bit then maybe I can settle Michael. We all get windy now and again. But you don't want someone who's windy around you. It spreads.

"I get Michael and four other men and we leave our packs and follow the support trench back. Captain Montfort's told me where to look, but when we get close we don't need to look for anything, the flies are everywhere."

He lights a cigarette from the end of his last.

"We climb out, and we have to keep down, because even though we're behind the line, we're not that far back. The ground wasn't too muddy just there. I don't know why. Otherwise they would have just slipped into it. But they needed burying. They were still sending shells over, and they were bloody loud, believe me, but the sound of the flies drowned everything else out." He stares into the empty space before him. "The last lot who were there had just left their mates in the open air to rot.

"So we tie scarves around our faces and we start to dig. We're digging just a bit away from where they're lying. It's too dark and dangerous to go far. We just had to bury them where they were. There were six of us, and we were digging one grave between two. I'm working with Michael and I keep asking him if he's all right. He says yes, but he keeps turning around to puke, but then we're all puking, so that's nothing strange.

"Every so often another of those lights goes up and we have to flatten ourselves to the ground and so we just jump down into the graves that we're digging. And I'm thinking, This is bloody lovely, isn't it? Anything happens to us and we're already buried. They're only going to have to come and shovel the earth over the top. But then there are the other poor fuckers that we're digging them for in the first place, and where are they going to go? And I don't fancy much sharing a grave with them.

"We're trying to look at their tags so as we can write on the crosses. You always had to do that, so they had a chance of being found, after everything, if they hadn't been blown to kingdom come. Michael's trying to look at this one's tag, but it keeps slipping out of his hands. 'Give over,' I say. 'Let's have a look.' I bend down and—"

He stops.

"It was a shell that came down. It must have hit about twenty yards from where we were. When I come to I can't see anything. I've got half a field stuffed up my nose and mouth and everything's blacker than it was before, and I just stand there, spitting, trying to get so as I can see.

"I turn on my torch. Everyone's standing around picking dirt out of their eyes and mouths. Michael's gone. I start shouting for him. I search all over, but he's not there.

"Everyone's there but him. I shovel a bit of earth over the body I'm supposed to be burying and leave him and I go back with the other men, to the bit of trench that was supposed to be our dugout. But he's not there. So I go to see Captain Montfort and tell him Private Hart has disappeared.

"'What do you mean, disappeared?' he says.

"'He's gone,' I say. 'There was a shell and now he's gone.'

"'I know full well there was a shell,' he says. 'Two of the cooks have been killed.'

"I'm shaking my head because I can't hear very well, and there's a ringing in my ears that's louder than anything else.

"'You've got blood on your head,' he says. 'You'd better go down the line and get it seen to.'

"I'm reading his lips as much as hearing him speak; the whistling's that loud.

"So I go down the line. And I keep looking out for Michael, seeing if I can see him, but he's nowhere."

"But surely . . ." Evelyn says.

"What?"

"Surely he could have been buried, too? By the shell? Did nobody think to look?"

He shakes his head. "I knew he wasn't," he says. "I got down to the casualty clearing post. They've got all sorts down there, the shelling's been so bad, and I'm not urgent, so it takes a while till they can bandage me up. And I keep looking out for Michael, thinking if he was hit, then he might have made his way back there. When they finally see me I tell them about the shell and ask if they've had anyone in. They ask me which company I'm from and when I tell them they say they had another of ours down there earlier, spouting nonsense and shaking. They'd put him on a stretcher but he'd disappeared. Had he reported back? they said. I said I didn't know. That's when I started to feel something really bad.

"When I get back up there to the line, I still can't see him.

"Night comes and he's still not back.

"When morning comes and we have a roll call and stand to, I haven't slept, and he's still not there, and everyone's looking at me as though I should know where he is.

"They call me in to see Captain Montfort. He starts screaming at me. He looks as though he hasn't slept, either. He's been drinking. You could always smell it on the officers, the whiskey." His voice is bitter. "We weren't allowed anything like that. Only rum ration in the morning before going over the top.

"He's screaming at me, did I see anything? Did I think he was dead in the shell or what did I think?

"And all I'm thinking about is the doctor down at the casualty clearing station and what he said. If it comes out that he told me then I'd be for it. So I tell him what the doctor said. And he goes straight down there, to the clearing station. He's gone all morning."

He shakes his head. "We were just hanging on in the trench that morning. It was worse than being in battle, being somewhere like that, because you couldn't move. You just had to hold it. You were stuck. I kept thinking that it was like the worst thing in the world had happened there, and we were just there to look at it. Just there in this hole to look at the worst thing in the world. Because if there was no one there to see it, then no one would ever believe it was possible."

He stubs out his cigarette. "Not that anyone's ever wanted to know."

"I want to know," says Evelyn. "That's why I'm here."

He hardly seems to hear her. "But it wasn't the worst thing," he says, lighting another cigarette. "Not in the end.

"Captain Montfort came back in the afternoon. I saw him walk past my dugout. I was on an hour's kip. But I couldn't sleep. I just had this feeling in me. Sure enough, he calls me straight in. Private Hart has been arrested. He was found at a farmhouse a few miles behind the line. He had built himself a fire there and an officer from another regiment saw the smoke and found him and put him under arrest.

"He kept me there for a long time. He wanted to know everything about Michael. I told him he was a good lad."

"Did he listen?" says Evelyn. "Did he listen to you?" She wants her brother to have listened, wants this suddenly more than anything in the world.

He shrugs. "He asked a few more questions. Then he let me go."

He sits back on the sofa.

"You'd see men," he says, "strung up on the sides of gun carriage wheels. 'Field punishment number one,' they called it. They looked like they were on the bloody cross, with their arms all strung up on either side; and they'd be left like that, on their knees, down by the side of the road. And we were supposed to look at them. The bastards that ran the show, that's what they wanted: They wanted us to look, to shame them. But we never did. We always turned our faces away when we went past, so as the poor buggers could get a bit of peace."

Evelyn nods. *That's what I would do. I'd do the same.*

"That night, if I closed my eyes, I'd see Michael, strung up. I thought that was what was coming, you see.

"Next morning Captain Montfort calls me in again. He says that Hart is going to be court-martialed for desertion. He says he's allowed someone to speak up for him at the trial. 'Prisoner's friend,' it's called. He says Hart's asked for me.

"I ask him when the trial's going to be and he tells me Thursday. I ask him what the day is today, he tells me Tuesday."

He looks up at her, and there's a silence before he speaks.

"And I know what's going to happen then, I swear. All of it, from start to finish. Like it's all written down in a book, like the Bible. Like I could skip through and see the last page already, and read the last line."

Evelyn clenches and unclenches her thumbs. Her missing finger is hurting her. "What happened then?" she says. "What happened at the trial?"

He stands up, walks over to the window, puts his hands in his pockets, and gazes out. "My bit was nothing. I didn't even get to see him. There was just me and two men with red on their uniforms in a small room. I was only in there a few minutes. I couldn't get my words out right. I wanted to tell them how they'd got it wrong, how he was in a bad way after the last bit of action he'd seen, but they kept asking about him shouting on the march. Your brother had already told them about it, so they had him pegged and there was nothing I could say and that was that."

He turns and steps to the fireplace, spits into the grate, and then rests his head on his good arm, leaning on the mantelpiece.

She watches him in the candle flame, guttering now; this small man, his shirt ridden up at the back, his braces hanging slack by his sides.

"You couldn't see him, then?" she asks softly.

He lifts his head toward her. He is silent for a long moment. "Not then.

"Next thing, when we were finally out of that bit of line, they round us all up and they tell us that Private Hart has been found guilty and he's going to be shot. And all I can hear is that phrase going round in my head: *Shot, shot, shot.* It's my fault, I'm thinking, I should have found him. Should have brought him back. And I'm thinking, Have they told him? Have they told him yet? Have they told his mum? Because judging from that cake she sent she's going to want to come out here and say good-bye."

He gives a short, bitter laugh.

"Did they let them do that, then?" Evelyn says. "The parents. Did they let them say good-bye?"

Rowan snorts, a look of utter contempt on his face. "What do you think? You think they bus them out to wave before their lads are going over the top? You think they're going to bring them over for something like this?"

Of course not. She feels bile rise in her throat. She lights a cigarette to try to force it down.

He shakes his head. "But all the time I've been thinking, Captain Montfort has been speaking, he's been reading off a list of names. I don't hear it properly, though. Afterward they say to me, 'Bad luck, isn't it?' 'What?' I say. 'About the firing squad,' they say. 'Bad luck to be shooting a chum.' And then I realize. I hadn't heard it. But your brother had read out my name."

He stares at her.

"Your fucking bastard brother read out my name."

He is shaking.

She prays it won't start. Not the fitting. Not now.

"They say to me, 'You can go and see him if you like. He might like that.' Like they're doing me a favor. Like they're doing *him* a favor, having me go to say good-bye. *All right, old chum? Sorry about the shooting. Bad luck it had to be me. Got any last requests? Anything I can tell your mum?*

"They said I was supposed to go and see him at seven o'clock.

But I didn't go. I went off into the woods instead. And I just sat there, thinking. What's he going to be thinking? On his own? I knew I should go there, to see him, but I couldn't go."

He stops in front of her, a look of utter anguish on his face. "Do you understand why I couldn't go? Do you?"

"Yes," she says. "Yes, I do."

He puts his head in his hands. His back heaves once, twice. When he starts to speak again the words come quickly, as if he, too, needs to get to the end. "In the morning they march us out to this place in the middle of nowhere. And there's a stump there." He stops. "There's a stump, just shoved there into the ground. And they line us up in front of it. And then they bring him out. They've covered his head in a sack and he can't stand properly and he looks like he's drunk. He might have been drunk. Someone told me that they fed them drink before it, so as they didn't know what was going on. He's got someone on either side of him, but he's not standing on his own feet. They're dragging him.

"Your brother comes down the line to check on us. And I've got my rifle in my hands and I'm thinking, I could shoot you instead." He looks at Evelyn. "I would have done it, too. Happily. But then I'd be shot myself. And I had my Dora already by then and I wanted to go back." His voice breaks. "All I wanted was to get back home.

"They're tying him to this post and I can see he's pissed himself. And the rest. You can smell it; he's that close. And we've been told that we have to be quiet. Standing so he doesn't know that we're there. It's so fucking quiet. And I'm thinking, Does Michael know I'm there? Can he tell?

"I wanted to say something to him, to let him know that he wasn't facing it on his own. But I couldn't. And I'd have been lying. Because he was on his own, wasn't he?"

He puts his hands over his face, so that his head is held in the net of his fingers.

"He starts saying something then. He's calling for his mum. *Mum, Mum, Mum.*"

Evelyn puts her hand to her mouth.

"And I start praying. Before, I always used to just move my lips a bit in school when they did the prayers. I'd never prayed properly in my life. I've got this one thing going over and over in my head. Forgive us our trespasses. *Forgive us our trespasses.* And as I'm praying I think, *What are you praying for, Rowan? There's no one listening to you, is there?* So I just stop. And then your brother goes over and pins a white handkerchief over his heart.

"I've got a plan. I know I'm going to fire wide. So as it can't be me, but then the man standing next to me, Private Jones—you could see why he had been chosen; he was a coldhearted bastard. But he just whispered to me. Shoot straight lad, he said. You'll be doing him a favor. Aim for the hankie. Shoot straight.

"And then the order comes and I lift my gun and I fire.

"Afterward he's slumped over and his head's down. Your brother walks over to him. He can't hardly walk straight himself. But he's got to shoot him if he's not dead, you see. He goes to take off the sack."

For a moment, he stares at the empty air. Then he shudders.

"I can't look. But there's no shot. So he must be dead.

"Then we walk out. And after that I start to shake. I shake and I don't stop. And I can't feel my arm. The arm that fired the shot. After that it stops working, and it never starts again."

He takes off his sling, so that his arm now hangs, wizened and useless by his side. He hits it. He hits it hard. He pummels it, over and over again.

. . . .

Ada shapes the dumplings carefully in her palms, humming as she does so—the snatch of a melody she used to love to sing. She lifts the lid off the pan. The stew has been bubbling for hours and is a rich, burnished brown. There is a good cut of beef in there, some of the last carrots from the allotment, and the squash that Jack gave her on Sunday. It felt wonderful to slice it, to see the orange skin giving way to an even brighter flesh underneath. She ladles the dumplings into the stew one by one, and when they are bobbing on the surface of the sauce puts the lid back and brushes the flour from her hands. Moving seems easy. She feels lighter somehow, at once less and more like herself.

She puts her hands to her hair, twisting the strands. Earlier, she boiled water and washed her hair and then pinned it when it was still damp. Later this evening, if she takes it down, it will fall in waves. Jack used to love it like that. He used to love her hair in waves to her back. She lights a candle and takes it over to the table with her. She has bought a couple of bottles of ale. She opens one and pours a glass for herself to keep her company while she waits.

. . . .

A family stands at an open window: a father, a mother, a daughter, and two small sons. The mother watches as the light spills onto the darkened garden below, illuminating the elm tree at the end of the grass, the swing that her children love. Beyond are the train tracks. The woman grew up in this village, in a house around the corner where her parents still live.

During the war, when she was standing in the garden, and her daughter was a baby, she would see the troop trains go past on their way to the coast. It was always exciting, at the beginning, to stop what she was doing—hanging washing, or playing with her little girl—and stand and wave, in the flower-filled garden. They loved it, the boys; they would wave back, furiously, shouting out, blowing kisses, their faces tight with pleasure and expectation. If the train stopped she would hold her daughter up, passing daisies and dande-lions through the windows, which the troops would grab and put behind their ears.

Trains would come the other way, too: hospital trains, laden with bodies, bound for the wards of London. If she had her daughter with her, and a hospital train passed, she would usher her inside. She felt awful but didn't like to think of it, the injured and the dying, so many thousands of them passing so close to her home.

Twenty-seven men from their village lost their lives. A memorial has been erected, just in front of the church. Twenty-seven names carved in stone.

But her husband came back safely somehow. She had never thought herself a particularly fortunate woman before. She knows that she is lucky now. Cannot escape it. On Sundays, in church, she can feel their eyes on her. Why her? Why him? What was so special about them?

The woman stiffens. She can sense the train before she hears it. Then the faint click of the wires. Click click, click click, click click.

"Here it comes," she whispers.

Her daughter puts her hand in hers. Her two sons clutch at her skirts. Her husband moves behind them all.

It is upon them before they can think, a chaos of steam and sound. Two ordinary carriages, and then, in the middle, a different one, its roof painted white. They have just enough time to see the coffin in-side, the purple lining of the carriage, the massive wreaths propped at either end, and then it has gone.

The woman exhales, leaning back into her family, into her hus-band's strong grip, into her luck.

. . . .

It's over an hour and a half before Ada hears the back gate clang and Jack's footsteps coming up the path. She stands and smooths her skirt and hair. Then the door opens and he is there, her husband, smelling of the pub and smoke and the cold outside air, the bulk of him filling the doorframe. It is as though she is seeing him for the first time. He catches in her throat.

He closes the door behind him, takes off his hat, and stuffs it in the pocket of his jacket. "What's up?" he says, looking around.

"I was waiting for you." It sounds silly, childish. "I mean, to eat," she says, covering her embarrassment by going over to the stove. "I made some stew."

"Stew?" He takes a seat, looking around suspiciously, as though sniffing the air for danger.

"And dumplings." She tries to make her voice light, unconcerned. The beer has made her heady; she's not used to drinking. "Are you hungry, then?"

"I am, yes."

She ladles food onto plates, puts one down before him, and seats herself.

"What's all this, then?" he says again.

"All what?" She pours him a glass of beer.

"This." He gestures with his hand. "What's it in aid of? And you. You've done something."

"Have I?"

He narrows his eyes. "Something's different. Your hair."

"Oh—well . . . I just—put it up." She can feel heat rising in her cheeks.

He takes a spoonful of stew, staring at her. "Why'd you do that, then?"

"I just—fancied a bit of a change."

He nods. At first he eats slowly, but then, when he has tasted it, he starts spooning it up in great mouthfuls and doesn't speak until he's finished. "It's good," he says, wiping his mouth. "Is there any more?"

She stands and dishes him out another bowlful. He watches her as she crosses back toward him. She has hardly eaten anything herself.

"Something's up," he says. "I can tell."

"I just—wanted to make something. For our anniversary. I wanted to mark it."

"That was Monday."

"I know. I just—today, I was passing the butcher's. I thought to get some meat. Make something nice."

"I thought you'd forgotten." He looks pleased.

"No." She shakes her head and takes her seat.

Look at your husband.

He wants to be seen.

She watches him as he eats, the width of his hands as they grip the spoon, the dark spray of hairs across the fingers.

She has the sudden thought that she should like to kiss him. Kiss him on the knuckles of his hands. She thinks about doing it— about catching him as he lifts his spoon. It would be easy. The distance is not far. The thought makes her smile and blush. He looks up and sees her staring.

"What?"

She shakes her head. But he seems to catch something of what she was thinking, because the air between them changes. It crackles. She can see an answering color in his cheeks. A different question on his face. He finishes and puts his spoon down on the side of his plate. There's a silence, then, "You look nice," he says. His voice is low.

"Thank you."

He holds her gaze, watching her as though she is an animal. She feels an old, renewed power in her. They sit like that for a moment, then, "Come here," he says.

She stands and crosses toward him.

He reaches for her hand, catches it, and rubs his thumb along her wrist.

"What have you been doing today, then?" he says, slowly. "Besides making stew."

"I was . . ."

"What?"

She is silent.

"Go on."

He keeps passing his thumb lightly over her wrist. His touch is turning her to liquid. She leans back against the table.

"I was . . . speaking with Ivy."

"Oh, yes?"

"She wants me to go down to the abbey with her, tomorrow."

"To watch the burial?" He presses lightly, his thumb on her pulse, and she can feel herself, beating against him. "And what did you say to that?"

"I just—" And suddenly it seems wrong not to tell him, not to share this with him, and so she reaches for him, clasping his hand. "I went to see a woman, Jack, earlier today."

"What woman?"

"Someone Ivy went to see in the war."

"Oh?"

"She's"—she gives a small laugh—"supposed to be able to talk to the dead." The air between them has changed again: It is stiller, but it is not a pleasant stillness. It is clenched, like a fist. She can feel his grip leave hers, the flesh detaching, drawing back. He lets go of her hand.

"She lives in Walthamstow. The most ordinary house—you'd never think it . . ."

"Think what?"

"Well—that—someone like that lived there."

He is silent, bringing his hands together in his lap.

"Are you all right?" she says quietly.

"Go on," he says. "You went to see this woman. Tell me what happened."

She feels a bit sick. *What did happen, then?* She can't remember. Her palms are damp. "I—took a photograph with me."

"A photograph? Of what?"

"Of—Michael. I took a photograph of him. To show to her."

"You took a photograph of *Michael*?"

"Yes."

"And what did she say?"

"She told me not to look at it again."

"What did she tell you that for?"

"She said it wasn't good for me."

In the force of her husband's scorn she can feel it wither, this feeling she has had all afternoon, feel it curl and die like a plant in the frost.

"Something lifted," she says. "And I felt lighter." Her voice peters out. She can hear how ridiculous, how stupid, it sounds.

There's silence again. The matting on his chair creaks as he leans backward.

"How much did you pay her?"

"I—"

"Go on," he says. "How much?"

She swallows. "Ten shillings."

He shakes his head and stands up. "You're mad," he says. He comes toward her, and for a moment she thinks he will hit her, but he doesn't; he puts his fingertip to her forehead instead, and presses there. "You've been mad for years. Living with the bloody dead. You might as well be dead. You think you're a wife? You think you're a real wife?"

She opens her mouth, closes it again.

"Do you?"

"I was going to—just then. I was going to—"

He takes his finger away, but she can feel where it was, burning against her skin. He grabs his hat and pulls it on.

"You're not a real wife," he says. "You're a ghost. You're nothing but a fucking ghost."

. . . .

Victoria Station. A mother stands against a barrier, her young son beside her. She has been here since eight o'clock this morning, determined to get a decent view. She has. She can see the empty platform that the train will come into: platform eight by the Buckingham Palace Road.

Since she read about it in the papers she has been determined to be here, to bring her son to see his father. Her boy is almost four now and looks just like him. The same blue eyes, the same strong brow.

She met him when she was fifteen. They were married two years later. He went away two months after that. Their son was born when he was away in France. She went and had a photograph taken, holding their baby up to the camera. She knows he had the picture on him when he died because she was sent his things. They arrived with the postman, a parcel of bloody uniform and, inside the jacket, a bundle of her letters and the photograph of her and their son. She was horrified, incredulous, putting her baby in the garden and locking the door. She rinsed the uniform, soaking out the blood. But not too much. She wanted it to smell of him still. Then she dressed a tailor's dummy in it.

She keeps it beside the bed.

It has been hard to keep her son amused for the long hours they have waited. They have played all sorts of games. She has told him all about his father—all of the stories she can think of. Whenever her boy has needed to pee she has held him up over the barrier so that he could do it on the platform. She got some funny looks for that, but she wasn't prepared to lose her place, and as the day has worn on, everyone has started doing it; most of the men have had a go. There was even a woman who squatted down on the ground, her skirts ballooning around her like a strange sea creature.

But all around her, now, she can feel the crowd stirring. The train is coming; it's time. She gathers her son, and he puts his arms around her neck. "He's coming," she whispers, to his neck, to his ear. "Daddy's coming now."

The boy looks around him. "Where is he? Where?"

"Shhh." She strokes his head. "He's coming on the train."

The train approaches, and there's a moaning in the crowd, and then they start pushing, jostling from the back. The woman is pressed hard against the barrier. Someone screams, "Stop it! There are children here. Stop!"

The woman holds her child tighter. The pushing gets harder. On the other side of the barriers, officials move with clipped, hurried purpose. Then, as the train pulls into the platform, the barriers fall and the crowd swarms out. At first, she cannot see anything, just smoke and the steam that billows high up to the roof of the station, until the smoke clears and she can see the carriage. There's an electric light inside. Some of the young men are trying to climb up onto the carriage roof, and everything is chaos, and all around women are sobbing, loud and unrestrained.

"There's your father," she says, pointing. "There he is."

"Daddy!" he calls. "Daddy?" Her son wriggles from her arms and runs forward.

Young men still pour onto the pavement. Policemen run here and there now, shouting at them to get back. The woman has a terrible vision of her son, trampled by running feet. She darts after him, but a large policeman holds her back.

She screams for her boy. She can see him, twenty feet from her, looking wildly to and fro. Then another policeman stops, leans down, takes her confused son by the hand, and leads him back to her. The

mother bends forward, gathering him up. She sobs into his neck,
holding him tight, tight.

. . . .

There seem to be no streetlights anywhere out here, only the
hunched, low shapes of buildings, and then scattered yellow lights
at the bottom of the hill. Evelyn cannot remember which way she
came. She walks a few steps forward and then remembers: Down
the hill is where the docks are.

Her feet are numb blocks at the ends of her legs. All the time
she was in Rowan's house, all the time he was talking, there was no
fire. She has no idea how long she was in there for. It might have
been two hours; it might have been six.

She passes the workers' café and sees the corner table where
she sat and ate her sandwich, the chair she sat in stacked neatly on
top. At the bottom of the hill she reaches the row of shops, deserted now, the costermongers all padlocked up, the benches
empty of their sullen men. She walks until she reaches the bus
stop. There is no sign of a bus, and only one gaslight stutters in the
distance; otherwise the street is dark.

The thought occurs to her that she could be stuck out here in
Poplar for the night. She would freeze to death surely, if she were.
Would she go back up to Rowan's house and beg him to take her
in? She shakes her head. It's as though everything is sluggish: her
thoughts, her blood. Of course she won't freeze. If it comes to it
then she can walk home from here, or at least to somewhere she
can get a bus or a cab. It can't be that far back to Primrose Hill—
five, six miles at the most?

There's a figure walking toward her. A man, his body braced
against the cold. She shrinks into the side of a building, unsure
whether he has seen her or not. He will pass close by her soon.
Rowan's words come to her, and she can almost hear the men now,

whispering across to one another in the hostile night: *Cushy, mate, cushy.*

The man passes her without a word.

She tries to light a cigarette but is shaking too badly to manage it. How long has she been shaking for? Has it just started? Or has she been like this since she left the house? Or before? While Rowan was speaking? She doesn't know. High, many-windowed warehouses tower over the road to her left. The street is silent, but it is not an easy silence; it is the silence of heavy things, of cranes and ships, stilled and waiting to move.

She'd asked him where the boy's grave was, just before she left. *They buried him there.*

"I went back out there, the first chance I got. Found the way. One Sunday morning. Found his grave. They'd buried him in the corner. I could tell by the dirt. It was fresher than the rest."

"They didn't put a cross?"

"No. But there were fields all around there. They were proper fields still, not like nearer the front. I went out into them and— they were proper fields with proper grass, and they were covered in flowers. I picked a bunch of them. Blue flowers. I didn't know what they were called. I left them there for him.

"But you know what was funny? When I came home, I found them growing in my garden. My wife had planted them. Borage, she said they were called. For courage. She'd planted them for me, to keep me strong. And so as I'd come home. What do you think about that?"

Courage.

She didn't know what she thought about that.

Standing here, now, in the cold street, Evelyn realizes something: that this meeting was what she has been waiting for—for someone to share their truth with her. After four years of war, and two more years of ex-soldiers, day in, day out, this is what she has wanted; this is what she has sought. Someone's truth. Not their cheer, not their bravery, not their anger, not their lies. And in four years of war, and two years of its aftermath, no one—not Fraser, not her brother, no one—has shared with her their truth.

And yet now she has heard it. Now she knows that somewhere, upriver in this city, is her brother, this man who ordered Rowan to fire on his friend.

Now that this truth is inside her, a part of her, it is not diamond hard and gleaming as truth should be but shadowed, rimed in fear and sweat and murk and grime. There is no elevation in it, no answers, and no hope.

Day 5

Thursday, November 11, 1920

Jack isn't there when she wakes; Ada knows this without opening her eyes, and when she pulls herself up in bed, even in the dark room she can see that his side of the blanket is smooth. Last night she stayed awake as long as she could, imagining him in the pub, drinking himself blind, rolling his cigarettes, speaking of her to the other men.

My wife.

My mad bloody wife.

Or worse.

But the empty space beside her fills her with thin fear. He has never, not in all their years of marriage, spent the night away from home.

Where did he go, then, when the pub closed? He must have found a bed somewhere. A thought comes to her, jolting her forward, as though someone has passed electricity through her back. What if he was with someone else? Another woman? A woman who had given him what she hadn't, or wouldn't, or had forgotten to? She thinks of the way he looked at her, last night; the contempt in his twisted face. *You're not a real wife. You're a ghost. You're nothing but a fucking ghost.*

She knows that there are ways to find women. Easily. A man has only to look. How much would it cost? Less than her ten shillings? Her ten shillings to speak with the dead?

She had been ready, though, last night.

Too late; she had been ready too late.

She pulls the covers off and gets to her feet, goes over to the curtains, and pulls them back a little way, peering out into the darkened street. Most of the windows have their curtains drawn, and though the sky to her left is a faint trace lighter, the dawn looks to be a way off still. The houses are all shuttered, except Ivy's window across the road, where a small light burns. The curtains are open and Ada can see her, in her bedroom, moving about. From this angle she can see only half of her face, turned away. One heavy arm is lifted behind her back, fastening her stays. When she has tied them, Ivy reaches over and picks something up from her bedside table and puts it in her mouth. Her teeth. Ada steps closer to the window as Ivy disappears, and although it seems wrong to be watching her like this, unguarded, unaware, she stays where she is, willing her to return.

When she comes back, Ivy is moving stiffly, all in black, in a high-necked old-fashioned dress from a different time.

Ada knows just how that dress feels, knows how heavy it is, how it smells. She has a similar one, packed in a chest at the end of her bed; she last wore it for her mother, twenty-three years ago.

Ivy lets down her hair and begins brushing the long white sheet of it, then twists it into a rope and pins it in place. She looks pale and aged and heavy, but, standing at the window, Ada can see the young woman she used to be: Ivy laughing, pregnant, holding her baby son in her arms, her small daughters clinging to her skirts.

Ivy finishes with her hair and walks over to the window, looking to the sky, as though to assess what the weather has in store. The sight of her—of her black dress and white hair, her upright carriage, dressed in mourning for her son—is so still, so arresting, that it makes the hairs on Ada's neck stand up.

And Ada turns, hurrying now, and lights the paraffin lamp by her bed. She brings it back over to the window, signaling out into the dark. She sees Ivy start, look across. The two women regard each other across the street. Ada lifts the lamp to her face. *"Wait,"* she mouths. *"Wait for me."*

. . . .

Thin remnants of mist drift over the streets as Evelyn leaves the flat, but she can already see the clouds separating to show the blue behind them and feel the surprising presence of the sun. She heads south toward her brother's house. He will not have left yet, she is sure of that; she has risen early to be sure to get him at home.

But however early she may be, the streets are already filling with black-clad people, walking toward town. They want to get a good position for the ceremony, she supposes. Good luck to them. Rather them than her. Still, there is a new-swept feeling about the city. Something of hope. The paths in Regent's Park look as though they have been sluiced clean. When she reaches the terrace of houses where her brother lives they are lovely in the morning light, which strikes off the cream stucco, turning them a mellow gold. She takes the rattling lift to the fifth floor, where Jackson, her brother's man, greets her at the door.

"Good morning, Miss Evelyn." He looks surprised to see her. "Are you here to see Captain Montfort?"

"Yes, I am."

"He's just getting dressed."

She walks past him into the dim hall. "Really? Then I suppose I'd better wait in here." And before he can do it for her, she opens the door to the living room and steps inside. The curtains are pushed wide and the bright morning is flooding the large room. She feels obscurely cross that her brother should be up already. It's as though he has beaten her to something, small but significant, like the games they used to play when they were children; the sort she always hated to lose. The room, however, is in some disarray, the carpet rolled back and the table pushed to one side, as though someone were just about to sweep the floor. The door to her brother's bedroom is closed.

"Ed?" she calls.

"Eves? Coming. Just give me a minute."

She circles the low table. She's never much liked this flat. It used to belong to their father, who lived here when he was in town. They used to visit as children, she and Ed, on trips up to the zoo with their nanny. They would be ushered in to greet him and stand, stranded in the middle of the floor, their nanny retreating to a safe distance, waiting for their father to make a pronouncement on their height, or the weather, as though they were the children of a family to whom he was distantly related and about whom he was distantly concerned. In those days the low table came up to her waist. The flat is Ed's now, and has been for years—ever since the middle of the war when their father retired.

The door to the bedroom opens and Ed stands there, hair freshly slicked, wearing a sober black suit. He is tying a black tie. Two medals are pinned to his chest, three stripes on each. "Eves." He crosses the floor toward her. "Glad you decided to come." He looks tired, as ever, the shadows beneath his eyes deeper and more purple, and as he kisses her she can smell alcohol and toothpaste mingled on his breath. It is strange, she thinks as she pulls away; he always smells of it, has done for years now, but she has never yet seen him drunk.

She shakes her head, impatient. "I'm not coming."

"Oh?" He pulls his tie tight. "Why not?"

"I can't think of anything worse."

"Really?"

"I think so, yes."

He finishes with his tie and puts his hands up. They are shaking a little, she notices. "I'm sorry to hear that. But let's not get into anything now, shall we? Not today?"

"What do you mean?"

"You're reacting rather extremely."

"Well, the whole thing disgusts me."

"*Disgust* is a strong word."

They are into it already.

"*Really?* This is supposed to make it all right, is it? This burial? This pulling a body from the earth in France and *dragging* him over here? And all of us standing, watching, weeping? Clapping at the *show*?"

"All right, Eves." He sighs. "Tell you what. Why don't you fix us both a drink?"

"What sort of a drink?"

"Whiskey should do it."

She thinks about making a comment about the hour, but from the smell of him, it's immaterial, and besides, she herself has hardly slept. Whiskey seems like a good idea. She crosses to the cabinet and pours out a couple of generous measures, hands a glass to Ed, and takes hers to the open window, where she lights a cigarette. Below, on the road that skirts the park, is a steady stream of people, moving right to left. She takes a sip of her drink. Above the terraces opposite, the sun continues to burn away the clouds. The people move in a sudden, bright light. She sees a few of them pause and lift their faces to the sky. She checks her wristwatch. Eight-thirty. She takes a swift drag of her cigarette. "I went to see Rowan Hind yesterday. The man you swore you couldn't remember." She turns to him. "He lives in Poplar. Have you any idea where that is?"

She sees her brother's eyes stray to the clock on the table beside him. It angers her. "You've plenty of time."

"I'm meeting Father at half past nine."

"You've still got plenty of time."

"The crowds—" There's a twitch of skin at his jaw as he grits his teeth. "All right," he says. "Go on."

"I went there yesterday. To Rowan Hind's house."

Ed nods.

"He told me something I think he'd been wanting to tell someone for a long while."

"And what was that?"

"It was about a private called Michael Hart."

Her brother's eyes flicker.

"Who was shot by firing squad in 1917."

He takes a mouthful of his drink. A strange expression crosses his face. She cannot read it. It is gone before she can even try. He holds the whiskey in his mouth before swallowing it down. "Yes," he says. "That's right."

"What do you mean, 'Yes, that's right'?"

"I mean yes, I remember. I was there." He says nothing more, just stands perfectly still, legs slightly apart, glass held before his chest, his body tense with a sudden military bearing she has forgotten he possessed.

"Is that *all*? Is that all you're going to say?"

"What, Evelyn?" He opens his hands. "It's hardly a secret. It's there in the military records, for anyone to see. Now why don't you tell me what this is really about?"

She swallows. "He told me that you sent Private Hart out on a burial party."

"Did I?" His jaw twitches again. "Well, I'm sorry, but I really don't remember."

"Rowan said that he was in a dreadful state. That his company had been decimated."

"*Rowan?*" He looks incredulous. "It's *Rowan* now, is it?"

She cracks her thumbs into her palms.

"Is that what Private Hind said?"

"Yes."

"Well." He gives a tight smile. "You've obviously been talking to the highest authority, Evelyn. Well done. You've found your little private in Poplar and you've constructed your little story and you've made up your little mind. And I have much better things to do than to spend precious minutes changing it for you. So, if you'll excuse me." He turns and goes into his bedroom, slamming the door behind him.

She stares after him, astonished. She kicks the table in front of her. The pain brings tears to her eyes. She goes over to the door and knocks on it. After a few seconds he comes out again. He looks as though he is barely containing himself.

"I'd really rather you'd leave, Evelyn. It's getting late and I have to go."

"Why didn't you write to his mother?"

"*What?*"

"Why didn't you write to his mother? Michael Hart's mother— Ada, she was called Ada. Did you know that? Why wasn't she told?"

"I think I probably wrote to his mother that her son died of his wounds. Which was the truth." He pushes past her, over to the cabinet.

"How can you live with yourself?" she says, under her breath.

"Excuse me?" He speaks quietly, his hand on the decanter.

"How can you live with yourself?" she says again, louder now. "How can you put on your medals and strut about like a *fool* when all the while you have blood on your hands?"

"You stupid, fucking *bitch.*" He flings the decanter at the wall in front of him, where it shatters into a thousand tiny shards and a dark stain spreads, horrible, on the wall. He turns to face her, his hands clenched into fists. "I'm not your *scab*, Evelyn. I'm not your fucking *scab*, here to be picked away at." He is shaking. "You know what your trouble is?"

"What's that, then?" She feels as though cold water is being poured down her spine.

"You *are bitter*," he says. "And you're alone. You've loved one person, in your entire life, and he was taken from you, and that was a desperate, desperate thing to happen and I'm so sorry. And I've always been sorry. But many people suffer much worse and remain decent human beings—perhaps even better human beings than they were before. But you've used that one death as fuel ever since to hate the world."

"No, I haven't. You're wrong."

"What, then? What don't you hate? Go on, Evelyn. Tell me." His face is twisted. *"What don't you hate?"*

"I didn't use to hate you."

For a moment he looks stunned, but then shakes his head, almost laughing. "For God's sake, Evelyn. You're utterly bilious. Look at yourself. You poisoned yourself in that ghastly factory and now you're poisoning yourself in that horrible job. And I fail utterly to see where this moral high ground comes from—you, who worked stuffing shells."

"That was different."

"Was it?" His lip curls. "Of course it was, Evelyn. Of course. Go on, why was that?"

She opens her mouth. "I—" Closes it again.

He shakes his head. "You look for the ugly and the rotten and you find it everywhere, and then you spend the rest of your time shoving it down everyone else's throats. And do you know what? Do you really want to know what? It's utterly selfish. Because all you care about is prolonging your own pain. Have you ever, Evelyn, just once, stopped and faced the fact that Fraser's death was something that happened to *him,* rather than something that happened to *you*?"

At first, she cannot tell which is stronger, the anger or the grief. The anger wins. "How *dare* you? Don't you *dare* speak like that to me." She storms across the room and hits him, as hard as she can, across the face. Her hand is half open and the blow is awkward, but when she pulls her hand back the pain feels astonishingly good.

"Come on, then." He grabs her wrists. "You want to hit me? Do it properly then, for Christ's sakes, come *on*."

Something surges in her, and then they are fighting, and he is hitting her back, and she is aware, somewhere in the back of her mind, that this is what she wants. That this, too, feels good. But then he has stopped—has moved away from her and is crouched in the corner of the room, and she is on her hands and knees gasping for breath.

A terrible noise fills the room.

His back is shaking. It is a moment before she understands that he is weeping. That her brother is crying in awful jagged sobs.

"Ed," she says. "Ed?"

He doesn't hear. He is lost in it.

"Eddie?"

A burst of cannon fire comes from outside. It rattles the windows in their sockets. Instinctively, Evelyn falls to the ground.

. . . .

They walk a couple more paces forward. The bus, which they had to wait so long to get on, since every one that passed them in Hackney was already full, dropped them off at the top of the Charing Cross Road. The conductor, red-faced and sweaty, shouted the news to the packed, expectant lower deck: "Can't get you any closer than this, I'm afraid. Trafalgar Square's already closed."

It has been slow going, in this thick crowd, walking in their heavy, unaccustomed clothes. Ada's hat, decorated as it is with flowers and marbled fruit, is heavy, too. The morning was proving so warm that they had to stop a little while ago and take off their coats, and as well as their coats, they both carry flowers, like all of the women around them, cut from their gardens before the sun was up. Ivy has the last of her roses, Ada, late-flowering Michael-mas daisies in her hands. But the morning has taken its toll on these, too, and they are beginning to wilt.

"We must be nearly there now," says Ada, more in hope than certainty. She has no idea where they are. The road they are on is opening to a great square, but in the packed crowd, it is impossible to see far in front—impossible to get any bearings at all.

"Oh, my goodness." Ivy grips Ada's arm. "Look!" She points to a large building with a tower topped by a bristling metal orb. "I know that place," she says. "I went there once."

"What is it?"

"The Coliseum. I saw a variety there, years ago. Bill took me when we were young. Oh, it's ever so nice inside. . . ." Ivy's face is pink with remembrance. "We saw these performing seals. And these swimmers, in tanks. Oh gosh, it was something. You should have seen it, Ada. You wouldn't have believed it!"

The sight of the theater seems to liven her up, and Ivy scans the scene in front of them with renewed vigor. "Let's go over there." She points to the steps of a large church to their left. "If we climb up there we might see a little bit more."

They push their way through the heaving crowd. The church steps, which are already thick with people, still have a little space at the back and they are able to squeeze their way through. The view is extraordinary: Spread below them the square is entirely black as far as they can see. Buses and motorcars are stranded in the middle of roads that are full of barely moving people, so it looks as though the vehicles are trapped in a river of tar.

"That's Nelson," says Ada, pleased to be able to recognize some-thing herself. The base of the column is thick with people. No stone can be seen.

"Doesn't look like much is going to be coming past on the road here, does it?" Ivy looks worried, confused.

Ada feels the edge of panic. "Where shall we go, then? Shall we stay up here? We don't even know where it's supposed to be coming past, do we?"

They look back to where they have come from, from where people keep coming. Soon that direction will be immovable, too. A sound, low and rumbling, like distant thunder, reverberates off the buildings, disturbing the crowd.

"What was that?" Ivy grips Ada's arm.

"I don't know. It sounded like guns."

"You think everything's all right?"

People are looking around, whispering, looking for confirmation, for comfort from their neighbors.

"It's fine." A tall, well-dressed man standing nearby addresses the crowd. "It's cannon fire. That's the beginning of the procession. They'll be leaving Victoria soon."

"Where'll they come from, then?" Ada turns, glad to find someone who knows something at last.

"Over there." The man points ahead of them. "That's the Mall; Buckingham Palace is at the end of that. They'll come out of that arch and turn down Whitehall." He points to a wide street, a little closer to where they stand. "Then they'll head down to the Cenotaph and the abbey from there. You won't get close to the Cenotaph, of course, that's tickets only, but you might get a place on the corner there if you're quick. We'll be staying here. My mother doesn't like the crowds."

Behind him, a young woman and an older woman nod hello, and two quiet children look at Ada with grave gray eyes.

"Thank you," says Ada.

The man lifts his hat. "Good luck."

They stare out at the multitudes, the slowed black human tide.

"Do you think we'll get there?" asks Ivy doubtfully.

"That's what we came for, isn't it?" says Ada.

"You're right." Ivy nods, steeling herself. "Come on then. Let's go."

. . . .

Eight soldiers from the Grenadier Guards enter the railway carriage and drape the coffin with a tattered Union Flag. The flag has been used many times before, as an altar cloth, at one of the makeshift services before battle, at Vimy Ridge, High Wood, Ypres, Messines, Cambrai, and Bethune. The soldiers place a steel infantry helmet and a webbing belt on the top.

The cortege forms—massed bands, pipes and drums, the pipers in their kilts, the gun carriage, the pallbearers: field marshals, admirals, generals. Then, behind them, a thousand ex-servicemen ready themselves, six abreast. In all the great vaulted space of the station only the odd clink of a buckle and the stray small scratch of cloth can be heard.

Then, from Hyde Park, a battery of nineteen guns fires a salute. The soldiers stand to attention. The echo of the guns lingers in the air as the band plays Chopin's Funeral March, and the cortege starts to move.

Standing in the crowd, just at the entrance to the station gates, a young man watches the cortege move past.

He is thinking of his best friend. The boy he grew up with on the streets of Battersea. He was eighteen and a virgin when he died; his life pooling onto the ground around him. The white shock on his face. A hole where his groin should have been.

The young man closes his eyes. He can feel the skin on his face tighten in the unexpected sun. Why him? Why was he spared? He wasn't the best of them. Nowhere near. He could reel off a list of better men. He can't even get a job.

But he has a wife—a girl who waited for him—whom he married just after the war. And a child now, too. A little girl. He watches them

sometimes, when they don't know he is looking. They are like mira-
cles, the pair of them: the smooth intactness of them. He loves to lis-
ten to the hushed voice of his wife as she rocks their child to sleep.

He thinks of what he will do tonight, when he gets home. He will
kiss his wife, he thinks, he will give thanks for her, and then he will
bury himself inside her, as far as he will go.

. . . .

When the rumbling has passed, Evelyn lifts her head.

Her brother is sitting on his heels, his back to the wall. His face
is lumpy and raw with tears.

"What was that?" she says.

"It will be a part of the ceremony," Ed says. "I'm sure."

"More guns?"

"Sounds like it."

"Can't they think of a better way to honor the dead?"

He opens his hands.

She wipes her sleeve across her cheek. Her hands are stinging.
"How could you do it?"

Ed sighs. He tips his head far back, as if the answer might lie
somewhere above. A raised red weal stands high on his left cheek,
and Evelyn sees now that he has a painful-looking bruise, too, on
his right eye.

"It was the most terrible piece of line," he says. "We'd been
wading in mud for months. And once someone goes, it spreads. At
least, that's what the generals thought. By the time they got their
hands on it, that was it. It was 1917. The Russians had gone; the
French were turning. They were absolutely terrified of mutiny. By
the time I got back from that clearing station it was already in the
hands of the tribunal. There was nothing that I could do."

Evelyn nods. She can see that. "But why pick him? Why pick
him to fire on his friend? It seems so—cruel."

"Standard practice, I'm afraid. It was meant to keep the men in order."

"And did it work?"

He looks away. "I should think it probably did."

"What about his mother?"

"Whose? Hart's?"

"Yes."

"We were told not to write the truth. And anyway, you really think the poor woman needed to know?"

"I think it was her right."

"Her right? I'm not so sure about that." Ed looks down at his hands. "What about Hind?" he says. "Do you think he'll ever go back there? Tell her?" He glances back up.

"I think if he was ever going to do that he'd have done it by now."

"And did he tell you? Where she lives?" Her brother's face is tight.

She shakes her head. "I thought about asking. But it's not my place, is it? Not my story to tell."

"Then why did he want to see me?"

She looks at her brother. Takes a breath. "I think he wanted to understand. But when he'd finished talking . . . he didn't ask me. Not for your address. Not anything. And I would have given it. But once he'd spoken of it once, and someone had listened, I think that seemed to be enough."

Ed nods slowly.

The air between them finally stills.

He takes two cigarettes from his case and hands one to her. She leans in to his light. They smoke in silence for a while.

"Do you want to know something, Eves?" he says eventually.

"What's that?"

He shifts back against the wall and wipes his face with his hand.

"In a minute," he says, "when I've finished this cigarette, I'm going to get up and go outside and walk as far as I can get toward the Cenotaph. And I hope that I am going to watch as they do this thing. I want to. And whatever you may think, I think it's a fine thing."

He rubs the point in between his eyes. It is the gesture of an exhausted man. It reminds her of someone. It reminds her of Rowan Hind.

"This might make people feel better, and it might help them to mourn. It may even help me. But it won't put an end to war. And whatever anyone thinks or says, England didn't win this war. And Germany wouldn't have won it, either."

"What do you mean?"

"War wins," he says. "And it keeps on winning, over and over again."

He draws a circle in the air with his cigarette, and it's as if he is drawing all of the wars, however many thousands of them, all of the wars past and all of them to come.

"War wins," he says bitterly, "and anyone who thinks any differently is a fool."

. . . .

Hettie sits on the edge of her bed, staring out into the small, sunlit room. She has been up since first light, has hardly slept. Her nose is blocked, eyes swollen, her chest scraped jagged and raw. She is sure her brother must have heard her crying through the walls.

Last night, walking home from the tube, her coat wrapped tight over Di's dress, she'd prayed that she might be lucky, that by some glorious stroke of luck her mother wouldn't be in.

But she wasn't lucky. It was not a lucky day.

She could feel the air, the anticipation keen as a blade as soon as she opened the door. Her mother was out of the kitchen before she had the chance to hide. "Go on, then," she hissed. "Tell me. You just tell me. What lies do you want to tell me this time?"

"I'm sorry, Mum—I—"

"You've been out since yesterday afternoon. *Where've you been?*"

"Di's."

"*Don't* you lie to me." Her mother came toward her, stopping halfway down the hall, her hand held to her mouth. "What've you done?"

"Nothing." She shrank back from her.

"You have. I can see it. Take off your hat. *What have you done?*"

It was only then Hettie realized that her mother was talking about her hair.

So she pulled off her hat and raised her chin.

Her mother turned pale. "When?"

"Yesterday."

"It's that friend of yours, isn't it? That filthy little friend?"

"No," said Hettie. "It was me. I wanted to. It was all my idea."

"*Don't* you answer back to me."

And her mother slapped her, then, hard across the cheek.

Hettie puts her hand to it now. Her face is sore. Everything is sore. It is as though she has shed her skin and there is only the soft painful inside left.

She takes a deep breath and looks down at her hands in her lap. In the room next door she can hear Fred stirring in bed. Soon he will go out for his walk. She hasn't got much time.

She stands up and goes quietly downstairs. Her mother is in the kitchen, sitting with a cup of tea. Hettie stands in the doorway and watches her. The bowed shoulders, and her face, unguarded, collapsed into its contours of disappointment and loss. It is not a face Hettie wants to inherit.

"Is there anything in the pot?"

Her mother looks up, surprised. She nods.

"Enough for two more?"

"I expect so."

Hettie takes a tray and two cups and pours out the tea, adding sugar and milk.

"What are you doing?" says her mother.

"I'm taking it to Fred."

She can feel her mother's incredulous silence follow her as she takes the tray out of the room. She climbs the stairs, puts the tea on the floor, and knocks on her brother's door.

She hears a rustling inside.

"Fred?" she says quietly. "Are you awake?"

Hesitant footsteps, and then her brother opens the door in his pajamas, his hair ruffled from sleep.

"Here." She bends down and holds out the tea. "For you."

He looks down at it, back up at her. Blinks, then reaches out and takes it. "Thanks," he says, his pale eyes questioning.

"I want you to do something for me, Fred," says Hettie. "Say yes. Please."

. . . .

The sun is surprisingly warm, surprisingly bright. Though the street she stands on, the one bordering the park, is quiet, to her left, down on the Euston Road, Evelyn can see a great moving mass of people. She turns away from them, taking the entrance to Regent's Park. But she doesn't escape the crowds; they come toward her, relentless, families carrying picnic baskets, children in their mothers' arms, women, everywhere women, old, tired-looking women, their hair pinned beneath hats from another century; younger women, their hair shorn and their black skirts short. The same fixed expression is on all of their faces, as though they have sewn themselves in, as though they are determined not to

spill before the appointed time, the time that the newspapers and
the politicians have decreed for mourning. Eleven o'clock.

Evelyn stares up at her brother's window, then pushes her way
against the tide, heading up the hill instead. They have a long way
to go, these people—a long slow walk until they are able to spill.

The eleventh of November.

Two years since the end of the war.

It was still a shock when it came, at the fag end of 1918.

She was in the office, filing invoices, when she saw a boy from
upstairs come running onto the factory floor below. She saw him
shouting, his arms moving up and down. From where she sat she
couldn't hear what he was saying, but she saw its effect on the
people below: saw them stand as one—the stunned pause as they
looked at one another and then walked out and left their machines
still running. She left what she was doing and went down the steps,
and by then she could hear the shouts, echoing up the stairwell:
"It's over; we've won. It's over; we've won!"

It was a damp, foggy day, and outside there was confusion,
women milling around, their voices ringing—shrill and useless. No
one seemed to know what to do. They were screaming, shouting,
crying, hugging one another. Others simply stood, staring into the
distance.

She saw a woman she knew from her days on the factory floor,
beckoning her from inside a taxi. Six or seven women were already
crammed into the cab and there was barely room, but she climbed
inside, half-sitting on someone's lap, her face jammed up against ·
the window as rain splayed across the glass.

The women kept stopping the taxi to try to buy champagne, but
all of the shops had sold out, and in the end they gave up and
bought bottles of cheap, acrid white wine and drank it leaning out
the windows, despite the rain, singing the raucous songs they had
learned on the factory floor. They were heading for Trafalgar
Square, but the taxi could only get as close as the Marylebone

Road, and so it stopped there and the women piled into the street. It was already nearly impossible to pass through the crowd, and Evelyn lost the other women immediately; but it was easier to move alone and she managed to push her way along Oxford Street, where the traffic was at a standstill, and then further down toward Soho. The pubs of the West End were packed; everywhere people were spilling out onto the pavement and streets, heedless of the rain. Drunken faces lurched in front of her. She passed an older woman, her long hair lank and loose, hanging on to the coat of a young soldier. "It's down to you," the woman was slurring. "It's all down to you." She fell to her knees in front of him, holding out her bottle of stout. The young man, embarrassed, was trying to pull himself away from her grip.

Evelyn pushed through the swaying crowds to the Charing Cross Road, where paper fluttered down from office windows as though the buildings had been turned inside out—and then onto Trafalgar Square. The sound of the celebration was a roar here, the traffic at a standstill, and people were dancing, stamping on the pavement and on the roofs of cars, running round and round in circles like broken mechanical toys.

Everywhere she looked she saw youth. Young people kissing one another everywhere, in various states of abandon; a couple wrapped around each other, the girl sitting on a wall, skirt hitched up, cutting into her white, bulging thighs. It felt as though, while she was in that factory, staring at machines and files, the world had left her behind. For two years she had sat at a bench, or at a desk, and looked only at what was in front of her. Now she would have to look up.

She skirted the square. Flags. Everywhere. Vendor after vendor, standing by little gray tables that had sprouted like mushrooms in the rain. A large, sweaty man in the midst of buying a job lot handed one to her. "There you go, love."

She stared at it, and then back up at him.

"You all right, love?"

When she didn't reply, he lost interest and began throwing the flags out to the appreciative crowd. She looked at the tiny flag: It was made of paper and wood and not much bigger than her palm, the end a sharp point, like a toothpick. She pushed the pointed end deep into her thumb. She felt the pain of it, but not enough, not nearly enough. She pulled it out again, and blood welled from the hole she had made. She smeared the blood across her mouth.

"Do what ought to have been done in 1914!"

A man beside her was selling lavatory paper. It had the kaiser's face imprinted on each perforated section. Evelyn blinked; for a moment she thought she was imagining it. "Do what ought to have been done in 1914!"

"Honey." There was a touch on her arm.

A young man in uniform stood in front of her. He was tall, his accent American or Canadian. "You okay?"

His face was broad and young and smooth; sweat stood out on his forehead. Was he really so young? It didn't seem possible for someone to be so young.

"Can I kiss you, honey?" he asked. "Can I give you a victory kiss?"

She said nothing, and so he pulled her toward him and kissed her. He opened his mouth and she could feel his tongue, taste beer, smell the thick wet khaki smell of his uniform and his sharp, salty sweat beneath. When he pulled back she saw that there was blood on his lip, and for a moment she thought that she must have hurt him—had bitten him—but then she remembered it was her own.

"Come on," he said. He took her hand and she let him lead her across the road, through the standing traffic, past a woman covered all over in Union Jacks who was riding a bicycle down the pavement, screaming, blind drunk, with two soldiers running along on either side. She followed him toward the church on the square, toward Saint Martin-in-the-Fields, where the steps were clogged with people, sitting, standing, sheltering from the rain. The young soldier pulled her around the side and down some shallow stone steps to where it was cool and arched and echoing and there was no one else.

"Here." He pushed her against a pillar. She felt the rough stone of it, pressing into her back. "Let's do it here." He began pulling at her blouse, not unbuttoning it, just tugging it out of her skirt and then passing his hands beneath it, under her camisole, until his hands were over her breasts. He leaned his face into her neck. She turned to the side, against the cold pillar, as he hitched up her skirt. He pulled down her knickers. She stepped out of one leg of them, letting them fall around her ankle to the floor. When he pushed himself up inside her she gasped.

She could hear the banging of the drums outside, the rattle and the screams and the singing, and the rasp of his uniform against her blouse. She lifted her face, up to the vaulted ceiling. It was over in five or six thrusts, and then he pulled away, turning from her to button himself. He looked like a child when he turned back. Part of her wanted to put a hand on his arm, to tell him it was all right. Part of her wanted to laugh.

They walked out together, and then, without speaking, as if they had already decided that this was what was to happen, they parted on the street without a word. She walked on, toward the river, away from the church, down Northumberland Avenue. The crowds kept coming toward her, ceaseless, swarming over the bridges from the south, packed tight now, a heaving, boozy mass. A song broke out near her, and the people started to sway, and the swaying spread until it was everywhere.

Finally she made it to the Embankment, where all along the length of the river the boats were moored, their sirens hooting. There was a crowd near to where she stood, gathered around a young boy who had shinnied to the top of a lamppost. At first she couldn't make out what he was doing, and then she saw he was scraping away the blackout paint. The lamp was lit, and there was an exultant cheer. Then another lamp blazed into life, and another, until there were lights all the way along the Embankment, all the way along the river.

She pushed her way to the low wall, where she stayed, gathering her breath. She could feel the cold, slippery residue of the boy in her knickers. Her stomach rolled in disgust. She stared out over the river, at the water, orange in the lamplight, and thought that she could easily climb the wall, climb it and jump. That no one would notice. That they were all looking up, at the future, and their places in it. And for a brief moment, she thought that she was brave enough, that she might have the courage to do it, but the moment passed, and she was still standing, staring out at the river, at the lit orange rain captured there, as if time had stopped and the rain was only held there, suspended, and wasn't falling after all.

. . . .

Fred is dressed smartly, in his hat and suit. Walking beside him, Hettie feels strange. Hollow. Like she used to after she was ill, when she was a child. That first day of getting up, and going back to school, walking on cotton wool legs, when everything would look different: The house she lived in. The people she passed. The street.

Today the street is deserted, and the people are all gone. The houses have an anxious look, as if unsure their occupants will ever return.

They will.

Today, she doesn't want the houses to be blown up, or the streets torn apart. She wants the bricks to be solid and sheltering. She wants things not to change. She wants her father not to be gone and the gardens to stay innocent and the heliotrope flowers to mean only summer and not swollen skin and quick, quick death. She wants there not to have been daughters lying down for man after man in their fathers' houses in villages in France. Or women on their last legs, waiting for the queues of men to end. She wants the sad parade of men at the Palais to disappear, or to be whole, or patched together again. She wants Ed to be unbroken. And Fred. She wants her brother back.

But she knows, in this warm, sun-bright morning, that none, or not all, of these things are possible. That Ed is right. That you cannot go back.

But her brother is beside her. He has done as she asked and come with her today. And they are walking, the two of them, their steps in time, side by side, one foot in front of the other. One in front of the other, walking down the street.

As they near the bottom of the street Hettie can hear the murmur of the crowd from Hammersmith Broadway. People are lining the road, three deep on either side. All of the shops are closed, their awnings still rolled, their shutters drawn down. Motorcars and omnibuses have pulled over to one side and parked. The clock on the little island in the middle of the road reads a quarter to eleven.

She and Fred skirt the back of the crowd, looking for a place to stand. But as they move further forward, to where the crowd is getting thicker and more difficult to pass, she can sense Fred's rising unease.

She reaches out and taps him on the arm. "Is here all right?" she says to him. "I don't think I can go any further in."

He looks down at her gratefully. "Yes." He nods. "It's fine."

They take their places. The crowd is already silent: hundreds of faces facing hundreds of faces across the empty street.

. . . .

They move through the crowd until they are wedged so deeply in among black backs that it seems as though they might never move again.

"Well, this won't do, will it," hisses Ivy. She is so close that Ada can smell her breath, slightly sour, the musty mothball smell of her dress, the roses she carries, and then, behind that, other bodies: thousands of them and thousands of other rapidly wilting bouquets. For a second, in the overwhelming, rank-sweet smell of the crowd, Ada feels she may faint. She steadies herself, twisting her neck to try to see around a tall man in front of her, but all she can make out is backs and heads and hats. They must be fifteen people away from the front at least. It is impossible to even see the barriers, the crowd is so deep. No one seems to want to speak it out loud, but plenty of people are grumbling about it under their breath.

She turns back to Ivy. "I suppose it will have to do," she says, with a brightness she doesn't feel. They should have stayed where they were. They could breathe there at least, and they had a view. It had been her idea to move.

Just then there's a scuffle in the crowd up ahead. Something is happening, closer to the front. For a long time it's not clear what, until voices start shouting, "Clear a space! Clear a space!" A narrow gangway is carved from the crowd, and two men carry out a young woman, feet first. The woman's hat falls off her lolling head, and Ada stoops to pick it up. She doesn't know what to do with it then, so she places it down on the woman's chest. The hat is a modern one, pretty, one of those that look like a bell, with a small spray of white fabric flowers on the rim.

She touches the young man on his arm. "Will she be all right?"

"She's fine. Just had a funny turn. Didn't you, Mary?"

The young woman is stirring now. "It's all right," says the man, leaning down. "We've got you, Mary love."

In the wake of the commotion the crowd churns and shifts back into place, then heaves suddenly from behind, as though people at the back had decided to push, all together. For a moment it seems that they will topple, like dominoes, until, as though on a wave, the part of the crowd where they are standing surges forward. Ada and Ivy hold on to each other, and to their flowers, as they find themselves traveling toward the front.

When the crowd has stopped moving, they are standing close to the barriers and have a clear view of the street: of the backs of the policemen, holding back the crowd, legs spread, arms behind their backs, the tips of their helmets shining in the sun; of the large expanse of empty road beyond; and then, on the other side of that, of all the many faces, ranged, expectant, staring back.

Beside her, Ivy is shaking. Ada touches her arm. "You all right, love?"

When Ivy brings her head up it's clear that she has been laughing. She nods, wiping her eyes. "Couldn't help it," she whispers back. "How about that, then? Someone wants us to see."

"That was funny, all right." Ada steadies herself. To their right stand a young couple, their young son between them, holding their hands. The man is speaking to his wife and boy in a low voice. "Look at the windows," he is saying. "Look up at the roofs."

Ada follows his finger, and what she sees astonishes her. Every window up above is packed with faces, and there are indeed people on the roofs: young men, mostly, though there are women, too, sitting in dangerous-looking positions on windowsills and out on the edges of small balconies. She taps Ivy on the arm and gestures up.

"Gracious." Ivy shudders.

In the distance, now, they can hear the slow, dull beating of the drums.

. . . .

The funeral cortege passes a young Irishman. He took the boat train over from Cork yesterday, landed at Southampton, and made his way here. He told no one at home he was coming—said he was going to visit his sister in Wexford. Things are changing in Ireland. It was necessary to lie.

The young Irishman joined up in 1915 and fought for Britain, but then, after the Easter Rising, he was spat at in the street whenever he was home on leave. Fucking Tommy, they'd say. Dirty fucking Tommy.

He is a Collins man now. A Sinn Féin man. He knows well whom he fights for. And there will be fighting. Of this he has no doubt. The lord mayor of Cork died while on hunger strike in Brixton prison not three weeks before.

And yet—he had to come. He had to lie and to come. For the lads he fought with and who died beside him, sometimes in his arms. Who, like him, were lied to, but fought like heroes nonetheless. Whose lives were thrown away, in their thousands, for scraps of land. He cannot forget them. He will not.

I'll remember you, he thinks, and as the gun carriage, with its coffin and its dented helmet, passes him by, he closes his eyes.

Nothing will bring them back. Not the words of comfortable men. Not the words of politicians. Or the platitudes of paid poets.

"At the going down of the sun, we will remember them."

No.

I will remember you when I pack my pipe.

I will remember you when I lift my pint.

I will remember you on fine days and on black ones. In the summer light I will remember you.

He opens his eyes and watches the military men march past. He knows who they all are; he read their names in the papers: field marshals, admirals, and generals. With a shock of recognition, he spots Haig; he's close enough to see the gray in his mustache. He would like to spit on him.

He knows the king stands somewhere not far from here. He has a
sudden image: of a man, a bomb strapped to him, running from the
crowd. A strike at the heart of empire. It would be easy, easy. He
shakes his head. Not yet, he thinks. Not yet.

. . . .

The sound of the drumming approaches, and with it a whisper
travels through the crowd: *He's coming, he's coming, he's coming.*
There's a surge from behind and Ada holds on to the barrier. Her
breath is constricted; ribbons of sweat roll down her back. She
wishes she hadn't tied herself in so tight. If she faints now, then
who will carry her out? Behind her, the crowd churns and then
settles again.

"Try to keep your feet wide," says the young man beside them.
"Don't worry. They won't move again now. That's it. You'll see."

Coming up the street toward them are four enormous chestnut
horses, the sound of their hooves deadened by the straw-strewn
pavement, and as the horses draw nearer, almost in one movement,
as though it were rehearsed, all the men in the crowd bare their
heads. The young man beside her holds his hat against his chest.

Behind the horses come drummers, their drums covered in
black fabric. The sound of their beat is hollow, muted. Pipers come
behind them, their pipes making a thin, high tone on the still air.
Behind there is space, a gap, then six black horses pull a carriage,
their eyes blinkered, coats gleaming. It bears a single coffin, a tattered flag draped over it, the colors faded, as though it has spent
too long in the sun.

On top of the flag Ada can see the dented helmet of a soldier.
It is the same helmet that Michael wore. For a stunned second
she thinks it is his—that it is the helmet that was tied around his
neck the last time she saw him, as he lumbered off down the road
in the lightening morning, bouncing against his back so that she

was worried it would bruise him; and for that second she is con-
vinced that the body in the coffin is his. Then there's the sound of
a woman's sob, sharp and uncontrolled. It echoes off the buildings
on either side of the road. Then there's another sob, and another,
and in the crowd opposite, hundreds of handkerchiefs appear,
stark white against the black. Beside her Ivy is convulsed with silent tears.

And then she understands: They all wore that helmet.

All of these women's husbands, brothers, sons.

The cortege passes them, moving down to the Cenotaph. Ada
watches it slow. Sees it come to a stop.

There is a hush before the silence, a settling.

And then the chimes begin.

. . . .

Breathless, Evelyn reaches the top of the hill. In exhilaration she
sees that no one else is up here, no one is sitting on her bench.
They have all been sucked down into the great gray magnet of the
city below. The air is so still that below her, the smoke from chim-
neys rises straight up into the air. It is a truly beautiful day.

She hears the chimes of eleven begin. The bells of Primrose
Hill, of Camden Town, and further into the city—many, many
bells, chiming together and apart. As the silence falls, she can see
it almost, traveling like a long rolling wave, up to where she sits on
the hill.

Then, what she thought was silence gives way to something
else. Something surprising. It is the sound of a city without people.
Without walking, speaking, running people; without buses, without cars, factories, offices, docks; but it is not silence, not here on
the hill, not at all. She can hear the wind, lifting through the last
brittle, tenacious leaves; hear the crows, calling to one another in
the trees; and then, in the distance, other calls: those of the animals

from the zoo. She hears the chattering of monkeys, the muffled roar of a big cat. She didn't expect this. It makes her smile.

Up here, there are still patches of mist clinging a little in the green hollows. Up here is land that has never been built on.

And this, too, is the city, she thinks.

And here she is, sitting on a bench in the sun.

It reminds her of another morning, a morning in summer, inside the flat in Primrose Hill, with the window open and the heat of the day outside. Lying beside Fraser, listening to the sounds of the city below. The feel of the sun through the window, hot on the soles of her feet. The close, warm smell of the man that she loved. Then standing, and stretching, her feet cool against the tiles of the floor, turning to him. *Shall we go outside?*

The slow break of his smile.

I loved you, she thinks. I loved you, Fraser.

In three weeks, she thinks, I will be thirty.

She breathes in, catches the faint scent of the earth, feels that same sun, the unexpected blessing of it—on a day in November—warm against her skin.

I am alive, she thinks. I am alive. *I am alive.*

. . . .

Beside her, in the silence, Hettie can feel Fred standing, held rigid.

She wants to ask him whom he thinks of. Who peoples this silence for him? Whose are the names that he calls in the night?

She cannot believe that she has not wanted to ask this before.

Facing her across the street are hundreds of men, their hats held to their chests, and hundreds of women. Many of them, both men and women, are weeping; and if hundreds stand here in Hammersmith then they are everywhere, all over this city, all over this country, and beyond, across the sea, in France.

And what of the girl with the long brown hair? Where is she

now? Standing on a street like this? In a village somewhere? Is her hair still long? Or has she cut hers, too? And the other women, the older women, the women who sold themselves over and over again. What has become of them?

They don't seem so very far from her somehow.

And Ed?

It is hard to think of him. It scrapes her heart.

Is he, too, standing on a street like this? Somewhere not too far away? Is he with his family? Or is he where she left him, bruised and alone?

She hopes not.

Beside her, Fred shifts. Hettie looks up. His face is calmer, his body less rigid. She reaches up and slips her arm through the crook of his elbow. At first he flinches, but he doesn't move, doesn't brush her off; he simply brings his hand down, to cover hers. They stay like that, arm in arm. She looks back at the faces, ranged across the street.

Bearing witness. This is what they are doing. They are witnessing one another, all of them. This is why they are here.

. . . .

As the silence stretches, something becomes clear. He is not here. Her son is not inside this. And yet it is not empty; it is full and loud with grief: the grief of the living. But her son is not here.

A bugle sounds, the "Last Post," tinny and distant from where they stand. As the final note dies away, the crowd exhales. For a long moment people stay where they are, as though reluctant to move. Then, very faintly at first, in the distance, comes the sound of traffic, the hum of life resuming, increasing. A known sound, and yet it seems like an affront.

Where they stand, at the front of the crowd, no one has yet

moved. Then, there is an easing; the crowd loosens, people are moving now, along the back of the pavement.

"Where are they all headed?" says Ada.

"To the Cenotaph," says a young woman to her left, holding a spray of lilies. "To lay their flowers for the dead."

"Shall we go, too, then?" Ivy says.

Ada turns. The queue is already twenty people wide, people shuffling forward step by tiny step. It will take hours to reach the end of the road.

"Do you want to?" she says to Ivy.

"Yes."

She hesitates. "Do you mind if I don't? There's somewhere else I want to go."

She doesn't elaborate, and Ivy doesn't push her—doesn't ask where, just gestures to the flowers in her hand. "Shall I lay those for you, then?"

"Yes, please," she says. "You'll be all right?"

"I'll be fine." Ivy nods, takes the daisies from her.

"They could do with a drink."

"Me, too. A stiff one." Ivy smiles. "When I get home. You come and find me if you like."

"Thanks." Ada smiles. "I might just do that."

They hug briefly.

"Go on with you now," says Ivy.

It is hard going at first, moving against the tide of people, but once she has fought her way to the back of the crowd and is able to find a bit of space to breathe in, Ada turns, to see if she can see Ivy in the crowd to wave good-bye.

It is then she sees him.

He is standing twenty paces away from her, his pregnant wife and little girl by his side. A small man: shoulders held against the world, pinched, pale blue eyes; thin little mustache barely covering his lip. He is standing in the queue for the Cenotaph. He has a bunch of blue flowers in his hand. He hasn't seen her yet.

She takes a step toward him. Just then, he looks up and he sees her. His hand tightens on his daughter's arm. The little girl cries out and twists from his grip.

At first, from the horrified look on his face, she thinks that he will leave his family and run. But he doesn't. He stands his ground, his face settles, and he holds her gaze. He seems to grow taller, as he pulls his daughter close again and holds his pregnant wife by the arm.

She doesn't call out to him. Doesn't go toward him. She just nods, as though to someone that she once knew, and then turns, and walks, slowly, steadily, the other way.

. . . .

After the funeral is finished, after the congregation has gone. After the king and queen and the prime minister and the mothers who lost all their sons, and the mothers who lost all their sons and their husbands, too, have gone. After the young girl who lost nine brothers—killed or missing—and wrote especially to be asked to come, and the hundred blinded nurses and the MPs and the lords who have lost a brother or a son have gone. After all of these have gone, Westminster Abbey is closed for a brief time.

Four wooden barriers are erected, and four lit candles are placed around the grave. They are expecting crowds.

A young chorister, relieved of his duties for the day, steals out of the room where his companions are changing from their robes. He doesn't tell anyone where he is going. The door into the nave has been left ajar. The young boy slides around it. No one is in the vast, echoing church. The candles are the only light. Above him the roof stretches into infinite space. He walks over to the wooden barriers, his heart thumping. Earlier, during the ceremony, from where he was standing in the choir, he couldn't see the coffin. Now he wants to see.

He ducks beneath the barriers, and on hands and knees crawls to the edge of the hole. In the grave, quite far down, he can see the casket, covered with a flag. From here, the candlelight hardly touches its red, white, and blue.

He thinks of his brother: of the last time he saw him, in his uniform; how tall he looked, how fine. He can remember him clearly, even though he was small then—can remember how much he wished that he were old enough to join him in the war.

War. Something in the word makes him shiver. A good shivering. The sort that tells him that someday, when he grows up, he might get his chance.

Then the great doors at the end of the abbey are opened again and pale November light floods the floor. The boy gets to his feet and crawls under the barriers, darting back into darkness. Before he slips away, he sees, coming toward him, a great procession of people, two abreast, flowing across the abbey floor.

. . . .

Evelyn stands in front of the mirror, holding a dress up to her chin, turning skeptically in the light. It is a deep red. She hasn't worn it for years, but it is well cut. She supposes it will have to do.

Behind her Doreen appears in the doorway, flushed from the outside air, her arms folded across her chest. "Going out?"

"Oh God. I don't know." Evelyn flings the dress down on the bed and sits beside it. "I'd forgotten what a fandango it all is."

Doreen sits down beside her on the bed, looking amused. "Am I allowed to ask where it is you're going?"

Evelyn reaches for her cigarette case. "Dancing. Supposedly."

Doreen raises an eyebrow. "Whereabouts?"

"Hammersmith."

"The Palais?"

"Mmmm."

"And with whom . . . ?" Doreen smiles.

Evelyn tips her head back. "A man."

"Well," Doreen says as her smile spreads, "that's a good start at least. What flavor of man might he be?"

"From work. He's a man from work."

"Well, isn't that a turnup for the books."

"It doesn't mean anything," says Evelyn, quickly, crossly.

"Course not." Doreen is still smiling.

"What?" says Evelyn. "*What?* Stop looking at me like that."

But Doreen doesn't stop. So Evelyn stands up, lifting the dress and holding it up to her chin. "What do you think?"

. . . .

Ada gets off the bus a couple of stops before home and walks down empty streets toward the canal. The mild sun is still hanging in the sky, and as she walks down the lichen-covered steps to the towpath, she feels a lift. She has always loved it down here, ever since she was a girl, when she used to come with her father to feed the ducks—loved the weed-and-water smell of it, the rampant scramble of green by the side of the path. She turns left, feeling the sun on her back, then tucks herself into the side to wait while a barge comes under the bridge. The bargeman lifts his cap to her. "Afternoon."

His boat is a shock of color, painted brightly in yellow, red, and blue. His bridled, blinkered pony's breath is sweet in the afternoon air.

She passes under the bridge and sees the gas towers ahead, half-full, their latticework etched gray against the sky. Nearing the allotments, she can smell woodsmoke. As she turns up the path that leads along the backs of the gardens, two fat wood pigeons

take to the air. She passes windfall apples, crisp, browned brambles, and empty, neatly tended plots.

Soon enough, she sees him. He has his back to her, kneeling by
a bed, trowel in hand. She stays just outside the gate, watching as
he bends forward, worrying something out from the soil. His
jacket is off; he is in his shirtsleeves, and patches of damp bloom
beneath his arms. There's a small pile of vegetables beside him on
the ground. To his right, a low bonfire burns. She bends and opens
the latch gate, taking a couple of steps toward him. He doesn't
turn at the sound, although she knows, from the way he stills, that
he has heard her. He stands slowly, wiping down his hands, and
walks over to a table, where he lays the trowel out. Only then does
he turn.

"Hello." She is the first to speak.

"Hello." He reaches up, wiping his face with his sleeve. "Been
standing there long, then?"

"I just arrived."

He nods. "It's not like you to come down here."

"Well." She holds her arms across her chest, self-conscious,
dressed as she is in her mourning. She reaches up and takes the hat
off, smoothing her hair. She holds the hat in front of her, looking
around at the other plots. "There's not many people about."

He shakes his head. "No one all day. I thought I'd take advan-
tage of it. I got a lot done. Set up for the winter now."

She can see that the beds have been freshly raked and covered
over with netting that is pegged into the ground. A large pile of
cleared brambles and leaves waits to go on the fire. There's an air
of quiet calm and order to it all.

"There's another squash just come through." Jack points to the
vegetables on the ground. "Thought we'd seen the last of them."

The squash sits surrounded by a small, muddy pile of vegetables. A bright orange, streaked with yellow and green, it is an even
deeper color than the one he brought her on Sunday. He goes to

the fire and kneels down beside it, leaning in and raking the embers until they glow with heat.

She comes to stand opposite him. "Were you here, then?" she says slowly, her throat dry. "Is this where you were last night?"

He looks up at her and nods once, slowly.

Relief floods her. "Where did you sleep?"

"Shed."

"Were you warm enough?"

"I was pissed enough."

She laughs at that. The air between them eases a little. She steps closer to the flames, holding her hands up to warm them. "Can I put some leaves on?"

He looks up at her, surprised, and gestures yes.

She goes over to the pile of leaves, gathers an armful of their red and yellow and brown, and throws them onto the flames, which lick them, until they catch and flare briefly, beautifully, before curling and spitting in the heat. Gray smoke curls into the still air. She breathes it in.

"I'm sorry," he says.

She looks across at him. His gaze is steady, watching the leaves burn, his face warping a little in the flames. His cheeks are reddened and his eyes look swollen, as though he has been staring into the fire for a long time.

"No." She shakes her head. "It's me who should say that."

"I'm not so sure." He looks up at her now.

"I didn't see you," she says. "All this time. I was looking somewhere else, for something else, and I didn't see you anymore."

He takes this in. Takes her in. Nods, as if acknowledging the truth of it.

"You go up to town, then?" he says.

"Yes."

"On your own?"

"With Ivy."

He grunts. Sits back on his heels, a challenge in him. "And was it worth it?"

Was it worth it?

She doesn't answer immediately. She thinks of the crowd. The press of so many bodies, so close together, the smell of them, of the silence, stretching: the noisy silence of grief. Of the boy, his wife, and his daughter and his blue flowers. Of turning away from him, and the feeling as she did so, as though she'd had her hand balled in a fist, held tight for years, and opened it, only to find that there was nothing inside. "Yes," she says. "It was."

He nods. "Well." He pushes himself to his feet and walks over to the remaining brambles and leaves, turning with a great armful, which he throws into the fire, where they pop and crackle, their thin stalks twisting and coiling in the flames, flaring briefly high, and then fall, and the blaze is quiet once more. He picks up his jacket and pulls it on. The sun is setting over the gas tower behind him, the sky purpling with evening light.

"Jack—"

"What's that?"

She goes to him then, and he lifts his arms to embrace her. She puts her head against him, her ear against his chest. She can hear his steady heart. She breathes him in. He smells of woodsmoke, his day's work, and of himself.

. . . .

At the station exit, Evelyn stops a young couple. "Excuse me. Do you have any idea where the Hammersmith Palais might be?"

The girl, dressed smartly in a cloche and woolen coat, stares at her as though she is touched in the head. "It's right here," she says. "We're going there, too."

They emerge to a queue that stretches fifty deep away from a building that looks like a tram shed.

"Thank you," says Evelyn, mortified. *Bloody hell.*

She doesn't want to stand near them, not on her own, not at the back of the queue, only to have them take pity on her and try to make conversation. "I just, must—go and buy some cigarettes."

She ducks into the little kiosk at the side of the station and buys a packet of Gold Flakes, then takes them around the side and lights one up.

What in hell's name is she doing here? She peers back around the corner. The young couple have already disappeared from view. People are streaming from the station to join the queue, which has lengthened until it is stretching down the block toward her, but it appears to be moving quickly at least, and it seems no one at the top is being turned away. She finishes her cigarette and grinds it out under her heel, and then, almost as if she isn't really doing it at all, Evelyn walks a couple of paces to join the line in the back.

They are young, most of them, horribly young.

She fingers her collar, aware of the red dress under her coat.

She has lost too much weight—it no longer fits. She wishes she weren't wearing it, wishes she had never put it on. The color is all wrong: too *red*. Whoever thought of wearing red? And it will gape. She knows this with a sinking certainty. She has no bust anymore and the dress will gape.

She wants to go home.

Is she early or late? She cannot tell. Will Robin be inside waiting for her? She cannot see him out here. Will he see her first? Or will she have to stand there, looking for him, trying to find him among this crowd? How in the hell are these things done? They should have arranged a place to meet, at least. Suddenly she's not even sure she can remember what he looks like, and everyone in this chattering, excitable queue seems so young, and this is why, this is *exactly* why, she doesn't come out: because places like these

are for the young, for those who have yet to understand that pleasure is not their right.

. . . .

Hettie can hear the chatter of the crowd massed outside as she files
into the Pen and takes her place as Grayson stalks the line.

There's a strange feeling about tonight—something bubbling
under the surface. It's in everyone: in the boys, sitting opposite
them, in Grayson, as his eyes sweep up and down, in the barely
contained excitement of the girls.

The Palais is looking its best. The cleaners have polished the
floor to a deep shine, the glass panels are gleaming, and the dust
has been dusted from the Chinese lamps. The doors at the back of
the stage open, and the band files out. A ripple runs through the
Pen as the musicians lift their instruments and start warming up.
Hettie and Di and everyone else sit a little higher in their seats.

The trumpeter does a little solo, a little scale, ending in a trill.
There's a confidence in the band, a swagger tonight. Still, Hettie's
not sure she wants to hear jazz. She'd like some music to match her
mood, this sweet-jagged melancholy mood that she's had all day.
This mood that, walking here, felt like carrying some precious liquid: something newly distilled that she didn't want to spill, that was
reflected back to her in the faces of the people she passed, in the
last of the day's unexpected sun.

The doors open and the punters flood the floor. Part of her re-
coils. She doesn't want this delicate feeling trampled on, not just
yet.

But the floor is already packed. Though the band has not yet
started, some people are dancing, and small eddies of movement
show where people are doing their own little rags. Hettie's eyes
light on a tall, fair man, wearing evening dress, standing alone. His
eyes scan the crowd, looking for someone. Then, as if he has felt

her staring, the man turns his head her way. When she looks again he is crossing the floor toward the Pen. An elbow digs her in her ribs. "There you go, Het," says Di beside her. "Now you're away."

The man is heading straight for her. A slight hesitancy interrupts his stride, a small roll, as though he has one leg longer than the other.

False leg.

The man comes to a halt just in front of where she sits.

"Hello," he says. He has an open face. A friendly smile. He reaches out and touches the metal gate with a finger, seeming to test it for strength. "Bit barbaric, this, isn't it?" He gives it a little rattle. "Why do they need to keep you locked up, then? Are you dangerous?"

She raises the ghost of a smile. She has heard the jokes already—heard them all.

"Do they ever let you out?"

"Sixpence," she says, pointing to the booth. "Over there."

"So I can release you for sixpence? That's cheap at the price."

The man turns, but then, as though something has just occurred to him, he turns back, hands in his pockets, a quizzical look on his face. "That is," he says, "if I may?"

Is he laughing at her? She cannot tell. "Of course," she says. "That's my job."

As he goes away from her, she sees again the slight pause, the tiny hesitancy in his stride that gives him away. He hides it well, she thinks, that leg; if you didn't know how to look you might not be able to tell.

"He's nice," says Di, leaning in. "How'd you manage to score that?"

Hettie shrugs. She can tell Di's trying to be nice. She's been nice to her ever since Hettie arrived earlier and just shook her head when Di asked her how it had gone Tuesday night. She hadn't pressed it, either, when Hettie had to explain that she hadn't brought the dress with her—that she'd gone down to the Broadway for the silence instead.

Di frowns now, putting her hand on Hettie's arm. "Are you sure you're all right, Het? You're ever so quiet tonight."

"I'm fine."

The fair-haired man is back in a minute with his docket. "There we go." He holds it out to her. "They say I've to give this to you."

Hettie takes it from him, puts it into her pouch, and lets herself out of the little gate. They stand, facing each other, he with his hands in his pockets, she with her arms behind her back. He makes no move toward her. They stand this way for a long moment, until she grows hot and cross. "Don't you *want* to dance?" she says eventually.

"*Dance?*" He raises his eyebrows. "Is *that* what you do? You just looked so forlorn, sitting there, that I thought I ought to set you free."

She glares at him.

"Sorry," he says, smiling. "Only joking." He takes his hands out of his pockets. "What's the next dance, then?"

"It's always a waltz. First and last."

Behind the man, she can see that the band has finished tuning up. The performers are straightening their ties, adjusting their music, and sitting forward in their seats. The conductor comes out from the wings to cheers and scattered applause.

"First and last," says the man, nodding, as if this is important, somehow, to note. "And how long are you free for?"

"Just one dance."

"And then what happens? Do you turn into a pumpkin? Or do I?"

"Then I go back in there." Hettie points to the Pen, where Di has been hired now, too, and where just three girls are left.

"Ah." He makes a small grimace. "I see."

All around them, couples are taking their places on the floor, and the raucous hubbub is dying, giving way to something else—an excited, expectant hush.

"Well, then," says the man, opening his arms. "I suppose I'd better make this count."

She lifts her arms and their palms touch, very lightly. His right arm circles her waist. "I hear the band is very good," he says.

She wonders how he will manage, dancing, with that leg.

The conductor lifts his baton, and the music begins. The band plays a low, pulsing beat. It is not an ordinary waltz. It is slower than usual and sounds mournful, a little strange. All around them there's the swish of cloth and the sound of feet on wood as couples start to move.

For two or three bars the man she is with does nothing. Then, just when she is thinking that he is going to stay that way all night, he pulls her a little tighter, leading her off, spinning her out across the floor. He leads well; his hold is firm, and his shoulders are open and relaxed as they turn around the room to this oddly accented beat.

The band stays with the strange, pulsing count for a long time, until its strangeness and hesitancy start to seem natural, a living thing, a fractured heartbeat. They stay on the beat until a lone trumpeter stands and starts to play over the top.

. . . .

Inside, everything is surprisingly lush and surprisingly Chinese; indecipherable signs are painted onto hanging panes of glass, and storks and pagodas repeat in patterns over the walls. It should be crass but it's surprisingly pleasant. Evelyn sees a sign for the ladies' cloakroom and goes inside, even though she doesn't really need the loo, but then she has to wait, in a torturous queue, while girls primp and preen themselves all down the long mirrored wall. When a stall finally comes free she locks herself inside, takes her brush from her bag, and pulls it through her hair. She wants to turn around and leave. This is no place for her. She should never have come.

Out of the stall, she faces herself reluctantly in the mirror, pulling at the dress so that it doesn't gape around her chest. Why, oh why, is she wearing it? Because she had nothing else, that's why. But if she moves, if she dances, then it *will* gape. That much is fairly clear. Perhaps she shouldn't dance, then? She's probably forgotten how anyway. And she certainly doesn't know how to dance to anything new. She'll probably only embarrass herself. She should never have come. *She should never have come.*

She hands her coat to the cloakroom attendant and takes the stub, then goes through the double doors into a vast hall, packed with swirling dancers. Large colored lanterns hang suspended from the ceiling, filling the room with their pink and blue and yellow light. In the middle of the polished dance floor is a funny sort of miniature mountain, water pouring down its sides, and over on the far side of the room, under what appears to be an approximation of a Chinese temple, is the band: twenty or thirty musicians in white suits.

So this is what a dance hall looks like.

All around the dance floor are tables. Evelyn decides that she will walk once around them, checking to see if Robin is sitting at one, and if she has not seen him by the time that she has done a circuit, she will turn around and leave.

She passes a little cabin selling drinks to her right. She joins the small queue, waits her turn, then, "Gin and orange, please," she says to the uniformed girl behind the bar.

The girl rolls her eyes. "No *alcohol*," she says, pointing to a sign dangling below her. NO ALCOHOL WILL BE SERVED. BY ORDER OF THE MANAGEMENT.

"Well," says Evelyn, eyebrow raised. "What do you suggest instead?"

"Tea, or fruit cup."

"Shouldn't fruit cup have gin in it?"

The girl stares at her.

"I'll have a fruit cup then, please."

"Twopence," says the girl, sloshing the drink into a cup from a large vat to her right.

Evelyn takes her fruit cup over to a table and puts it down briefly so that she can light her cigarette. She is standing close to the band, near the conductor as he comes out onto the stage, and as he lifts his baton and the band starts to play, she begins walking around the dance floor, keeping her gaze as light as possible, trying not to miss any of the tables, trying not to appear as though she is looking; but Robin is nowhere to be seen.

When she has traveled halfway around the room, the thought occurs to her that he may well not have come. It has been days since they made this arrangement. He may have forgotten. Is it only her arrogance that supposes that he will be here—that he will be waiting? Does she even want to see him at all? She stops, turning to lean against the barrier and look out over the floor. There must be four or five hundred couples moving out there, and yet, despite this, the move and shuffle of their feet is light; despite this, she can still hear the single trumpeter over the top, playing his solo, while the band keeps up a fractured, pulsing rhythm underneath.

. . . .

The man is an extraordinary dancer. As Hettie spins in his arms to this halting, sad music, with his palm splayed on her back and the steady, sure step of him keeping time, she can feel herself, her skin, her blood, right to the smallest part. And the parts of her feel different, charged, rearranged.

She is not the same as she was.

It is Ed. It is as though some of his brokenness has entered her. It is Fred, and standing with him in the silence and the sun. It is the thought of those women in France. It is the sadness of this waltz.

But though she can feel all of this sadness, something is holding her up; it is this man. It is in the way he holds her, in the steady but constant distance between them—a distance he doesn't seem to want or need to cross. The way he makes her know from his movements that he wants to dance with her, and that dancing is enough.

The trumpeter stops, his last note lingering in the air, and the music is slowing now, coming to a close.

"Thank you." The man brings her gently to a stop. "That was a very fine sixpence indeed."

She wants to ask to dance with him again; she wants to tell him that she would happily dance with him all night, wants to ask him how it is that he can dance so beautifully when he—

But the man has seen something over her shoulder. His face has changed, and color touches his cheek. He releases her with a funny little bow. "Excuse me," he says.

Every part of him is concentrated on something just behind her head. She knows without turning that it is a woman; that it is the woman he has come here to meet.

Of course he has come here to meet someone. Of course.

Hettie bites her disappointment down and turns to see.

A woman stands, in a red dress, on the far edge of the dance floor. She is leaning on the barrier, staring out and smoking a cigarette. She has wavy brown hair cut short to her chin. She is not too small and not too tall, and she is beautiful. Not beautiful in the manner of those women who want people to stare; this woman looks as though she would be happy if no one were to look at her at all. The woman reminds Hettie of someone, though she cannot think of whom.

The woman has not yet seen him looking at her, and so the man's face is still unguarded, and his eyes are free to roam. Hettie watches him. Perhaps, she thinks, this woman will sense that she is being stared at, and will turn to meet this man's gaze.

She wonders if this woman thinks of this man the way he so obviously thinks of her. She knows, without even thinking it properly, without even really forming the thought, that this man loves this woman. And she knows, too, that this man is a good man; that he is a good man to love.

Hettie steps away from the man, moving back toward the Pen, so that when the woman turns she will not be in the way of her view.

The woman turns . . .

Author's Note

Accounts differ as to the selection process of the body of the Unknown Warrior. For the purposes of this book, I have stayed close to Brigadier General L. J. Wyatt's contemporary account, quoted extensively in Michael Gavaghan's *The Story of the British Unknown Warrior.* This states that there were four bodies taken from each of the main areas of British involvement on the Western Front—the Somme, Aisne, Arras, and Ypres—and that the bodies were taken from the battlefields themselves, not simply from cemeteries, as is sometimes suggested. The idea that the chosen body originated from the fields around Arras is my own.

Acknowledgments

. . . .

I read widely while researching and writing *Wake,* but returned to several books many times:

For insight into post–World War I British society: Juliet Nicolson's *The Great Silence: 1918–1920* and Robert Graves and Alan Hodge's wonderful *The Long Week-End: A Social History of Britain, 1918–1939.*

For the impact of the war on women of Evelyn's generation: *Singled Out* by Virginia Nicholson.

For contemporary accounts of the war and its aftermath: *Women of the Aftermath* by Helen Zenna Smith, *The Virago Book of Women and the Great War,* Vera Brittain's *Testament of Youth,* and Mary Borden's stunning *The Forbidden Zone,* which, even though it didn't directly influence the text, makes for essential reading for anyone interested in women's experiences of World War I.

For the conditions for soldiers on the Western Front, Paul Fussell's *The Great War and Modern Memory* and *Death's Men* by Denis Winter, a desperately moving account of the reality of life for Kitchener's soldiers.

For monuments and mourning: Jay Winter's *Sites of Memory, Sites of Mourning,* and Geoff Dyer's brilliant *The Missing of the Somme.*

Marek Kohn's *Dope Girls* is a fantastic book and deserves to be better known. It taught me about the phenomenon of the dance instructress and gave me the background and inspiration I needed for the characters of Hettie and Di.

Michael Gavaghan's *The Story of the British Unknown Warrior* and Neil Hanson's *The Unknown Soldier* were both invaluable to me.

Further thanks are due:

To my fantastic agent, Caroline Wood, and everyone at Felicity Bryan Associates.

To Jane Lawson, a great editor, and my ideal reader.

To Susan Kamil, for her insightful notes on the text.

To the teams at Transworld and Random House U.S.

To Thea Bennett, Martha Close, Pippa Griffin, Keith Jarrett, Olya Knezevic, Philip Makatrewicz, Josh Raymond, David Savill, Matthew Weait, Ginevra White, and Cynthia Wilson, a.k.a. the Unwriteables, a phenomenal bunch of writers, for inspiration, friendship, and support.

To Philip Makatrewicz and Toby Dantzic, who very kindly read this manuscript and offered invaluable help at a critical period in its gestation.

To Christine Bacon, for giving me a break when I needed it most.

To Allan Mallinson, for clarifying military matters.

To Cherry Buckwell, Jennie Grant, Hazel Sainsbury, Beth Weightman, Lou Rhodes, and Emma Darwall-Smith.

To Sandy Chapman.

To my lovely, loopy family—Dan, Emily, and Sophie—and all the extended crew.

It would take another book to acknowledge all the things I am grateful to my parents for, but for now:

To Tony Hope, for his kindness, his generosity, and for giving me my love of books.

To Pamela Hope, who read to me before I could read myself and was the indefatigable and enthusiastic reader of so many different versions of this book.

And finally to Dave—for your utter support, your joyous love, for building the shed, and for telling me to get on with it. You're the best.

Thank you.

ABOUT THE AUTHOR

ANNA HOPE was born in Manchester. She was educated at Oxford University, attended the Royal Academy of Dramatic Art, and has a master's degree in creative writing from Birkbeck College, University of London. She lives in London. *Wake* is her first novel.